ASHTON'S SECRET

Liana Laverentz

A KISMET® Romance

METEOR PUBLISHING CORPORATION
Bensalem, Pennsylvania

To Marilyn, who was the first to believe,
and her son, Darrell, who makes it possible
for me to write.

LIANA LAVERENTZ

Liana Laverentz is an avid romance reader who got
halfway through her MBA before deciding she'd
rather spend her time writing romances. She thought
it would be easier. She was wrong. Six years, several
false starts, and umpteen revisions later, her first
manuscript was accepted for publication. She hopes
you enjoy it. Liana welcomes mail from her readers:
P.O. Box 7367, Erie, PA 16510.

PROLOGUE

Chalking it up to city-bred paranoia, Heather shook off the feeling someone was following her and dropped two letters into Ashton's solitary corner mailbox. She'd decided against waiting until morning to mail them, afraid by then she'd come up with yet another weak excuse not to let her family know where she was.

The deed done, she turned and meandered toward the lake, her thoughts on the letter to her younger sister. The one that had been hard to write.

Dear Cassie,

I'm sorry I missed your wedding. I thought long and hard about it, but I just couldn't face the D.C. crowd again, not after Mother's last visit. I don't know how you stand it. Her lies, her relentless social climbing. Sometimes I think it's her fault I ended up in detox in the first place.

Now that you're successfully married, I know she's going to start on me again. I can't take the pressure. I'm tired of being told who to see, what to wear, where to go, who I can and can't talk to or go out with. I'm twenty-six, for heaven's sake.

I'm sure she's managed to convince everyone I'm still vacationing in Cancun, but the truth is I left the clinic last month. I've sent Mother and Dad a letter telling them where I am and that I'm not coming home, but wanted you to hear it from me.

I came to Ashton to apply for a teaching job. One of the high school's English teachers retired, and I answered an ad for a replacement. I got the job. Lucky for me, teachers aren't beating the doors down to get a position at Ashton High.

Ashton's a world apart from D.C. It's as small as they come. But I like it. I think you would, too. It's so peaceful, especially with the lake nearby. The sunsets are gorgeous.

I've also met someone. He's different, as in not in the least like the Ivy Leaguers Mother's pushed at us since we were debs. His friends call him "Hawk." It suits him. He's my age, tall, dark, and unbelievably handsome . . . but then, I'm biased.

He's got a Harley and takes me riding. Mother would choke on her Valium if she knew. I know what you're thinking—lonely new schoolteacher in town falls for leader of the local hoodlums. Sounds like something out of one of our favorite oldies.

It's not like that at all. He's funny, kind, and gentle—and straight. He doesn't even drink. I'm meeting him after work tonight. Between you and me, I think tonight's the night. By this time next week, I could be a married woman, too.

There's another man who's been trying to romance me, but he's the kind who'll go after anything in a skirt. His family owns Lakeland, a local resort, and the Smuggler's Wharf, the night spot where Hawk works. Mother and Dad would approve of him, which means he has two strikes against him already in my book. Besides, there's Hawk.

Be happy for me, Cassie. I've finally got my head on straight. I'd love it if you'd come to visit. Think about it. New York in the fall. The colors will be spectacular. You could bring your camera. At night we can go across the lake to The Wharf and jitterbug to our heart's content—just like old times. Write back soon. I love you.

Sassie

Heather picked up speed as the church bell chimed eleven. Hawk had asked her to meet him on the Ashton dock at ten after. He'd said he had something important to ask her. As she approached Lake Ashton's dark shoreline, the cool night breeze rippled through her ebony hair. Her gaze focused on The Wharf across the water. It appeared brilliantly lit when there was no moon to compete with, like tonight. She smiled and hugged herself in anticipation. It was a perfect night for lovers.

She was standing at the water's edge lost in romantic fantasies when a large hand covered her mouth from behind. A damp, sweet-smelling rag was pressed to her nose, and her world turned as black as the night surrounding her.

ONE

It was a hell of a homecoming.

No sooner had he rented the slip at the Ashton Marina than people had gathered on the dock. People he'd known most of his life, people whose expressions ranged from surprise to wariness to outright hostility.

Not one had offered to help as he'd backed the trailer holding his twenty-seven-foot ketch into the water. Not that he'd needed help, but a show of welcome would've been nice. Instead he'd berthed the boat alone and driven away without a word spoken by anyone.

Now, ten minutes later, Nicholas Hawkinson surveyed the abandoned property he'd inherited while he'd been away. His professional contractor's eye didn't miss a single telling detail. The beige and brown Victorian farmhouse he'd been raised in showed every one of its fifty years—and then some.

Seeing the overgrown yard and neglected house, with its forlorn barn off to the side, he felt like Rip Van Winkle. Passing a hand over his beard-stubbled face, he sighed in resignation. It would take more time to fix up the place and sell it than the local citizenry was willing to give him. If his reception at the marina was any indication, it was still obvious nobody in Ashton wanted to rub elbows with an accused murderer.

Easing out of the truck, his muscles kinked from four days on the road, Nick wanted nothing more than a shower and a round-the-clock nap. Instead he headed for the barn. Crossing the dirt threshold, he strode to the narrow wood stairway at the back, ignoring his stomach's churning. The sooner he faced the past, the sooner he could put it behind him. With silent steps he climbed the stairs to the loft, where the nightmare had begun.

An almost suffocating heat engulfed him as he closed his eyes and braced himself against the memory of Heather, her delicate features distorted in agony. Pain washed over him as he relived the moment he'd found her still warm body. The smell of decaying hay made his trip into the murky past seem almost real. He recalled the sirens, the shouting, the chaos when he'd resisted arrest, and more. Much more.

When his trembling subsided, he opened his eyes, half expecting to see Heather's ghost pointing an accusing finger at him. Instead he found himself staring at a different woman.

Too shaken to speak, he kept staring. She stood in the corner, her attention absorbed by a massive spiderweb above her head. Late afternoon sun struggled through the dirt-covered window at the apex of the back wall, bathing her in soft light. Dust motes meandered in the hazy summer air around her.

She had to be a mirage. He shook his head and blinked several times. The mirage remained. He studied her profile: a smooth, unblemished cheek, a slim nose with aristocratic lines, soft, full lips, slightly parted. Her shining blond hair was twisted into a loose topknot. She wore a denim skirt, pink blouse, ballerina-type shoes, and ankle socks with little ruffles.

Inexplicably she reminded him of Heather. His scrutiny intensified. Neither her coloring nor her shape was the same, but . . . Nick looked into the rafters. He had to get a grip. Heather Morgan was dead.

The woman made a soft, inarticulate sound, reclaiming his attention. With a slender hand she reached inside a large bag hanging over her shoulder and withdrew a crumpled tissue. The sight of her sniffing and pressing it against her nose stirred a discordant note of compassion in him and reminded him why he'd never allowed sentimental females in his loft. Not even Heather. The loft was Nick's private domain. His sanctuary. A well-known fact of which Heather's killer had taken ruthless advantage.

At the thought of the bastard he'd see behind bars well before he posted the SOLD sign in his front yard, Nick's anger returned full force.

"What the hell do you think you're doing in here?"

Meghan's head snapped around at the angry male voice behind her. At the sight of the big, imposing body that went with it, she instinctively stepped backward, only to trip over some unidentified piece of lawn-care equipment. With a startled yelp, she landed on her rear in a pile of fetid hay, her camera bag sliding off her shoulder and tipping over.

The man started toward her, and she held up a hand. "Come any closer and I'll scream bloody murder."

He froze in his tracks, surprising her. Running a hand over his shadowed face, he muttered something unintelligible, then said, "All right. I'll stay put if you promise not to scream. Deal?"

She nodded, breathed deeply, and took stock of her situation. Nothing hurt, but she knew it was best to move cautiously when dealing with a large, angry man. Releasing her breath slowly, she tried to make out his features. Unfortunately, since his back was to the loft's only window, the sunlight filtering past his shoulders forced her to squint at his silhouette instead.

Broad shoulders, narrow hips, hard thighs. Over six feet tall. He wore faded jeans and a black T-shirt. His stance was nonthreatening. He held no weapon. Maybe she'd misjudged the situation. Still, an offense might be her best defense.

"Didn't your mother tell you it's not polite to sneak up on people?"

The man stiffened. "Didn't yours tell you it's not polite to trespass? Not to mention illegal."

Surreptitiously she gauged the distance to the exit. "Have you come to make a citizen's arrest?"

He snorted. "Hardly."

The irony in his response didn't escape Meghan. He shifted, and the latent power she sensed in him renewed the idea she needed to proceed cautiously. Lifting her gaze heavenward for guidance, she spotted a huge, rusted pully-operated pitchfork suspended from the ceiling, hanging above the man's head like a guillotine awaiting its next victim. She shivered, despite the sweltering heat.

"Are you all right?"

"I'm fine. It's just that . . ." Light flooded her eyes as he stepped forward. She blinked rapidly.

"I'm sorry if I startled you. I wasn't expecting to find anyone up here. You . . . took me by surprise."

Her smile was shaky. "My sentiments exactly."

His shoulders relaxed a bit. "You're not from around here, are you?"

Neither was he if he had to ask. Her wariness returned. "What makes you think that?"

"The hay you're sitting on. It's loaded with mule worms and other parasites."

Meghan started. Trying not to panic, she furtively searched the hay, unobtrusively snagging her dropped tissue in the event she needed it as a weapon against the hidden creatures. The man closed the distance between them and held out a large hand.

"Come on, I'll help you up."

A creepy, crawly sensation started up her calf, and Meghan hastily chose the lesser of two evils. Grabbing Nick's hand, she popped up onto her feet, but overbalanced in her haste to escape the unseen bugs. With a muffled gasp, she stumbled headlong into his chest.

Unprepared, he caught her awkwardly, his arm grazing her breasts as she clutched him for support. She heard his sharp intake of breath and looked up to find his face, covered by the dark stubble of a new beard, inches from hers. Their eyes met in startled awareness, man meeting woman, hard meeting soft, and he exhaled slowly, his breath fanning her face and smelling of spearmint. The rest of him smelled faintly of road dust, fresh air, and interested male.

It was hot in the loft, but not nearly as hot as she suddenly felt. Her hands came up to lever against his broad chest. "I'm sorry. I . . . overstepped."

"No problem." His low voice held an element of regret as he released her. She backed away and steadied herself against a nearby wall, putting distance between them, then brought the tissue to her nose to fight back a sneeze. The hay she'd tumbled into was sending up the most noxious fumes. "Are you sure you're all right?"

She looked up, embarrassed. "I'm fine. Just catching my breath." And collecting my wits. Extending her hand, she stepped forward. "Meghan Edwards."

The man hesitated noticeably. Meghan wondered if he'd heard the name before—from Heather. But no, Heather had always called her Cassie. Cassie and Sassie, the Motown Mimics. Childhood nicknames they'd never outgrown, even though they'd taken very separate roads to adulthood.

"Nicholas Hawkinson," he said quietly, folding his hand around hers.

Her heart skipped a beat. "Hawkinson? Do your friends call you Hawk?"

Abruptly he dropped her hand. "No. They call me Nick." His gaze grew sharp and assessing. "I think it's time you told me what you're doing in here."

She sent him an almost rueful smile. "I'm not sure myself. But I'm a sucker for old houses and barns."

"Why is that?"

"They appeal to my sense of home and tradition. I travel a lot. If I'm in one place more than three days— I've been here almost a week—I start calling it home, so most of the time I use the term loosely. But there are some places that—" her brow furrowed as she searched for the right words "—call out to me."

"And this is one of them?"

She smiled at his skepticism. "I like to think I can tell the difference between a house and a home from a mile away. For instance, this property might be abandoned, but it was never anything but a home. I can see the love and tradition that went into it. The house is solid and sturdy, there's a rose garden in the front yard, a vegetable garden in back. But that's not the best part." She lowered her voice to a conspiratorial whisper. "If you peek in the windows, it's like looking into another era."

Assuming a connection between the property and Nick—a relative of the owners, perhaps, come to check out her snooping—she wondered if she'd said too much. But he didn't seem annoyed. Instead he seemed pleased, maybe even a bit nostalgic.

"You seem to have a talent for seeing beneath the surface of things," he said quietly.

Except when it came to her family. But that was changing. She shrugged. "I try."

Nick leaned against a support beam, one of six spaced evenly on either side of the loft, and crossed his arms. "What's in the bag?"

Meghan hesitated. For some reason she felt uncomfortable telling him the practiced lie she'd used to explain her presence in Ashton. To everyone else she'd implied she was on assignment to capture the town's picture-postcard beauty on film for a layout in a national magazine. But she couldn't very well blurt out she was looking for her dead sister's lover.

"My camera."

"Are you on vacation?"

She grinned. "A photographer never takes a vacation unless she leaves her camera at home."

"What do you photograph?"

"Whatever pays the rent. Mostly homes and gardens."

"Any good?"

"My brother's a photojournalist. I trailed around the world with him for two years and picked up a few tips."

She smiled impishly. "Last year I had a six-page feature in *Life*."

He raised an eyebrow. "Which month?"

"September."

He didn't comment for a long moment, then asked, "Why would a world traveler like yourself come to a one-stoplight town like Ashton for a vacation? There's nothing within miles of here that even resembles a tourist attraction."

Meghan had no alternative but to retreat behind the curtain of her alibi. "I'm not on vacation. I'm on assignment to—"

Nick swore sharply.

"Excuse me?"

"Who told you to come up here? Into this loft?"

He'd gone rigid. She fought the urge to step backward, not wanting to fall again. "No one. In fact, I was warned against exploring the property." But no one had told her why, other than murmuring it was unsafe.

"But you didn't let that stop you, did you?" He moved closer, his voice ominously calm. "No, you barged right in with your camera to invade—" He stopped and scrubbed a hand across his face, muffling another curse. Wheeling around, he strode to a set of double doors in the front wall and threw them open. As afternoon sun lit the loft, he looked outside, one arm resting on the wall, his long, lean body a study in coiled tension.

"I'm not a photojournalist, if that's what you're thinking. Just a photographer who's interested in old houses and the people who live in them."

"Oh? Then it comes naturally for you not to have any respect for other people's privacy?"

"I repeat, I'm no reporter. But if I were, what would be the harm in giving Ashton a little recognition? It's a beautiful town."

He turned to face her, his eyes hard. "I don't give a damn about the rest of this 'beautiful town,' but you're not going to photograph so much as a tree on this property."

So. Nicholas Hawkinson owned the house, the barn, and all that went with it. Interesting. "Why not?" she asked, wondering why he was so vehemently protective of his neglected holdings.

"That's none of your business."

His militant expression reminded Meghan of herself, four years earlier, during the most abysmal point in her life. Not that the man was so transparent. To anyone else he would've appeared to be simply hostile. But—owing to her "talent for seeing beneath the surface of things," as he'd put it—she sensed he was bitterly unhappy, and hiding his unhappiness behind a deep, yet controlled, anger. Intrigued, she studied his face for clues to the man beneath the angry exterior.

Her gaze drifted across his face, obscured by bristly hair. No clues there, other than lines of exhaustion. She registered a nose that had been broken once, maybe twice, then encountered the most sensual lips she'd seen on a man, despite their tightness at the moment. Hard, yet full, tinged with a promise of gentleness. She shivered again.

"I think you'd better leave."

Meghan lifted her gaze to his. "I think you're right. But first, I'd like to know—"

"I meant leave Ashton."

She was stunned; he was serious. "Is that before sundown or after?"

"The sooner the better, since I'm sure you've collected enough shots for a magazine layout in the last week and you can't take pictures here."

Meghan didn't take kindly to the word "can't." It hadn't been in her vocabulary for the past four years. "Excuse me, Mr. Hawkinson, but what makes you think I can't take pictures of this property?"

He looked startled for a second, as if he wasn't used to having his orders questioned, then said evenly, "If I understand the law, Miss Edwards, it's advisable to get permission from the owner when you photograph property for publication."

There were loopholes in his knowledge, ones she didn't care to point out. She nodded once. "Go on."

"I'm not giving my permission."

She widened her eyes innocently. "You own the whole town?"

He was not amused. "I own this property, as you well know. And you, Miss Edwards, are trespassing."

So they were back to that again. Reluctantly she confirmed her first impression of Nicholas Hawkinson: When provoked, he could be a dangerous man. Clearly he ached to speed her on her way, preferably by tossing her through the set of double doors. But his obvious capacity for restraint told her she was safe—as long as she didn't push him any further.

She tried a different tack. "I understand how you feel. I wouldn't like it either if I found some stranger poking around my home. With a camera, no less. All I can say is, I thought the place was deserted, and couldn't resist taking a look around."

"Despite being warned against it."

She offered her most disarming smile. "I'm stubborn that way sometimes. But I am sorry for trespassing. If you'll accept my apology, maybe we can start over."

He looked at her long and hard. "You're a tempting piece of work, all right, but I'm not interested in starting anything with you."

Meghan's cheeks flamed, but she held her tongue. Stepping past him, she retrieved her camera equipment. As she hefted the bag onto her shoulder, her gaze touched on the hanging pitchfork. She pictured Nick standing under it, her hand on the rope that released it. The image soothed her bruised ego.

She turned, smiling sweetly. "Thank you for your time. If you change your mind, I'm staying—"

His dark eyes narrowed. "Good-bye."

"Of course. Good-bye." Making her way across the loft, Meghan descended the narrow wood steps into the dry, dusty garage. At the bottom of the steps, she paused. Hidden in a corner stood a half-covered motorcycle. She'd missed seeing it earlier, her attention focused on the steps to the loft. Her heart beat faster as she recalled a line from Heather's letter.

He has a Harley and takes me riding.

"He" was Hawk, the man she needed to find. The man who could answer her questions about what Meghan had believed until about a week ago to be an open-and-shut case of suicide. Despite the coroner's report and her mother's firm conviction that her eldest daughter had committed suicide, after reading Heather's letter, Meghan couldn't help but wonder if her sister's death had been an accident.

Heather had mailed the letter from Ashton the day she'd disappeared. Three days later, she'd turned up dead. But by then Meghan had been on her honeymoon in Australia, too far away to make it back in time for the funeral. Her mother had collected her mail. Then deliberately kept Heather's letter from her. Why, Meghan intended to find out . . . in Ashton.

Slowly she drew back the motorcycle's oilcloth cover and brushed away layers of grime obscuring the manufacturer's name. Her heartbeat accelerated when she saw the distinctive black and orange bar-and-shield Harley Davidson emblem that appeared.

If Nicholas Hawkinson wasn't Hawk, he sure as hell knew who was.

TWO

Heart hammering, Meghan stared at the bike, torn between returning to the loft to demand information about its owner and letting common sense rule. The man was already angry with her; approaching him now with a barrage of questions could only be a losing proposition. Her own state of mind wasn't exactly placid, either. She might have more success if she gave them both time to calm down.

Forcing herself to leave the barn, she spied a battered pickup parked on the street. The license plate read "Texas." The truck's cooling engine pinged at her accusingly. She recalled Nick's unkempt appearance, the exhaustion she'd seen in his face.

No wonder he'd been in no mood to entertain her curiosity. He'd obviously been on the road a few days.

"Damn."

Her timing had been disastrous. Meghan looked up and down the maple-and-oak-lined street, her disappointment at her latest failure to obtain information about Hawk leaving her feeling as wilted as an unwatered plant. The weatherman predicted another week of record high June temperatures for western New York. A second case of bad timing. She sighed. At least the air wasn't steaming with humidity, as it was in D.C. Just oven-hot and relentlessly dry.

The hairs on the back of her neck prickled. She knew without looking that Nick stood at the loft door, watching her. The sensation of dark eyes burning holes in her back made her want to turn around and wave out of spite, but she squelched the impulse. She couldn't antagonize the man, not when she needed his answers.

She broke into a smile, imagining the look on his face when he realized she was staying in the bungalow across the street.

The telephone rang as Meghan entered the bungalow.

"Meghan, it's Tom Saunders. I was wonderin' if you'd like to keep an old man company for dinner tonight."

She laughed. Tom, the owner of The Farmer's Market, Ashton's quaint country store, might have thirty years on her, but wasn't close to approaching "old man" status. "I'd love to. But it has to be my treat."

"Meghan . . ."

"Uh-uh, Tom. I owe you for finding me a place to stay and introducing me around town. Let's call dinner my way of saying thanks."

Several hours later, Tom, a Sherman tank of a man with silver hair, helped Meghan out of his car at the Smuggler's Wharf. When he'd picked her up, he'd asked if she had any preference, and she'd practically pounced on the chance to visit the night spot where Heather's letter had stated Hawk worked.

As they left the parking lot, Tom pointed out a yacht-, cabin-cruiser- and sailboat-filled marina, the atmosphere bustling with the camaraderie of people bringing in their boats after a busy day on Lake Ashton. They crossed a walkway over the water to the main buildings, situated on a pier large enough to hold a football field. The night spot consisted of two gray wood and glass buildings, separated by a courtyard with wood benches and potted plants. The lattice-covered courtyard formed a breezeway between the shoreline and Lake Ashton. The boardwalk surrounding the buildings teemed with people enjoying an evening stroll. Tom and Meghan approached the building on the right.

"Why two buildings?" she asked.

"Dinin' here, dancin' over there. Keeps the noise level down in the dinin' room so folks like me can eat their meals in peace. Music gets a little loud sometimes."

"Has the Smuggler's Wharf been here long?"

" 'Bout seven years. Folks around here just call it The Wharf. Half of Ashton works here or at Lakeland."

Meghan had heard of Lakeland, a resort community a few miles away, but her explorations hadn't yet taken her there. "What's that?" she asked, indicating a two-story gray duplex at the edge of the parking lot.

"Condominium sales office. Got three model apartments for Lakeland inside. Real nice. You should check 'em out sometime."

They entered the restaurant, decorated in red and gold, a spectacular sight in the sunset's soft glow. Once seated, Meghan was delighted to find the tall glass wall overlooking Lake Ashton framed the picturesque hamlet across the lake. It took her only a minute to identify the redwood deck behind her bungalow.

"There's a rumor goin' round you're not really takin' pictures for a magazine article," Tom said after the waitress had brought their drinks.

Meghan tensed. She'd told the friendly storekeeper the white lie upon her arrival in town in hopes it would enable her to unobtrusively conduct her search for Hawk. The fabrication had seemed to appease the natural curiosity of the townspeople, but now she had to live with the guilt of deceiving people she'd come to like and respect.

"What do people think I'm doing?" If her instincts were on target, the minute the Ashtonians discovered her true reason for descending on them, they'd close up tighter than clams. Incredible as it seemed, Meghan suspected a silent conspiracy to eliminate the stain of her sister's suicide from the town's past.

"They say you're gonna put those pictures you been

takin' all over town in a book. You been takin' too many for just one article in a magazine."

Meghan relaxed and smiled. "Maybe I am." Tom beamed, and she realized who was the source of the rumors. On one hand she could've cheerfully wrung his beefy neck, but on the other, he might just have saved hers. The book idea would buy her more time in Ashton if her investigation into Heather's death continued to proceed at the frustrating snail's pace it had so far.

Tom was finishing his second cup of coffee when the sun disappeared over the horizon. Meghan sipped hers and idly scanned the room, wondering if any of the employees she'd seen could be Hawk.

He's tall, dark, and unbelievably handsome.

The one person she'd seen who *might* qualify for Heather's brief, subjective description was Nick. A disquieting feeling came over her at the image of Heather and Nick together. She shrugged it off and smiled at Tom. "I met someone new today."

"Oh? Who? I didn't think there was anyone in Ashton who hadn't come to you with their two cents worth by now, not after I told them what you were takin' pictures for."

How true. But their combined two cents worth hadn't been worth that much when it came to her sister. Why did people think if they didn't talk about the suicide, it couldn't have happened?

Meghan knew better. Heather was dead. Her letter had made it hard to believe she was unhappy enough to take her own life. Quite the opposite. But until Meghan found Hawk, she couldn't be sure.

"Nicholas Hawkinson," she said.

"I heard he was back in town. Where'd you run into him?"

"In his barn this afternoon."

Tom stared. "You were in his barn?"

"His loft, to be exact."

"Meghan, that wasn't a very good idea."

Her instincts went on alert. "Why not?"

"You know how people feel about that property. It's unsafe. And Nick . . . well, he has a reputation for being . . . temperamental."

"So I noticed."

Tom's eyes narrowed. "Oh? What happened?"

"He told me to get off his property. Said he wouldn't give me permission to take pictures."

Tom leaned back in his chair and rubbed his chin. "Wonder if Benson knows he's back, yet."

"Benson?"

"Speak of the devil." Tom nodded toward the kitchen door. Meghan turned to see two well-dressed men talking with a couple seated several tables away. Father and son, without a doubt. The father, trim and gray with sharp blue eyes, wore an expensive suit and carried himself with a confidence that was hard to miss. The aura of understated power beneath his obvious charm told her that, like Nicholas Hawkinson, this was a man who expected to be obeyed without question.

The son, taller and blond, lacked his father's sense of presence, but she had to admit he wasn't hard on the eyes—despite his choice of attire. In his white slacks and shirt, navy blazer, and red handkerchief in his breast pocket, he looked every inch the wealthy weekend sailor. Not her type at all.

The older man disappeared into the kitchen, leaving his son to entertain their guests. "Donner and Coleman Benson," Tom said, as Meghan turned back to her coffee and arched an inquiring brow. "Donner owns The Wharf, Lakeland, half of Ashton, and the local newspaper." He chuckled. "Come to think of it, Cole's the one you should be sittin' here with. Good-lookin' buck. Don't hurt that he's young, rich, and single, either."

Meghan had had her fill of rich men, no matter how attractive. She'd been burned by one of the richest, her ex-husband, Carter, and had the bank account to prove it. Guilt money, she called it—and refused to touch it.

She smiled warmly. "I've got no complaints about the company I'm keeping."

Tom grinned, and waved hello to two men being seated across the room. Meghan saw the younger Benson move toward another table, smiling with cool, urbane charm. She swiveled her head to look at the now inky lake. How could she get the conversation about Nick back on track?

"Good evening, Tom," a honey-smooth voice said at her shoulder a moment later. "I hope you enjoyed your meal."

Tom looked up and smiled—a bit too brightly, Meghan thought. "The best, as usual, Cole. I'd like you to meet a newcomer to Ashton, Miss Meghan Edwards. She's from Washington, D.C. Meghan, Coleman Benson."

Startling pale ice blue eyes captured Meghan's attention. "Washington? How interesting. I'm pleased to meet you, Miss . . . Edwards, is it?"

"Yes. It's a pleasure meeting you," she responded with the grace she'd acquired as a diplomat's daughter.

Something flickered in Coleman's eyes before he turned to Tom. "Ashton had another beautiful visitor from Washington a few years back. Isn't that right, Tom?"

Tom looked stunned for a moment, then murmured, "Can't say as I recall."

Benson laughed. "Come now, Tom. Surely you can't have forgotten already. It's only been what? Five years? I believe her name was Heather something or other." He looked back at Meghan. "It certainly wasn't Edwards."

Meghan stopped breathing. This man had known Heather, and wasn't afraid to talk about her. She waited, but Tom stoically refused to continue the conversation. Coleman offered a put-upon sigh. "Tom must be getting on in years if he can't remember. After all, it isn't as if Ashton attracts a lot of big-city visitors—not like Lakeland. So, Miss Edwards, what brings *you* to Ashton?"

The lie she'd told all week came automatically. "A working vacation."

"Vacation? Then by all means, you should be staying at Lakeland. We've got everything for vacationing Washingtonians."

Like Heather? she wondered. A woman in search of

herself, using drugs to keep her company along the way? But no, Heather had put all that behind her, according to her letter. She'd planned to settle in Ashton—and marry a man named Hawk. A man who had worked for this Coleman Benson.

She offered him her best embassy party smile. "I'm sure you do, but I'm perfectly happy where I am."

"Still, Ashton must seem a bit mild compared to what you're used to," Coleman persisted amiably. "If you get bored, give me a call. I'd be happy to show you what we—and I—have to offer you on this side of the lake."

Recognizing Coleman as simply a salesman at heart, Meghan relaxed and favored him with an easier smile. "I'll keep that in mind."

He nodded in satisfaction, then addressed Tom. "Will you be staying to dance?"

"Hadn't thought of it, to tell you the truth. I hung up my dancin' shoes about twenty years ago. But if the little lady wants to give it a try, maybe we will."

"I hope you do." Coleman's pale eyes settled on Meghan again, the appreciative look in them making it clear he'd like another chance to sway her with his sales pitch. Meghan wasn't averse to letting him try, but outside of any information he might be able to provide about Heather and Hawk, she wasn't the least bit interested in Coleman Benson or his property.

Now, Nicholas Hawkinson was another matter entirely. Both the man and his house intrigued her immensely.

"Looks like you caught Cole's eye," Tom commented when Benson was out of earshot.

Meghan pulled her thoughts away from Nick and smiled dryly. "I'm not here for romance, Tom. Just a little R and R."

Meghan and Tom sat at a table in the smoke-filled dance lounge, taking a break. They'd spent the previous two hours sharing moderate-paced dances after Tom's good-natured pronouncement, "Dancin' too fast with or too close to such a pretty young thing might strain my poor old heart.''

The band eased into Johnny Rivers' "Slow Dancing." Meghan swung her foot in time to the music and spied a couple on the dance floor gazing into each other's eyes with love. A twinge of envy went through her. She'd never been in love like that, and probably never would be. Carter had seen to that.

"Tom, would you mind if I asked your date to dance?"

Meghan looked up to see Coleman Benson smiling at her. If she'd been the least bit attracted to him, his smile might have melted her. Instead, she felt mildly annoyed by it. It made her feel like a possession to be coveted.

"Go right ahead." Tom sent Meghan an I-told-you-so grin.

"Would you care to dance, Miss Edwards?"

Dismissing her annoyance, she returned Coleman's smile. Since she'd botched things with Nick, Benson was probably her best bet for information about Heather and Hawk. Although she preferred not to openly ask him about Heather for the time being, perhaps she could find out if Hawk still worked for him. If she could find Hawk, she needn't discuss Heather with anyone else.

"I'd love to. And please, call me Meghan."

"I'm Cole," he said, sweeping her onto the dance floor.

Meghan let the languorous beat, the romantic mood, the expertise of her partner, carry her through the dance. The song ended, and with a grin, Cole asked, "Shall we do it again?"

She looked over at Tom, who'd been joined by the two men she'd seen earlier in the dining room. They were engrossed in what appeared to be a friendly conversation. A waitress set three fresh beers on their table. Meghan accepted Cole's offer.

The lively dance tune was one of her favorites. She didn't stop smiling as she followed Cole's lead with little effort. Meghan was better than most at dancing. She and Carter had won countless country club dance contests before the accident. But when she could no longer walk, much less dance, he'd left her. Even so, their marriage had been over long before then. It never should've taken place, if she was honest about it. She'd been too naive to see through her mother's ambitions.

Cole and Meghan rolled along until Meghan noticed Tom canvassing the room with concern. His friends had left. "It looks like Tom's ready to leave." A trace of reluctance colored her voice. She hadn't had a chance to ask Cole about Hawk.

"I hope you enjoyed our dancing."

"I did. I haven't danced so much in ages. I've missed it. Thank you."

"My pleasure. You're an excellent dancer."

"It has more to do with my partner's skill at leading."

Cole almost preened, reminding Meghan irritatingly of Carter. A perfectionist to the core, Carter had needed a steady infusion of compliments to battle his insecurities. Pushing the memory aside, she smiled a farewell to Cole and started away.

He caught her arm. "Why don't you stay? The night's just beginning. I could take you home later."

Meghan was not a patient woman. But her accident and painstaking recovery had taught her the value of patience. She could wait to talk to Cole again. "I can't. Not tonight. I'm a girl who makes it a policy to leave with the man I came with."

"Some other time, then? Say, Thursday night? That's when the old-time rock and roll band plays." He winked and sent her a conspiratorial grin. "Something tells me you're a bona fide jitterbugger at heart."

She laughed, delighted. With Cole's invitation, she'd gained her entrée to The Wharf. "I'll be here."

Pleased with the evening's outcome, she threaded her way through the crowd to rejoin Tom. But one thought still bothered her. Why had Tom reacted so strangely to Cole's mention of Heather's name? Something odd was afoot here, and Meghan suspected it didn't bode well for her investigation. Ashton obviously wanted to keep Heather's memory buried with her. Why? Was it possible her death had been, not suicide, but an accident? Had the town closed ranks to protect whoever was to blame?

Meghan shivered at the thought, knowing how close-knit country communities operated. She'd have to step carefully or her investigation might be over before it had begun. She couldn't afford to be run out of town before she had her answers.

In two days time she'd be better prepared to ask Cole the right questions. In the meantime she wouldn't be idle. She'd work on improving neighborly relations.

Watching The Farmer's Market for the afternoon as a favor to Tom, Meghan lounged on a stool behind the cash register, a magazine in one hand and the last of a Popsicle in the other. The bell over the door jingled and she looked up with a welcoming smile on her face. Then did a double take.

It was Nick. He'd shaved and combed his hair back. The difference in him was just short of overwhelming. He still wasn't what she'd call handsome, but his aloof, almost arrogant expression held a certain indefinable appeal. Every female cell in her body screamed hello. She took advantage of the few seconds his eyes needed to adjust to the store's dim light to regain her composure, then slid off the stool. This was her chance to recover from yesterday's fiasco.

"Hi."

It was ninety-five degrees in the shade outside, but the coolness that entered Nick's eyes when he recognized her made her want to put on a sweater. "Have you changed careers since yesterday?" he asked, referring to the white shopkeeper's apron she wore over her jeans and T-shirt.

She smiled, determined to coax from him a likewise response. "No, I'm just helping out. Since Mrs. Weaver's on vacation, Tom was going to close the store while he went to Buffalo to get supplies. I convinced him he could trust me to hold the fort for a few hours."

If she'd hoped Tom's vote of confidence would soften

Nick's distrust of her, it didn't work. "And then, when he returns?"

"I'll go back to my project."

"You've decided to stay. Why?"

Meghan dropped her smile. "Let's not start that again. You'll only be disappointed."

"Tell me, how many pictures of this backwater town do you need to fill a few pages?"

"The last I heard, this was a free country." Nick opened his mouth, and Meghan held up a hand, silencing him. "Arguing won't solve anything. You've made your position clear, and I'll respect your privacy. Beyond that, you're out of luck. I'm staying." So much for winning him over.

"If you're worried I'll be a nuisance, don't be," she added. "I'm not a borrower, I don't play any musical instruments, and I don't give wild parties. I'd offer to give you references, but I'm afraid my neighbors in D.C. don't know I exist."

He released a resigned sigh, as if she'd missed the point. Undaunted, Meghan rested a hip against the counter, crossed her arms, and slanted him a sideways glance. "Maybe I should be the one to worry about noisy parties."

"Why would you think that?"

"You've been away. Naturally you'd want to catch up on what's been happening while you were gone. What better way than with a housewarming party?" She thought of his neglected farmhouse. "Or better yet, a house-fixing-up party."

"I wouldn't count on it," he said dryly.

"It's that bad, is it? Is there anything I can help with? I'm pretty handy with a hammer and nails, or a paintbrush."

When he didn't immediately decline, her hopes snowballed. But before they could gain momentum, he said, "Thank you, but I don't need your help." His voice was sharp, almost as if he were annoyed at her for offering and angry at himself for considering her offer.

"I'm beginning to get the picture. You're a loner."

"You've at least got that much right."

Meghan didn't dwell on what he thought she'd gotten wrong. "What a shame. I was hoping we could be friends."

"Then you're the one who's going to be disappointed."

Shrugging, she opted for a bit of reverse psychology. "So be it." She made a show of rearranging the candy display on the counter. Nick didn't turn away. "Is there something else I can do for you? Do you need a tour of the store?"

He shook his head as if to clear it. "I know the layout. It's changed some, but not much."

"How long have you been away?"

His look told her he'd had enough chitchat for one day.

"Sorry." She held up her hands. "Occupational hazard. For both photographers and shopkeepers." She picked up her magazine and plunged her nose into the latest issue of *Home Decorating Ideas*. "Let me know if there's something you can't find."

After reading the same paragraph six times and absorbing none of it, she looked up to find Nick hadn't moved. He was watching her with a strange, half-lost expression. She wanted to reach out to the loneliness she sensed in him, but knew he'd rebuff any attempt to do so. "Don't let me keep you."

Muttering to himself, Nick turned and strode through the store. He had no trouble finding what he was looking for. He dropped a load of groceries onto the counter and turned away in search of more. After the second load, the counter overflowed.

Using the list of taxable items Tom had left with her as a guide, Meghan began ringing up and bagging the groceries. Produce, dairy products, staples. Apparently Nick liked his meals fresh and well balanced. He was also planning to stay a few days. She tried to appear disinterested in his forays up and down the store's four aisles, but when he removed a box of instant baby food from the shelf and examined it, she dropped all pretense of discretion.

Baby Food? Something akin to disappointment rattled around in her brain as he stuffed the box under his arm and headed for the rear of the store. "Do volunteer shop-keepers work the meat counter, too?" he called over his shoulder, interrupting her moment of loss.

"We do whatever the job requires."

He paused. Meghan braced herself for a sharp come-back. He already thought her an insensitive reporter who would go to any lengths for a story.

"Then how about wrapping up a couple of steaks for me?"

Meghan smiled and chalked up another point for her neighbor. Underneath his hard exterior, Nicholas Hawkin-son was a gentleman. "Be right there." She stepped be-hind the meat counter, eyed the steaks on display, and decided they were much too skimpy for a man of Nick's size. He'd need half a dozen for a decent meal. With a flash of inspiration, she remembered Tom's special reserve.

"I think we've got what you're looking for in the back." Casting Nick a quick smile, she slipped past the curtain that led to the cooler. She returned holding two prime examples of beef as if they were trophies. "Best in the house and over an inch thick." She wrapped them and handed the package over the counter. "There you go."

He reached for the package, and his callused fingers brushed hers. Tiny sparks ignited in her fingers and danced up her arm. Startled, Meghan looked into his eyes. They were a mesmerizing deep brown, almost black, and housed an unfathomable question. She suddenly felt like a moth trapped under glass by his gaze, and thought it was a wonder half of Ashton didn't hear her heart thudding against her chest.

"How about wrapping up one of those chickens?"

Lord. How could he make asking for a dead *chicken* sound like the sexiest proposition she'd had in years? Meghan's tongue darted out to moisten her suddenly dry lips. "Sure," she croaked, and could've kicked herself. Maybe her brother, Jason, was right. She'd been too long without a man, and it was starting to show. She handed Nick the chicken wordlessly, not about to try any more playful repartee.

Someone entered the room behind her. "Meghan, I'm back," Tom called from behind the armload of boxes before setting them down. "Oh, there you are. Thanks for watching the store. I . . ."

Nick pulled his gaze from Meghan. The air suddenly crackled with tension as Meghan looked back and forth between the men. Tom's gray eyes were defensive, while Nick's hard gaze reflected . . .

Betrayal? It didn't seem possible, but there it was. Lurking in Nick's dark eyes. She'd become well acquainted with the bitter, angry emotions betrayal aroused four years earlier. Starting the night her husband had told her she was the coldest fish he'd ever taken to bed, and the complete opposite of Heather.

While she was still reeling from the shock of his drunken confession, he'd overshot a curve on the sleet-slick highway, and they'd careened over an embankment. In the space of two minutes, Meghan's heart and legs had been left paralyzed, while Carter had walked away without a scratch. Six months later, he'd walked away from their marriage, a nubile debutante on his arm.

Meghan knew betrayal when she saw it.

Had Tom betrayed Nick? How could that be? Tom was the most generous and kindhearted person she knew.

"Hello, Tom."

"Nick. Heard you were back in town."

Meghan waited for the hearty handshake she'd seen Tom offer other customers. None came. Nick apparently caught the slight. His face became as impassive as stone, yet a determined light burned in his dark eyes. Meghan was again reminded of herself after the accident, when her consuming goal had been to prove her family and faithless ex-husband wrong.

Whom did Nick feel the need to prove wrong? And why?

"For how long?" Tom asked.

Nick speared him with a look. "As long as it takes."

Tom's face flushed, then tightened, his stance becoming more rigid and defensive. "Meghan, there's some stuff by the back door that needs to be brought in. Take care of it, would you?''

What was going on? Tom looked like a grizzly preparing to defend his territory. Nick's expression was both hostile and mocking, as if challenging Tom to make the first move. He showed every sign of being willing and eager to take the older man on—and trouncing him in the process.

Prudence warred with protectiveness inside her. Tom had been good to her, introduced her around town, found her a place to stay, given her his trust. Nicholas Hawkinson had been rude, insulting, uncooperative, and ill tempered. She owed it to Tom to do as he asked, but not at the expense of seeing him hurt.

"Not until I know you won't tear each other apart," she announced, looking directly at Nick.

"What's between Tom and me is none of your business."

"Maybe not, but I doubt either of you wants to do something you'll regret."

"I don't recall anyone asking for your opinion," he snapped.

She held his gaze for a long, confrontational moment, then turned to Tom, planting her fists on her hips. "Are we going to stand here all day?"

Looking more than chagrined, Tom plowed a hand through his silver hair. "Meghan, you don't understand."

What? Now he was *defending* Nick? "You're damn right I don't. Why don't you fill me in?"

Nick exploded with profanity. "I'm leaving. Tom, next time you take on help, find someone who'll listen to you instead of sass you and stick her nose in places it doesn't belong." With a final disgusted imprecation, he strode to the cash register, tossed his baby food, steaks, and chicken into the waiting bags, threw several bills on the counter, and scooped up his groceries.

The screen door's slam echoed behind him for a full minute.

THREE

Meghan turned to find Tom regarding the front door sadly. "He hasn't changed a bit. After all this time, I'd hoped . . ." He trailed off wearily, his voice filled with regret.

"Hoped what?" Meghan prompted.

Tom smiled ruefully. "You've just seen firsthand what I tried to tell you last night—Nick's got the devil's own temper."

"Sorry, Tom. Five minutes ago, none of us were winning any awards for congeniality. What you tried to tell me last night has nothing to do with that man's temper. Now, will you please tell me what's going on around here?"

Tom's unwillingness to discuss the subject was painfully clear. Meghan hated pressing him, but she needed to know what had pushed this gentle, easygoing man to the brink of violence. "Please, Tom."

His troubled gaze drifted around the store, as if taking stock of all he owned and held dear—or all he had to lose. He sighed, then met her gaze. "I have to warn you. People would get mighty upset if they knew I was talking to an outsider about this. But with Nick back in town, it's all gonna come out sooner or later, so you might as well hear it now before things get all twisted and tangled up in gossip again.''

Meghan nodded slowly, anticipation fluttering in her breast.

"We had some trouble in Ashton about five years ago. A young woman your age, the one Cole mentioned last night, died of a drug overdose. Cocaine. It tore the town apart. Some people think she committed suicide, and some think . . ." He looked at the front door again, his expression pained. "Some think—"

"Nicholas Hawkinson is responsible for her death," Meghan finished for him in a burst of clarity.

Tom nodded grimly. "They say he gave her the overdose that killed her."

Meghan sagged against the meat counter, drew a steadying breath, and forced herself to stay calm. She couldn't believe it. She wouldn't. The man was innocent until proven guilty, wasn't he? There hadn't been a trial. There must've been a valid reason for not having one. And what about the coroner's report? It hadn't mentioned anything about the possibility of murder.

"Did he?" she heard herself ask.

Tom met her eyes steadily. "He's the only one who knows."

Meghan wanted to break into a run. She wanted to charge after Nick and demand answers to her questions before he could leave Ashton again. Instead, she braced her hands on the refrigerated counter behind her and let its numbing chill help her retain her grasp on reality.

"Do *you* believe he was responsible?" she asked.

Tom looked away. He appeared to be torn between his loyalties to some unknown force and his innate honesty. Slowly he brought his eyes back to hers. "No," he said firmly. "But I'm about the only one in town who thinks that."

"Surely there must be *someone* else."

"If there is, I never heard tell of it."

"Maybe they're simply keeping their own counsel."

Tom shook his head. "Not after Cole's dad called a

town meetin' to clear the air the day after the girl's family came to get her.'' At Meghan's confused look, he explained. ''Donner was chairman of the town council at the time. The Bensons still lived in Ashton back then. So Donner called a special meetin', and anybody who had something to say on the subject showed up. I guess he figured it might help the sheriff with his investigation if everybody told what they knew right up front.''

Meghan's heart tripped faster. ''And what did they know?''

''Not a whole hell of a lot.''

''Was Nick there?''

''No, he was still sittin' in jail.''

And unable to defend himself. Small-town justice at its finest, Meghan mused, meted out by a man who owned the local newspaper and half the town. She recalled seeing the elder Benson at The Wharf, the aura of power he so effortlessly exuded. No wonder Heather's death hadn't made a splash in any papers. Between her mother and Cole's father, they'd wrapped the story up tight and buried it along with Heather.

Her mother's motive, Meghan knew. It would create a scandal and tarnish her ambassador husband's sterling reputation if word got out his eldest daughter had died of a drug overdose, especially since a month before her death, Heather had been discharged from a drug rehabilitation clinic no one but the family knew she'd been admitted to. But why would Cole's father want to suppress such news? Probably because everyone in town knew it already, and he saw no need to leak it to outsiders. Might be bad for business on both sides of the lake.

''So what was the upshot of that meeting?'' she asked, pretty sure she already had a good idea.

''That Nick was guilty.''

''Whether the authorities found him so or not.''

Tom nodded. ''When they found out cocaine killed her, people said she had to have gotten it from Nick, 'cause everybody knew he'd had some drug troubles before, and with her living right there in the house with him—''

Meghan's jaw dropped. "She was living with Nick?" Tom looked at her sharply. "That must not have gone over too well with the townspeople," she murmured weakly. From what she'd seen of them, she didn't think they were the type to approve of one of their schoolteachers living in sin.

"Anyway, the town decided they didn't want a man like Nick running loose in Ashton anymore. When he got out of jail, they made sure he knew it."

"How?"

Tom shifted uncomfortably. "People have their ways."

"And you were forced to go along with the general consensus or risk having your business boycotted."

"Things were pretty tense there for a while."

"What happened with the sheriff's investigation? I assume they never formally charged Nick with murder." Not that it made any difference once the town had made up its mind.

"Nick had an airtight alibi. He was takin' inventory over at Lakeland in the supply warehouse the night she died."

"Nick worked for Cole?"

"Cole's dad. Worked in shipping and receiving. The work schedule showed he was alone, but that night he . . . had company."

Had Heather killed herself because Hawk was seeing someone else? Was that what he'd wanted to tell her that night he was supposed to have met her after work? The night she'd vanished? Had he broken up with her and asked her to move out?

"He used another woman as his 'airtight' alibi?"

"Hell, no. Nick didn't say nothin' one way or another. He sat there in jail for a week until she came forward and told the sheriff she'd been with Nick."

"Why did it take her so long?"

Tom put his hands in his overall pockets and looked at his shoes. "She was married. To the mayor."

"Oh." No wonder things had gotten a little tense.

"Everybody knew she and Nick had had somethin'

going before she got married. I guess . . ." He shrugged helplessly. "I really don't know the story there, either."

Meghan didn't know what to say. "Was it the same mayor you have now?" Somehow she couldn't see Nick involved in an illicit affair with the jovial but doughy-armed mother of four who ran Cookson's Bakery. Then again, this had been several years ago.

Tom grinned wryly, as if he knew her thoughts and found the idea just as humorous and improbable. "No. Sam died a couple of years back in a boating accident. Mary Lou moved to California shortly after the funeral." Sobering, he focused his attention on the street beyond the front door. "So now people just want to forget the whole thing happened."

They sank into a contemplative silence. Meghan spoke first, frowning. "There's still something I don't under-stand. If you think Nick is innocent, why were you so hostile to him? Because of his supposed affair with the mayor's wife?"

Tom shook his head. "I wasn't tryin' to be hostile. Nick's got a big chip on his shoulder, and I just reacted kinda bad to it—maybe out of guilt. What I meant to do was let him know he's got a rough road ahead of him, but I couldn't say a whole heck of a lot with you standing there. Bein' as private as he is about his business, well, he wouldn't have liked that at all."

Understanding dawned, and with it came guilt. "So you asked me to leave so you could speak to him alone."

"That, and I saw the way he was lookin' at you. You know, like he wanted to . . ." Tom colored.

Nick? And her? Together? "You can't be serious."

"Temper and all, Nick always was a heartbreaker. Since you're new in town, with no one to tell you these things . . ." He again shrugged his massive shoulders helplessly.

Meghan didn't know whether to laugh or cry. Had Nick broken Heather's previously unbreakable heart by taking up with his old flame, the mayor's wife? She had to admit the man didn't seem to do things by halves. "Thank you for the warning. But I don't think you have anything to worry about. He did order me off his property, and after what just happened, it's not likely he'll be setting out to charm me."

"I've taken such a likin' to you, Meghan. I wouldn't want to see you hurt."

She snorted. "By that man? I've got the feeling if he never sees me again, it will be too soon."

Which didn't explain why, two hours later, Meghan stood on Nicholas Hawkinson's front porch, a plate of brownies in hand as she nervously waited for him to open the door.

Maybe the bell didn't work. She hadn't heard it ring over the pounding in her heart when she'd touched her finger to the buzzer. She'd half expected it to shock some sense into her.

What was she doing on the doorstep of a man who'd made it abundantly clear she wouldn't be a welcome visitor? Getting to the bottom of her sister's death. Though he'd denied he was Hawk, the pieces fit too well. Nicholas Hawkinson had been Heather's lover. He might also have two-timed her and thrown her out of his house, providing the catalyst for Heather to slip back into her cocaine habit. Meghan didn't for a minute believe he'd actually killed her, but she wouldn't rest until she'd uncovered the truth about what had happened between them.

Meghan knocked on the door. No answer. She looked over her shoulder at Nick's pickup. Maybe he'd gone for a walk or was in the backyard. Her foot was poised over the porch steps when the door opened behind her with an eerie groan.

Banishing thoughts of ghosts and haunted houses, she turned. Nick leaned with deceptive casualness against the doorjamb on the other side of the screen door, his arms crossed. His eyes expressed what could only be described as bored detachment.

At least he wasn't stiff with hostility. She hazarded a smile and held up the plate of brownies. "I brought these over to apologize . . . for trespassing on your property yesterday, and for sticking my nose where it doesn't belong today.''

A long moment passed as he studied the plate in her hands. ''Don't tell me you're the Welcome Wagon representative in Ashton, too. For a city girl, you certainly have a flair for community involvement.''

''Are you telling me my good intentions were wasted?''

He didn't look bored anymore. If she didn't know better, she'd swear she saw amusement lurking in his eyes. ''Not at all. I like brownies. Did you make them yourself?''

''Yes.''

He eyed her speculatively from head to toe. ''Why?''

''I told you, I wanted to—''

''Haven't you figured out yet I'm the black sheep of Ashton, Miss Edwards? Maybe you should think about shopkeeping as a permanent career change. You're slipping up as a reporter.''

''I'm not a reporter. And yes, I know people consider you a troublemaker.''

''Does my bad-boy image appeal to you?''

''No.''

''Then why are you here?''

''I told you. I came to apologize.''

''Or to get me to do the same?''

Ignoring the lazy challenge in his voice, Meghan offered a cool smile. ''I hadn't thought of that. But now that you mention it . . .'' She arched a mildly expectant brow.

Several heartbeats passed before he slowly pushed the screen door open. Looking into his enigmatic eyes, Meghan saw a door was opening to her. The door to what, she had no idea, but was more than game to find out. With a nod, she stepped inside.

Nick brushed past her and started up the staircase a few feet beyond the front door. He climbed three steps, crossed a landing, and started down the other side. ''Kitchen's this way. Excuse the mess. I haven't had a chance to do much cleaning.''

The cozy kitchen was a masterpiece in aged oak. Oak cabinets, oak window frames, oak trim, oak doors, all polished to a warm patina. A *Country Living* photographer's dream and a far cry from Jason's state-of-the-art counterpart in D.C. The homey scent of lemon oil tickled her nose, and Meghan fell in love. Forgetting about the brownies, she let her gaze travel the room, absorbing each detail before meeting her reluctant host's gaze.

"It's beautiful."

He didn't smile, but his eyes glowed with proud ownership. "Glad you like it. Why don't you put those on the table?"

His low, husky voice made Meghan think of candlelight, champagne, and satin sheets. Slowly she set the brownies on an oak drop-leaf table for two in the center of the room. Get a grip, Edwards, she admonished herself. There's no room in your life for candlelight and champagne. Or satin sheets. Especially with this man. Drop off the brownies, ask your questions, and leave.

Nick turned to stir something in a pot on the stove. "What would you like to drink with them?"

Meghan stared at his broad back. An invitation? She hadn't expected that. She remembered the two gallons of milk he'd bought at the store. The thought of a man with such an unsavory reputation drinking vast quantities of something as wholesome as milk fostered a quick smile. "Milk would be nice."

He moved, and she noticed the box of instant baby food on the counter. Turning off the stove, he removed the pan from the burner. "First I have to take care of a friend of mine." He filled a plastic dime-store doll bottle, no longer than five inches, with something resembling farina, then set the bottle on the counter to cool and rinsed the pan in the sink.

Sliding into a chair, Meghan watched him go through the door to the mud room as closely as she would a magic trick, half expecting him to vanish. He returned carrying a shoe box. Placing it on the table, he eased into the chair opposite her. In one large hand he scooped up a furry little animal; with the other he reached for the small plastic bottle.

Cradling the baby squirrel in his hand, he placed the bottle's nipple in its mouth and gave a gentle squeeze. Miniature paws wrapped around the bottle's head, and the six-inch-long creature, mostly tail, claimed its dinner.

Nick looked up. "Meet Fred."

Meghan was fascinated. "Its eyes are still closed. How did you know what to feed it?"

"I didn't. He seems to like the formula."

" 'He'?"

Nick held the feasting squirrel toward her, cupped in his broad palms. "See if you can figure it out."

Meghan flushed. "It's as good a call as any."

Nick moved the squirrel closer to his stomach and gave Fred his full attention. Meghan sat back in her chair and studied Nick's profile. She was glad he'd shaved. A beard would've hidden the gentleness and strength of character in his features. He didn't look at all like the kind of man who would betray one woman with another, and a married one at that. Such cruelties were more Carter's style. She returned her gaze to the squirrel, surrounded by capable hands and long fingers. What would those fingers feel like running through her hair? Trailing across her skin?

Meghan blinked and shook her head sharply. What was she thinking? Even if Nick hadn't been unfaithful to her sister, Meghan had no intention of getting involved with him. That he'd slept with Heather was enough. She refused to make a fool out of herself a second time.

Fred grew restless. Nick settled him in his newspaper-lined box and returned the squirrel to the mud room. "Now, where were we? Ah, yes. Milk and brownies." He seemed amused.

His denim-clad hip brushed her shoulder as he reached to open a cabinet door behind her. Meghan held her breath to avoid inhaling his subtle male scent. "So, are you here to stay?"

Nick returned to the counter to fill two tumblers with

milk. "On a fact-finding mission for the good citizens of Ashton, Miss Edwards?"

"No. Why?"

He placed her glass and paper napkins on the table and took his seat. "I'm sure they'd be interested in my answer."

Impasse. They stared at each other for a moment, the brownies waiting on the table between them.

"After you," Nick said.

Meghan accepted the temporary setback, then smiled, unable to resist temptation any longer. She dug in to her brownie with alacrity, reacting to its rich sweetness as she always did, with the rapture of one enjoying a spiritual experience.

"Mmmm. Thanks for inviting me in. Once I smelled these, I was afraid I'd have to bake another batch for myself." She closed her eyes for a moment and savored the dark, moist chocolate square. "They're like that, I guess."

"What? Or should I ask who?"

She had to hand it to him, he was quick. "The people of Ashton. They like to know the who, what, when, where, and why of things. It took some getting used to. No one gives a second thought to new people in town where I come from. It'd be a full-time occupation if they did. Mind if I steal another one?"

"Go ahead." His teeth flashed white as he bit into his brownie.

"How did you meet Fred?"

"I picked him up while I was cleaning the yard. He must've fallen out of the nest in the silver maple out front."

"I can imagine the look on Herman's face if I brought home a wild, furry little creature. My orange tabby," she explained at the sudden narrowing in Nick's eyes. "He'd be thinking 'dinner.' "

"Who's watching him now?"

"My brother." And roommate. Jason had offered her a place to stay after the divorce, and they'd gotten along so well, she'd never left. Between his job and fiancée, he wasn't there half the time, anyway. She reached for another brownie, wondering if Nick lived with someone. Did he have a wife? Children? A pang of something startlingly close to envy went through her. "Did you leave any special . . . pets in Texas?" Warmth flooded her cheeks. "I noticed you have Texas plates."

"That's right, and no, I don't have any special . . . pets."

Meghan felt her flush deepen. Nick leaned forward, his napkin in hand. "You've got a moustache."

He touched a corner of her mouth. Meghan felt his hand's heat through the thin paper napkin, and her stomach somersaulted. She sat motionless as he dabbed at one side, then the other, and then, in an utterly sensual movement, drew a gentle finger across her upper, then lower, lip.

His hand left her face, and she knew regret. Her eyes met his across the table. They were dark and unreadable. Feeling awkward and off balance, Meghan crumpled her napkin. "I'd better get going. I just wanted to drop these off and apologize for my rudeness." She couldn't talk about his relationship with Heather when her insides were fluttering like this. She needed to regroup. Her chair scraped backwards as she stood, and she winced at the harsh sound.

"You didn't have to apologize. I was pretty rude myself, but . . ." His voice trailed off, and he surprised her by asking, "Would you like to see more of the house?"

She smiled, delighted. "I'd love to."

Nick's fingers whispered across her back as he ushered her through an open archway leading to the dining room. Meghan's nerve endings, already in a state of unrest, rioted. Her mind raced to outdistance her pulse. Maybe she could use the subject of his house as common ground. Would he show her his bedroom, the room where Heather had slept? If so, would she be able to ease into her questions about his relationship with Heather? Direct questioning was impossible. Nick would boot her out in a flash if he suspected her true motives.

She moved around the dining room, avoiding the cobwebs, trailing her fingers in the dust covering the table. "I can imagine how gorgeous this will be when you get it cleaned up."

Her gaze rested on a built-in china cabinet. A subtle hand-carved French country design graced the cabinet doors beneath glass-encased shelves. The hardware was antique brass. Meghan had to restrain herself from asking permission to photograph it.

"Who made that? The craftmanship is exquisite."

He seemed surprised by her remark, as if he doubted she knew anything about cabinetry and woodworking. "My father and I."

Meghan moved closer to inspect the cabinet. "You make a wonderful team."

"Made a wonderful team. He's dead."

Her pause was respectful. "I'm sorry."

"He died ten years ago, when I was twenty. He used to make furniture in a workshop in the barn."

Meghan sensed the sadness beneath the pride in his words. "What about your mother? Is she still alive?"

"No." The topic was closed.

They moved through French doors into the living room, Nick silent as a shadow behind her. Oak columns flanked an open archway to the foyer. The room's focal point was a brick hearth with an oak mantel and beveled-glass mirror above it. The furniture was covered with sheets, which were in turn covered with dust and cobwebs. Meghan offered more appreciative comments, but Nick no longer seemed to be in a receptive mood. The pauses between her comments grew lengthier, and she caught him glancing at the telephone more than once. Her tour was obviously over.

Near the fireplace she bent, ostensibly to admire the engraved iron plate that converted the hearth into a wood-burning stove. From the corner of her eye she studied her host instead.

Such a solitary man. He stood at a side window, looking into the yard, absently fingering a dust-laden drape. Meghan shivered as she remembered his gentle touch on her mouth. Straightening, she shoved fidgeting hands into her pants pockets.

"I guess I'll go now. I left the kitchen a mess. Mrs. Weaver would probably ask for damages if she could see it."

He looked over at her. "She's not there?"

"No. She's in Colorado, visiting her grandchildren."

"And you're . . . renting her house?"

"More like house-sitting."

"How did you meet her?" He moved to the center of the room, filling it with his presence. Meghan couldn't imagine him living anywhere else. This was his home. He belonged here, no matter what anyone else in Ashton thought.

"I drove into town the day before she left. I needed a place to stay, and she was looking for someone to watch the house. She works for Tom, so he introduced us. I spent the first night with her."

"I'm sure that was an experience. She probably talked your ear off."

Meghan grinned and eyed him mischievously. "Yep. Unlike other people I've met."

His face remained expressionless, but his eyes filled with a dark, disturbing glow that Meghan felt to her toes. "I never was much for talking."

Bedroom eyes. She had no other way to describe them. Zeroed in on her mouth. Meghan was suddenly glad he *hadn't* offered to show her the upstairs rooms. Tom was right. Nick was a born charmer. If he'd looked at her like that in the bedroom and touched her again . . ."

She blanked out the erotic images that came to mind. "I guessed as much," she said as he stepped in front of her, blocking her view of the room. Meghan suddenly felt very much the prey to his hunter. "But I wanted to be sure it was by choice, and not because of the way you've been received around town."

His eyes narrowed. "Is that what this visit is about?"

"No, I—"

Her shoulders bumped the mantel behind her as he advanced. "Let's get one thing straight right now, Welcome Wagon lady. I don't need your sympathy."

"I'm not offering it."

He perused her with slow, deliberate precision. "Then what *are* you offering?"

She drew a deep breath to calm her erratic heartbeat— a mistake. His gaze dropped to her breasts, which immediately responded to the attention. The smell of his woodsy cologne, mingled with the heat of his anger and the desire she saw rising in his eyes, assaulted her in a way more debilitating than any physical blow.

His anger, she could deal with; his blatant masculinity, she couldn't. She had to get out of there. "Friendship," she snapped. "Something you obviously know nothing about. So if you'll step aside, Mr. Hawkinson, I'll see myself out."

He shook his head and placed his hands on the mantel, trapping her. Meghan's heart went into overdrive. "I don't think so. This conversation isn't over yet."

Meghan lifted her chin with fast-fading courage. "In the past half hour you've spoken very little. Why the sudden change of heart?"

"Because you intrigue the hell out of me." He moved closer, his body heat warming her. "I've never met anyone who'd put up with as much crap as I've given you and come back for more. When most people would be running for cover, you dig in your heels and stay put. Half the time I feel like you're reading my mind, and, lady, I don't like that at all. So tell me, what gives?"

Meghan didn't move a muscle. She couldn't move if she'd wanted to. Her gaze fastened on his face, roughened by a five-o'clock shadow that magnified his dark appeal. "I understand what you're going through."

He didn't speak, but she caught the compelling mixture of vulnerability, yearning, and molten desire that entered his eyes. No longer afraid and feeling a deep need to comfort, she slid her hands behind his nape to pull his head down to hers.

He didn't resist. She sighed with pleasure as a low groan escaped him when their lips broke contact a moment later. His head dipped to hers again, his mouth warm and mobile. Her fingers exploring the corded tendons in his neck, she opened to him and answered his need, submerging herself in the exhilaration of man meeting woman.

His tongue touched hers, drawing her into an astonishingly deep kiss that suddenly got very hot, very fast. At the precise moment that fireworks exploded in her brain, Nick abruptly pulled back, his breathing as rough and ragged as her own. Meghan waited, staggered by the emotional fire storm he'd evoked in her. She'd never responded to a man so instantaneously before. Or enjoyed a kiss so much.

"Clever, Miss Edwards, very clever. I'm beginning to understand the secret behind your journalistic success."

Meghan drew back as if he'd slapped her. "What?"

"You don't know me from Adam, and you haven't got a clue as to what's happening here or what I'm going through. And as enjoyable as it might be, I'm not interested in tumbling some nosy, stubborn reporter who obviously isn't above sleeping with someone to get her story."

"Sleeping with someone to get her—? Now, listen here, buddy, the *last* place I want to be is in your bed, and I am not a reporter! How many times—"

"Then what the hell are you doing here?"

Vibrating with adrenaline and anger, Meghan brought her nose to within inches of his. "Trying to find out why Heather Morgan died."

A look of pure pain crossed Nick's features before they tightened in dark fury. "You scheming, conniving witch. Heather was more woman than you'll ever be, and I won't let you dredge up her ghost and smear her name across some sleazy tabloid. Don't let me hear you say her name again or so help me, I'll—"

"Do what?" Meghan exploded as floodgates of resentment at having once again come in a poor second to Heather burst open. "Get rid of me like you did her? Because I'll have to be as dead as she is before you can stop me!"

FOUR

Nick blanched. Meghan's hands flew to her mouth, too late. "Oh, God, Nick. I'm sorry. I didn't mean—"

His arms dropped to his sides. "Get out."

His voice, as cold and cutting as an arctic wind, told Meghan what she needed to know. Nicholas Hawkinson, alias Hawk, had cared for her sister deeply.

"No."

She braced herself for the inevitable eruption, but it didn't come. Instead Nick turned and ran a shaky hand through his hair, mussed minutes earlier by her own fingers. "How much do you want?"

"Pardon me?"

"Money. How much do you want to leave Ashton? I'll pay you triple whatever your fee for this assignment is to forget you ever came here."

Money? He was offering her *money*? She glared at him in contempt. It seemed the man wasn't so different from Carter, after all. "Why do you want the details of your relationship with Heather kept quiet? To protect her—or yourself?"

"Damn you! Name your price!"

The anguish in his voice seared Meghan's soul. She backed off quickly, realizing she'd made another mistake.

Swallowing hard, she met Nick's eyes and spoke quietly. "I'm sorry. But there isn't enough money in the world to make me drop this," she said, praying she wouldn't start crying. "Because I'm not here for any magazine or newspaper, or to take any photographs. I'm here . . . because Heather . . . Heather was . . ." Hot tears rose in her eyes, and she knew she couldn't tell him. Not until he admitted he was Hawk. She looked away, blinking. "She was my friend. I thought maybe you were her friend, too, and we could—"

"Could what? Trade stories and laugh together?" Nick stared at her, incredulous. "In case you haven't noticed, what happened to Heather is no laughing matter. Her death put me through five years of hell, and it's not over yet."

"Is that why you came back to Ashton?"

He straightened and scowled. "Damn straight. I grew up here. This is my home. I've got just as much right to be here as any law-abiding citizen. To walk down the street without being looked at like scum, to—"

Meghan's frustrations overflowed. "Oh, for— Will you *listen* to yourself? You practically drip belligerence and hostility!"

Nick blinked. "What's that got to do with . . . ?"

"How can you hope to convince people you're innocent if—"

"Innocent? Who says I'm innocent?"

Suddenly too tired to go on, Meghan shook her head and stared at the floor. Nick grabbed her by the arms and shook her once, hard. Her head snapped up, and sharp, almost desperate black eyes bored into hers. "I repeat, who says I'm innocent?"

"Tom."

"Did he send you here to tell me that?"

"No," she said wearily. "He has no idea I'm here. In fact, he warned me to stay away from you for a different reason."

"Which was?"

"Your charming personality."

Swearing, Nick released her and stepped back. "Give

me one good reason I should believe you, a woman who's lied to everyone in town at least once already.'' Feeling drained and defeated, Meghan remained silent. Nick started for the front door. ''Time's up, city girl. Go find someone else to welcome to town.''

His dismissal cut deeply, and she lashed out in pain. ''Dammit, Nick, you've wrapped yourself in such a hard shell of bitterness, you can't give an inch, can you? But it's that same bitterness and stubborn pride that's keeping you from seeing there are people out there who'd be willing to go to bat for you if you'd give them half a chance,'' she practically shouted, sounding more like her brother, Jason, than she realized. He'd hammered the same message into her four years earlier, after the accident.

Nick swung around. ''Including you?''

The question landed like a thrown glove between them. Meghan looked away first. ''As of five minutes ago, yes. Now I'm not so sure.''

He exhaled heavily. ''You don't pull any punches, do you?''

She had to get out of there before she broke down. She wasn't nearly as strong as Nick made her out to be, but she couldn't let him know that. It was her only defense against him.

''If you plan to stay in Ashton, you owe it to yourself to talk to Tom. That's all I have to say.'' She pushed past him to the door, which groaned as she opened it. Nick remained in the cobwebbed living room, looking bewildered. Meghan turned and saw him, and her heart went out to him. He'd lost so much. His parents, his home, his reputation . . . her sister. Suddenly she didn't want to leave without a small attempt at reconciliation.

''Needs some oil,'' she said quietly.

His eyes met hers. ''I'll take care of it.''

She knew he would. She had the feeling he'd take excellent care of anything that was his. Especially his woman. So why had Heather killed herself? It was obvious Nick had cared deeply for her. The whole business about the mayor's wife had probably been blown out of proportion. Small towns were like that when it came to sex and scandal. Then again . . . *No!* Quickly Meghan reached for the screen door latch before she said something else she had no business saying. She'd caused them both enough pain for one day.

"Meghan?"

Her heart skipped a beat. "Yes?"

Nick crossed the room. "Would you like to take pictures of the house after I've fixed a few things and cleaned it up? Not for your nonexistent assignment, but for me?"

She couldn't stop her genuinely pleased smile. She looked up at him, a mixture of gratitude and relief filling her heart. "Yes, I would."

He hesitated, then slowly reached up to trace her smile with one long finger. Heat flooded her body, and she trembled deep inside. He dropped his hand, but continued staring at her mouth. "Thanks for stopping by," he said quietly.

She tried for nonchalant. "Any time."

The telephone rang. Neither of them moved. The phone rang twice more before, with dark regret in his eyes, Nick turned to answer it. The moment he did, Meghan fled— on legs that shook like jelly. Another two seconds and she'd have been back in his arms.

Through the front window Nick watched Meghan scoot across the street as he lifted the receiver to his ear. "Hello? Jesus, Ralph, what took you so— Of course I'm alone. What did you find out? No. Not good enough. See if you can get the blueprints. Yeah, both offices . . . the apartment, too. I don't know. I'll come up with something. Okay. Call me tomorrow. Same time."

The call hadn't brought the information he'd hoped for, which left Nick with a lot of time on his hands that night. Time in which his disappointment at Meghan's departure set in like fog over the lake on a cold, damp day.

He'd never been any good at making conversation with women. He'd never had to be. There wasn't time for idle chitchat on a construction site, and the women he employed wanted to be treated like the men. Fine by him.

The women he occasionally dated weren't much on conversation, either. By design.

Heather had been his first and only female friend, a rare experience he'd cherished, and had since avoided scrupulously. Now this Meghan Edwards had volunteered for the job. Why? He peered into the beveled mirror above the fireplace. He didn't see the words "lonely man" written on his forehead.

There had to be a connection between the two women, stronger than the one Meghan claimed. Nick strained his memory, sifted through conversations he'd had with Heather. She'd once mentioned a younger sister, but she'd called her Cassie, and described her as a docile child, as different from herself in looks and temperament as night and day. Other than that, she'd said very little about her family.

Meghan Edwards was no docile child. She was a woman who knew what she wanted and didn't hesitate to go after it. If Meghan was Heather's sister, why didn't she want him to know? Why were their surnames different? Were they stepsisters? Or was Meghan using an assumed name?

Maybe she was married. He frowned. She'd had no telltale indentation or pale circle around her left ring finger to indicate the absence of a wedding band—he tended to check that sort of thing out automatically. Divorced, maybe? No, he'd called her "Miss" several times, and she hadn't corrected him.

What difference did it make? The question was, if Meghan Edwards was Heather's sister, why had she waited five years to come to Ashton? Her timing couldn't have been worse.

Still, if Meghan and Heather *were* sisters, the information might be useful. Coleman Benson wasn't blind. Once he saw Meghan, he wouldn't waste time. The similarities between the two women were too strong. Both were intelligent, classy ladies with a hell of a lot going for them.

Just the kind of woman who had little use for Benson.

Just the sort of challenge Benson enjoyed.

Maybe Meghan knew what she was doing, keeping her identity secret. She could find herself in serious trouble if the wrong people got wind of her relationship to Heather. He'd hate to see her run out of town the way he'd been, or worse. She might be an annoying complication in his life, but she didn't deserve to be hurt.

He'd have to keep an eye on her until he had this damn mess straightened out. In the meantime he'd play her game. Miss Meghan Edwards might play her cards close to the vest, but Nick held the one she was looking for.

Hawk.

Nick wasn't sure what he'd done right the night before, but he must've stumbled onto something, because at eight o'clock sharp the next morning, Meghan stood on his doorstep. He opened the door, wondering if she'd noticed its groan was gone.

She did. The smile she sent him outshone the sun. "Hi. I brought some breakfast." She held up a bag from Cookson's Bakery, and he noticed she wore loose army-surplus-type fatigues and an old, baggy T-shirt. Whoever she was, Meghan Edwards certainly wasn't picky about what she wore in public. She also looked about sixteen, and too young to have ever been married.

He decided to test his theory anyway. "If you're after my heart by way of my stomach, *Miss* Edwards, you're setting yourself up for disappointment. I haven't got one."

"Tell that to Fred."

Taken aback by her firm, unruffled response, he asked sharply, "Do I look like I'm not eating well?"

"Hardly. I've never met a man who looked so . . . healthy." A faint blush stole into her cheeks as she held out the bag. "Here. I didn't want to come empty-handed. It's croissants, so if you've already had breakfast, you can save them for lunch."

He opened the door and retrieved the bag, but decided against inviting her inside just yet. Instinct told him to play this hand slowly or Miss Meghan Edwards might soon be the one holding all the cards. She had a way of making a man do and say things he wasn't planning on without even trying.

"Listen . . . Nick," she began, and he fought a smile at her earnest expression. "I've already photographed just about everything there is to see in Ashton. I couldn't just sit across the street and wait while you get your house ready for me all by yourself. I'd like to help."

That explained her clothes. She'd come prepared to work. He smiled inwardly. This might work out after all. If he could keep her busy for an hour or two, she was sure to let something slip. After that, he'd find out what she wanted, give it to her if he could, and send her on her way. The woman might be willing and eager, but he didn't think she knew her way around a carpenter's tool kit. He wasn't about to subject either of his projects— nailing Heather's killer or restoring his beloved home—to an amateur.

"Then I'd be a fool to refuse your offer twice. Come on in and help yourself to some coffee. I've got to finish hanging one more sheet of wallpaper in the upstairs bathroom."

In the kitchen Meghan allowed her smug smile free rein. She'd done it. She was going to spend the day with Nick, and by nightfall, she'd have her answers. Beaming, she reached for the coffeepot. Three minutes later she heard a clatter, a loud thump, and a steady stream of swearing.

She ran to the foot of the stairs. "Nick? Are you okay?"

He didn't answer. She sailed up the steps, braced against the bathroom door to catch her breath, and almost laughed. Nick sat in a claw-footed bathtub sideways, his long legs hanging outside, a strip of wallpaper partially applied to the wall twisted at the middle and covering him, sticky side down. He was trying to extricate the wallpaper from his hair. The stepladder he'd been using to get the wallpaper into the corner lay on its side. Apparently he'd overreached and lost his balance. Meghan stifled her mirth. His temper was close to the boiling point.

She walked into the room and placed her hands over his. "Sit still. I'll get it." Nick reluctantly lowered his hands. Any second now she expected him to growl at her for pulling his hair, but he remained stoic as she removed the wallpaper without damaging Nick or the paper. Lord, but his hair felt good. Softer than she remembered. She could've easily spent an hour or so running her fingers through it, wallpaper paste or no.

"There. I've got it now," she murmured. Nick raked a hand through his hair, grimaced as it came away sticky with paste, and muttered another colorful comment. "Don't worry, it'll wash out. But the sooner you get to it, the better. Are you hurt?"

He scowled. "No, I'm not hurt."

Meghan smiled. Except for his pride. He took the hand she offered and pushed out of the tub. Meghan stepped back but could only go so far with the wallpaper in her free hand still half-attached to the wall. She got caught between Nick and the sink, gingerly holding the wallpaper in both hands.

For a long moment they stood in silence, only inches apart. Meghan focused on Nick's Adam's apple, which seemed to have developed a pulse all its own. She didn't dare look higher.

"You smell awfully good today, Meghan. Good enough to eat."

Her toes curled at the low, intimate note in his voice. The wallpaper crinkled in her hands. She looked away and found herself staring at an invitingly rumpled bed through a doorway across the hall.

Nick's room.

Nick and Heather's room.

An image of them together flooded her brain, and she nearly crushed Nick's last sheet of wallpaper. Looking down at her clenched hands in surprise, she recalled her reason for being there. "Why don't you let me hang this? I'm lighter than you. I can stand on the edge of the tub to reach the corner."

Without waiting for an answer, she expertly covered the

back of the wallpaper with another coat of paste and handed it to him. "Hold this while I climb up." She stepped onto the tub's rim and found her balance. "Okay, now hand me the paper."

With the professionalism of a veteran wallpaper hanger, she lined up the paper and matched the delicate pattern perfectly. She held out her hand, and Nick placed the smoothing brush in it. He settled his hands on her waist, and she nearly dropped the brush. One hand left her briefly to exchange the brush for the seam roller. A few minutes later, she finished the job, but knew the memory of Nick's firm, warm touch would linger indefinitely.

"There. It's done," she announced primly.

He released her slowly. Avoiding his eyes, she studied the small room, decorated in muted beige and rose colors. "I like it. You have excellent taste, Nick."

"I'm beginning to think so." His voice was rough and husky.

She hopped off the edge of the tub with a seemingly casual hand on his shoulder. In reality she had to restrain herself from squeezing to test its hardness. To maintain distance between them, she collected Nick's wallpapering tools—paste brush and container, smoothing brush, scissors, scam roller.

"I'll meet you downstairs when you're ready to get to work."

Nick entered the kitchen wearing a pair of faded cutoffs and a clean, pale blue T-shirt. Tanned biceps flexed as he toweled the remaining droplets of water from his hair. Meghan lowered her eyes, only to encounter his exposed legs—twin trunks of solid bone and sinew, covered with dark, curly hair.

The sight of such strong, masculine limbs, the clean smell of damp hair, soap, and woodsy cologne, gave Meghan an unwanted jolt of sexual adrenaline. She had to bite her tongue to anchor her thoughts in reality. Nick could never be hers.

"Do I have my pants on backward?"

Meghan quelled the warm flush creeping into her cheeks. "No . . . no, you managed to . . . Oh, hell." She dropped her gaze to her coffee, mortified.

Chuckling, Nick poured his own coffee. "I thought I'd get started in the living room. Move the furniture into the dining room and clean from the top down."

"What do you want me to do?"

He paused. "You're serious about this, aren't you?"

"Of course I am."

"You squeamish about cobwebs?" She dreaded them, but shook her head. "Good. There's a broom hanging inside the closet." He pointed to a door behind her with his mug.

Once they started working, Nick seemed disinclined to talk. They worked in tandem, their furniture-moving efforts punctuated by words like "Ready?" and "Got it." Grunts of exertion peppered the air as they lugged the living room's contents into the dining room. Spying an antique cathedral-style radio on a stand in the corner, Meghan asked, "Does the radio work?"

"Don't know. Haven't turned it on. Go ahead."

She tuned in a classic oldies station, then smiled as the familiar bass beat opening to the Temptations' "My Girl" wafted across the room. "I'm partial to oldies," she explained when Nick looked over at her in mild inquiry. Grabbing the broom, she headed for a cobweb-filled corner. "In fact, one of my favorite radio programs is *Solid Gold Saturday Night*."

Nick began rolling up an oriental carpet destined for a thorough cleaning. "Somehow I don't see you as a woman who spends Saturday nights at home listening to the radio. Not in a city like D.C. You must know an awful lot of people there."

Meghan glanced at him over her shoulder. Was he fishing? She couldn't tell, as his back was to her. "I do, but by the time Saturday night rolls around, I'm usually more than happy to spend a quiet evening alone with a glass of wine, a good book, and some favorite tunes." She stabbed at cobwebs with an upended broom. "Listening to the oldies revives me somehow. They play the same songs over and over each week, but at the end of a long week, it's nice to come home and settle down with something familiar.''

The silence behind her was suddenly so acute, she had to look over her shoulder again. Nick stood beside the rolled-up carpet, studying her thoughtfully.

"What?"

He seemed to give himself a mental shake, then bent and hefted the carpet onto one broad shoulder. Looking like Paul Bunyan, he scanned the room, now empty of furniture. "If you've got things under control here, I'll go out and trim the hedges."

Frowning, Meghan watched him carry the carpet away, then shrugged and turned up the radio's volume to drown out the hedge trimmer. Hours later, she was dancing and singing along with Diana Ross and the Supremes when she whirled around, bellowing the lyrics to "You Can't Hurry Love," and spotted Nick standing in the foyer watching her.

She blushed beet red. Nick smiled broadly. It was the first full-blown smile she'd seen bless his face, and it turned her insides to pure mush. "You don't just sit back and listen," he said. "You dance."

Grinning, Meghan covered her eyes with her hands in mock guilt. "My secret's been exposed. I confess. I'm a closet dancer." He laughed, and they smiled at each other for a long moment, before Meghan realized they were staring and cleared her throat. "I didn't hear you come in."

"No wonder." He nodded at the radio. Sheepishly she hustled over to lower the volume. "Ready for lunch?" he asked.

Lunch? Meghan looked at her watch. One-ten. Where had the time gone? She followed Nick into the kitchen and was startled to find two place settings ready and waiting. A bowl of cold fried chicken and another of what looked like homemade potato salad were on the table, along with her croissants and a jar of home-canned peach jam. Sliced tomatoes were on their plates. This meant Nick had heard every word of her emotion-packed rendition of the Righteous Brothers' "Soul and Inspiration" before the Supremes tune. She felt her cheeks heat up again.

Nick set a glass of iced tea next to her plate and joined her at the table. "You're quite a performer." Meghan stilled, and he arched a brow. "I meant that as a compliment."

"Thank you. My . . . sister and I used to . . . to work up routines to our favorite songs and put on shows for our friends. We liked the Motown hits especially."

"Where's your sister now?" he asked, salting his tomatoes.

Meghan was taken aback by his casual demeanor, having forgotten no one in Ashton knew she was Heather's sister. She managed to keep her voice steady. "She's dead."

"I'm sorry," he said quietly, and she knew he meant it. Guilt swept through her. If she wanted to gain Nick's trust, she had to be honest with him. But she couldn't bring herself to confide in him just yet. Their truce was still too fragile.

She changed the subject. "How about those Mets?"

FIVE

Evening found Meghan on her hands and knees, washing the last of the hardwood floor. Soothing strains of a classical guitar arrangement echoed through the empty room. Sitting back on her heels, she swiped her forehead with the back of her hand, then idly massaged a thigh, smiling. Her muscles were sore, but she welcomed the minor discomfort. There had been a time in her life when she couldn't feel anything below the waist. A time when washing a floor would have been an impossible feat for her. She felt thankful to be able to do it now.

"It looks great."

She looked up to find Nick watching her again. Her smile brightened. "Thanks." Standing, she picked up the bucket of pine-scented water. As she walked past Nick, heading for the kitchen, his hand circled her wrist.

"I'll take that," he said softly. "Why don't you go home and take a cool shower? Come back and I'll feed you one of those 'best in the house' steaks you sold me."

Meghan grinned, delighted. Her plan, somehow forgotten during the course of the day, was working. "All right, but if I'm not back in an hour, give me a buzz. I have this tendency to nod off without warning after a day like today, when I've been constantly on the move. I'd hate to miss out on a steak dinner."

Nick chuckled. "I'll see you in an hour."

When Meghan emerged from her bathroom wrapped in a fluffy towel, it was twilight. Sinking onto her bed, she released the towel and reached for the lotion she used to smooth over the network of scars covering her upper thighs and abdomen. Tracing her fingers over the myriad bumps and indentations, she recalled how they'd once been ugly, jagged crisscrosses, marking her like a topographical map.

The sight of them didn't bother her so much anymore. She'd adapted. To more than the fading scars. She'd adapted to the upheaval a few terrifying seconds had brought into her life. She'd risen above her anger and bitterness during intense months of painful therapy, both physical and mental, and regained control over both her legs and her shattered emotions.

Lying back on the bed, she let the warm breeze skittering through the room like a playful chipmunk dry the lotion's moisture from her skin. Her eyes drifted shut, and the soft sounds of a small-town summer evening filtered through the open window, lulling her into a light sleep.

An errant wind carried to her the subtle scent of a man's woodsy cologne. Her drowsy mind had no trouble conjuring up the image to match the scent. Tall, dark, and sexy. With deep brown velvet eyes smoldering with passion.

She felt his burning gaze travel over her, and her body's response. Her nerve endings ignited one by one. The weariness in her limbs faded. She saw Nick standing at the foot of the bed, staring at her hungrily. Possessively. Their eyes met, and she opened her arms. He came to her, bringing with him all the passion and promise she'd lived without these past four years.

When their lips met, hard against soft, the results were as explosive as a keg of dynamite touched by a flaming match.

Meghan awoke with a start, saw she was alone in the

room, and felt extremely silly. She also noticed she could use another shower. A cold one. Two minutes later, the telephone rang.

"Just checking to see if you're awake," Nick said, his voice oddly strained.

She looked at the clock. Her hour was up. "I'm sorry. I was . . . sidetracked. I'll need another fifteen minutes, okay?"

"No problem. I'll start the coals."

Meghan returned to Nick's to find he'd set up two lounge chairs with a small table between them on the backyard patio. The coals in the grill were almost ready. A frosty pitcher of iced tea and two tall tumblers sat invitingly on the table.

Nick emerged from the barn, and Meghan's grip tightened on the bowl of salad greens in her hands. No man had a right to look that good. He, too, had showered and changed. He'd also shaved for the second time that day.

"I hope you like salad. I think I made too much."

He grinned as if they shared a delicious secret. Meghan had the feeling he was mentally undressing her, and the territory he traversed was familiar. She found the feeling exciting.

"We'll manage." He took the bowl. "Have a seat. I'll get the steaks and pop the potatoes in the microwave."

Meghan sighed as he bounded up the steps to the mud room off the kitchen. Where did he get his energy? With a bone-deep contentment that came from putting in a hard day's work, she sank into one of the lounge chairs. She poured a glass of tea, took a long swallow, leaned her head back, and closed her eyes. When she opened them again, it was to find Nick grinning down at her.

"Would you prefer something stronger? Something to keep you awake?"

Meghan wasn't much of a drinker. She remembered Hawk wasn't either. She took another sip of tea. "No, this is perfect."

Dinner was a verbal extension of their day, spent talking about Nick's plans for renovating the house, which, to

Meghan's horror, he announced he was going to sell. As they finished their meal, he summed things up with, "So I'll probably strip the wallpaper and redo all the upstairs rooms, put new insulation in the attic, maybe finish the basement."

"After I polish the living room floor, what do you want me to do? The dining room?"

"Meghan, you're on vacation. Why would you want to spend your time working yourself to the bone on this place?"

"Simple. I can't wait to photograph it."

He gave her a mildly exasperated look. "All right. The living room and dining room are yours, but the upstairs you'll leave to me. Deal?"

"I can wallpaper and paint as well as you."

"Has anyone ever told you you're a very stubborn woman?"

She met his eyes, hers half-teasing. "Matter of fact."

Nick studied her face, then looked away and sighed resignedly. "Oh, Meghan. Do you always get what you want?"

She wasn't sure, but she sensed he was asking more than a simple question. He seemed to be battling something inside himself. She answered honestly, seriously. "Not always."

It was more than a minute before he turned back to her, his expression grave and maybe even just a little bit sad. Easing her empty plate from her lap, he placed it on the table, then sat on the edge of her chair. "What or who is eluding you this time? It's certainly not me. Not anymore."

Her pulse rate picked up. "I'm not sure what you mean."

"Think about it, Meghan," he said, his voice low and lulling. "I'm not stupid. There's a reason you're helping me, and it's not because of your work. Oh, I know you want to take those pictures. Your eyes shine when you describe a shot you'd like to take. But you want something more from me, don't you? Something that has to do with

Heather. And it's not because she was your friend. Your relationship to her runs deeper than that, doesn't it, Meghan?''

"No," she whispered, dismayed. She wasn't ready to reveal her identity yet. Not until she had her answers.

"You're lying, sweetheart." He leaned forward, lightly kissing her nose, cheeks, and forehead. "But that's all right—for now. I don't want to talk about Heather tonight, either."

His lips covered hers, and her brain ceased to function. Her senses took over instead, as Nick's warm, mobile, curious mouth traced a tickling path of kisses along her jawline to her ear. Smiling, she turned to give him better access to her neck. It felt right being here with him, sharing kisses as the end of the day, looking forward to sharing the night as well. . . .

Whoa. What was she thinking, sharing the night? That wasn't part of the plan at all. Not with this man. Not with any man, ever again. With a determined effort Meghan regained control of her languid limbs and pulled back, pushing lightly at Nick's chest. He stopped nibbling her earlobe and looked down at her questioningly.

Taking a deep breath, she plunged in. "You're right. I did come here to talk about Heather. Why did she have to die, Nick?''

She barely caught the flash of anger in his eyes before his features went completely blank. For the longest moment, absolute silence surrounded them, as if all of Ashton awaited his answer.

Then his telephone rang.

"Excuse me. I think that's the call I've been waiting for."

As he strode into the house, Meghan leaned her head back and closed her eyes in self-recrimination. What was happening to her? Heather was the reason she was spending time with Nick. The only reason. How could she have lost sight of that?

Nick's absence stretched into minutes. Needing something to do to occupy her troubled mind, Meghan collected their dirty dishes and went inside. Nick was in the living room, speaking in hushed tones. She started rinsing the dishes. His low voice filled an unintentional empty spot and she heard, "The murdering bastard doesn't know I'm here yet, but I think I've found just the right person to flush him out. I'll have to tell you about it later, though."

Meghan's hands stilled. *Murdering bastard?* Had she heard right? And what did he mean about having found "just the right person" to flush him out? Who was "him," and what exactly did Nick do for a living? With what sort of people did he associate?

She shook her head to clear the sudden dark, sinister images filling her mind. Nick, the man who'd rescued a baby squirrel, couldn't possibly be involved with the likes of murderers. The idea was ludicrous. He'd simply been using a figure of speech.

Plunging ahead with the dishes, Meghan refused to further analyze the snatch of conversation she'd overheard. It wouldn't do to have Nick think she'd been eavesdropping. She had to convince him he could trust her if they were to continue their friendship. She'd put the last bowl in the dishwasher and was wiping the sink when she heard, "You didn't have to do those."

She turned to find Nick leaning against the doorjamb, arms crossed, his eyes alight with an unreadable emotion. "I know."

"I'm sorry I took so long."

"I'm sure it couldn't be helped."

Nick seemed to have forgotten the conversation they'd started outside, and the drugging kisses that had interrupted it. He reached for the plate of brownies covered with plastic wrap. Of the dozen or so she'd left him with, three remained. A warm feeling washed over her at the thought he'd enjoyed her brownies.

"Ready for dessert?"

Meghan recalled the time he'd asked for the chicken at The Farmer's Market. His voice now carried that same low, sexy tone. She shook her head. "I think I'll pass and go home. I'm almost too tired to stand." She turned to finish wiping the counter. They could tackle the discussion about Heather in the morning, after she'd had a chance to sort out what she was going to say.

Strong hands settling on her shoulders brought her own hands to a standstill. "I appreciate what you've done, Meghan."

She stared out the window, at the barn. What did he mean? The dishes? The cleaning? Not asking about his phone call? Not pursuing the topic of Heather? All of the above?

"I didn't mind."

Nick's agile fingers slowly massaged the base of her neck. She sighed in appreciation and tilted her head from one side to the other. "That feels wonderful."

"You're going to be stiff tomorrow from cleaning cobwebs from the ceiling and washing the floor," he murmured, sliding his hands to her shoulders, continuing his gentle kneading. "You've worked so hard, the least I can do to repay you is this."

Meghan knew she should protest. Knew she should tell him she'd done nothing she wouldn't do for any friend. But her body was sending her brain a different message, her senses urging her to forget about friendship and simply lean back and enjoy Nick's soothing gentleness, his confident, masculine touch.

The dish towel slipped from her fingers as her shoulders filled with a warm lassitude beneath his work-roughened hands. She closed her eyes and gave in to the rhythmic pressure, feeling his calluses through her thin cotton shirt. Her body began to hum as she imagined his hands sliding lower, beneath her arms, and covering her swelling . . .

Her eyes flew open and she straightened. Good Lord, what was she thinking? Hadn't she sorted that one out already?

Nick's dark gaze met hers in the window's reflection. "Easy, Meghan. I'm not going to hurt you. You deserve this. You worked your fanny off today."

She took a deep breath to calm her racing heart. He was right. She did deserve this. She'd worked long and hard today. It was only her overtired, overactive imagination that had her so touchy. She'd had massages before. He wasn't doing anything strange or threatening. Exhaling, she closed her eyes and slowly relaxed, telling herself she'd leave in a few minutes.

But when she opened her eyes again, she was face-to-face with Nick. Before she realized what was happening, he loosened the pins holding up her topknot. She felt her heavy hair cascade past her shoulders and forgot to breathe as Nick threaded gentle fingers through it. His dark brown eyes captured hers, and she thought she might drown in their warm sensuality.

"Why do you put it up?" he whispered, his thumbs stroking her jawline.

"It . . . it gets in the way when I'm working."

"You're not working now."

His lips descended. Hers lifted. Strangely, as he had earlier, he seemed content to nibble at the corners of her mouth, as though he were only sipping, tasting of her. His kiss was immensely pleasurable, but not at all what she would've expected after the explosion of passion between them the night before.

It wasn't long before she wanted more. She wanted to recapture the fire, the heat, the need. She leaned into him, moaning softly when he thrust his tongue past her parted lips. His strong arms encircled her as he deepened the kiss, his large hands sliding over her hips and pulling her firmly against him.

Need took over as she wrapped her arms around his neck. It had been so long since she'd been held in a man's arms; much, much too long. She responded to Nick's increasing demands with demands of her own, drowning in the strong current of passion evoked by his mouth's velvety possession of hers, his warm, rough hands on her body.

Nick pulled away to trail fevered kisses down her neck. Meghan arched against him, reveling in the feel of his lips on her skin, his palm caressing her breast through her blouse, the hard evidence of his desire for her against her hip. At the base of her throat, he buried his face in her hair.

"Ah, Meghan, you feel so damned good. Come upstairs with me," he breathed against her skin, stroking her back with smooth, urgent caresses, pressing her tightly against his erection.

Meghan's heart dropped to her toes. She wanted to. Lord, how she wanted to. She'd never experienced such intense desire. Not even with Carter.

Carter. An unwanted image of him rose in her mind's eye. Looking at her in revulsion after the accident. Serving her with divorce papers, telling her he'd never wanted her, only Heather.

Heather.

Meghan stiffened. She couldn't make love with Nick. He'd been Heather's lover, for God's sake! The devil alone knew what else he'd done. She sure as hell didn't.

"Honey, what is it?" Nick's voice was hoarse.

"I can't do this."

Confused eyes devoured her face, asking unspoken questions. Meghan had no time to decipher them. She was too busy asking questions of her own. How could she have thought she could compete with her sister's ghost—in the bed Nick had shared with Heather? How could she have thought to compete with Heather at all? Hadn't Nick already told her she'd never be the woman Heather was?

"I mean I don't want to."

"You don't want to what?"

"Dammit, I don't want to go upstairs with you."

"Fine. Where do you want to go?"

"Home. I want to go home."

"All right. If you'd feel better—"

"*Alone.*"

Nick withdrew slowly as her meaning registered. The dark pools of desire she'd thought she could drown in earlier grew as hard as coal. "I see." His face was expressionless, his body rigid with suppressed desire. "Playing games, are we?" He shook his head, his voice rough and cutting. "Sorry, baby. I don't jump through those kinds of hoops. It just isn't worth it."

Stepping back, he opened the door. "I'm sure you know your way home."

SIX

High noon, and the heat was stifling. Meghan, seated on the sofa in her bungalow, dressed in a T-shirt and her underwear, listlessly flipped through the lastest issue of *Outdoor Photography*, trying to convince herself her mood would improve if she went out to photograph. But the heat was conspiring with her heart to keep her motivation level low.

She couldn't stop thinking about Nick. About how she'd wormed her way into his home, managed to get them both all hot and bothered, then put up almost no resistance when he'd kissed her. Hell, she'd practically lost her mind when he'd run his strong, callused hands over her body.

How could she have done something so stupid? She was a twenty-seven-year-old woman. She knew better than to play with fire like that. Nick might've let her off the hook once—in her saner moments she considered his anger almost justified, since she'd openly admitted she was there to talk about Heather—but he wouldn't do it again. Not when she knew he wanted her as much as he wanted her.

The sensible thing to do would be to steer clear of him from now on. But that was impossible. She still needed to talk to him about Heather. She sighed resignedly. Somehow she'd have to shove her personal feelings aside and see him again.

Dammit, why hadn't she done that last night? If she had, she might be on her way back to Washington by now. Now, the longer she stayed, the higher the odds of Nick kissing her again. Something intensely chemical was happening between them. It was only a matter of time before the explosion. But once the dust from the explosion settled, the fact remained that no man wanted a woman who was a failure in bed. Carter hadn't, and he'd promised to love, cherish, and honor her for the rest of her life.

The doorbell rang, interrupting her morose thoughts. Meghan sprinted to the bedroom for a skirt. Relief washed over her as she pulled the front door open to find Nick standing there. Maybe she wouldn't have to grovel her way back into his good graces after all.

He looked down. Her gaze followed his. In his large hands, hands that barely had to touch her to make her ache with need, were Mrs. Weaver's stoneware plate and salad bowl.

Quietly he cleared his throat. "Thought I'd return these."

"Oh." He hadn't come to see her, but to return the dishes. "Thank you." She retrieved the stoneware, taking care not to let their fingers touch. Nick seemed leery of the same thing. She straightened and backed away, then stilled at the look in Nick's eyes. He wanted something from her. What, she had no idea, but it didn't appear to be sexual. At least not blatantly so. Swallowing, she asked, "Would you like a glass of lemonade?"

Minutes later, they sat in identical flowered print chaise lounges, facing the lake, tall, cold glasses of lemonade in their hands. Maples shaded the deck, but didn't obscure their view of Lake Ashton and The Wharf across the water.

Nick looked over at Meghan, his gaze slowly traveling the length of her reclining body. She glanced down at her pink T-shirt and denim skirt, thought of her scars, and wondered how fast his ardor would've waned last night at the sight of them.

"How are you feeling today?" he asked.

"Fine," she lied. She'd hardly slept at all.

He leaned back and closed his eyes. His ebony hair reflected the afternoon sun peeking through the trees. The little crinkles fanning from his eyes and furrows in his brow showed in stark relief on his rugged, weary features. Nicholas Hawkinson was apparently a man with a lot on his mind. But after last night, Meghan knew she'd be the last person he'd confide in.

"Are your muscles sore?" he asked.

"Oh no. Never felt better." Another lie.

"Good. I would've felt responsible if you'd been too stiff to move today. I thought maybe that was why you didn't show up this morning."

Meghan's head came up. He'd expected her to return this morning? After the way he'd tossed her out the night before? "Somehow I thought . . . I mean . . . after the way I left . . ."

Nick's eyes opened slowly, piercing her with their directness. "It was just a pass, Meghan. Admittedly a clumsy, heavy-handed one, but a pass all the same."

Just a pass? Did all his passes include kisses that dissolved a girl's defenses and words that sliced to the bone? Meghan forced a smile and tried to look on the bright side. Nick was here; she hadn't had to go looking for him. If he was willing to forgive her for leading him on, she could damn well forgive him for his anger when she'd backed away.

"You're right. I overreacted."

He studied her face closely, but Meghan kept her smile firmly in place. She'd had lots of practice at smiling when she didn't want to.

"No. I did. When you said no, I lashed out like a frustrated male who'd spent all day lusting after a beautiful woman. But you've made it clear you aren't interested in anything more than friendship." His eyes caught hers. "I'm sorry, Meghan. I overstepped my bounds," he said quietly.

His bounds or hers? she wondered, then wondered what

difference it made. The result was the same. They'd both gone too far. "Apology accepted," she murmured.

"If I promise to behave, will you come back this afternoon?" He moved to the edge of his chaise, resting his forearms on his thighs and loosely clasping his hands. "It's too quiet working alone. Things just aren't the same without the sounds of Meghan Edwards and the Supremes filling the house." He grinned crookedly. "Besides, you're much better at cleaning than I am."

This time Meghan's smile was genuine. "I doubt that. But I'll take your attempt to butter me up for what it's worth."

"Does that mean I'll see you later this afternoon?"

She laughed. He sounded half-desperate. "Better than that. Give me ten minutes to change and I'll be over."

Nick stood, drained his glass, and set it on the railing. "I'll be working in the back. You can go right into the house when you get there."

Moghan was warmed by the wink he threw over his shoulder as he descended the steps off the deck and rounded the corner of the house. Smiling, she picked up their empty glasses. As she opened the back door, a flicker of movement in the window of the house next door caught her eye. She turned her head in time to see a dainty lace curtain fall back into place.

Interesting. Apparently Miss Abigail Peabody, formerly Ashton High's most fear-inspiring English lit teacher, now five years retired and the town's resident busybody, was keeping close tabs on her temporary neighbor.

Meghan waved to Nick, clearing debris from the edge of the yard, as she climbed the steps to the mud room. Inside, she discovered he'd been busy in her absence. From the looks of it, he'd worked the night through. The living room floor was polished to a warm patina, and the furniture had been replaced; the oriental carpet had been beaten clean, its rich reds and greens now giving the room a welcoming glow. The dining room furniture was neatly stacked just outside the French doors.

Taking a deep breath, she got busy. First she attacked the cobwebs, then washed the windows and wiped down the sills and oak trim, then washed—and this time polished—the hardwood floor.

"I knew I could count on you to work another miracle," Nick said hours later, peering through the dining room window.

"Flatterer," she returned dryly. "Are you ready to come in for a while?"

"I could be. What's up?"

"The floor's dry. I thought we could move furniture back in here."

"Don't move anything by yourself. I'll put the wheelbarrow and tools up for the night and be right in."

Meghan returned to polishing the built-in china cabinet Nick and his father had lovingly crafted, the smell of lemon oil giving her a warm feeling of tradition and domesticity. Belatedly realizing what was happening, she tried to shake it off. She couldn't afford to feel that way. She didn't belong in Ashton. She was leaving as soon as she found out what had happened to Heather, and would do well to remember that.

Maybe tonight she'd unearth some clues at The Wharf. She wouldn't have time to delve into the subject with Nick before she had to leave. A part of her still wasn't sure she wanted to know what he'd shared with her sister. After last night, the thought of Nick holding another woman in his arms bordered on painful.

Nick came in, and they moved the furniture with ease. When everything was back in place, he stood in the double doorway between the living and dining rooms and admired the results of her handiwork. "This room needs a special dinner to christen it."

Meghan looked around, smiling with pride. The room sparkled. Gleaming brass candlesticks with ivory tapers flanked a cut-crystal vase on a handmade lace doily. She'd slipped out to the overgrown rose garden in the front yard, clipped three perfect yellow roses, and arranged them in the vase. It looked as if important company were about to arrive any minute.

"You might be right," she murmured, thinking along the lines of a traditional Thanksgiving dinner.

"Unfortunately," Nick said, "I don't have any more food in the house. I don't think takeout Chinese or a delivered pizza would do the trick." He paused. "Have you been to The Wharf?"

Meghan experienced a slow, sinking feeling. "I went with Tom Tuesday night," she said, hoping that would be the end of it.

"Feel like going again?"

When she didn't respond, he pointed out quietly, "There aren't a whole lot of options in Ashton, Meghan. This isn't like Washington."

That wasn't the problem. "I don't think so, Nick."

He studied her carefully. "Are you still mad at me for last night?"

Meghan sighed. "No, I'm not mad at you."

"Then what's wrong?"

"Nothing. It's just that . . . well, I already have plans."

Her quick flush gave her away. Nick nodded and smiled slowly. "I see. Miss Edwards, is it possible you have a *date* tonight?" His smile broadened as her flush returned, deeper this time. "Anybody I know? Think he'd mind if I tagged along?"

She didn't appreciate his teasing, or the irrational guilt she felt. "Yes, I think he would." Abruptly she collected her cleaning supplies. "Now, if you'll excuse me, I have to be going or I'll be late."

Nick's amusement faded. "Who is he?"

She looked him in the eye. "Coleman Benson."

Nick didn't say a word. Meghan wished she could pick up the phone and cancel. Instead she strode into the kitchen to put her cleaning supplies away. Nick followed, poking his head in the refrigerator. She avoided him as she took her cleaning rags out to the laundry basket in the mud room. When she returned several minutes later, her composure restored, the kitchen was empty.

Having decided sneaking out the back way would be cowardly, she left the kitchen and cut across the small landing leading upstairs, determined to call out a breezy good night and exit by the front door. But as she crossed the foyer, the jingle of the oldies station she'd listened to the day before caught her attention. She looked into the living room, where Nick had settled in on the sofa next to the radio, a large, glossy magazine in his lap and a glass of chilled wine at his elbow.

Frowning, she said the first thing that came to mind. "I thought you didn't drink."

He looked up from his magazine and smiled innocently. "As a rule, no. But a glass of wine sounds good right about now." Returning his attention to the magazine, he idly flipped a page, and Meghan's frown deepened. Slowly she moved closer. The magazine looked suspiciously like the previous year's September issue of *Life*—the one she'd told him she had a six-page spread in. Scenes from rural South America. She'd accompanied Jason on a journalistic assignment and taken a few pictures of her own.

Nick flipped another page, and her suspicions were confirmed. Meghan stared. Where had he gotten ahold of *that*? The radio commercial ended, and the Ronettes' "Be My Baby" filled the air as Nick looked up again, his dark eyes beckoning.

He patted the seat next to him and smiled again. "In thirty seconds I could have a glass poured for you, too. I'd love to hear the stories behind these pictures of yours. They're great."

It was tempting. Oh, so tempting. A cozy setting, a relaxing glass of wine, the chance to have her questions answered once and for all. But she'd made a promise to Cole, and Meghan wasn't one to welsh on her promises. She knew all too well how it felt to be on the receiving end when they were broken.

"Damn you, Nick. You don't play fair."

His eyes and smile grew cold. "Not when I intend to win."

Meghan arrived at The Wharf's dance lounge after eight to find the lights still on and the band setting up. Cole sauntered into the room two minutes later, dressed like a *Miami Vice* clone in a pastel, collarless shirt, a white suit, and Italian shoes without socks.

"Meghan. I'm glad you came. Let's walk the dock. The band doesn't start until nine."

They strolled the huge pier, Cole in top form as he extolled the virtues of the Smuggler's Wharf and Lakeland. At the end of his barely disguised sales pitch, they admired the setting sun over the lake. Leaning one arm on the railing, Cole turned to her and asked, "So . . . how are you getting along in Ashton?"

Meghan smiled at the incongruous halo around Cole's blond, almost white hair. He was too smooth to be an angel. "Fine."

"Are you finding enough to do over there to keep you from dying from boredom?"

"More than enough. I'm a professional photographer. Ashton's turned out to be a photographic wonderland—from both sides of the lake. I've snapped quite a few shots of The Wharf. You have an impressive layout here."

As intended, her remark pleased him. But the quiet light of proud ownership didn't surface in his eyes as it had in Nick's when she'd praised his home. Cole's expression was mercenary.

"How about a drink in the bar?" he asked.

Cole was greeted with waves and nods as he hustled Meghan to a reserved corner table in the red and gold bar. She noted the location afforded them a clear view of anyone entering The Wharf. "You're pretty popular around here," she remarked.

He shrugged and rested his arm on the back of her chair. "Comes with the territory." A buxom waitress in ruby red hot pants materialized at his side. "What would you like to drink?"

"Mineral water, please," Meghan told the waitress, who eyed her with open hostility.

"You heard the lady, Beth. Bring me my usual." The waitress sent Meghan another withering glare before turning away.

"You have the most incredible eyes."

Meghan returned her attention to her date. "Thank you."

"I've only seen eyes like yours once before. They were so fascinating, I haven't been able to forget them."

Was he speaking of Heather? Both sisters had inherited their mother's eyes. They tilted at the corners, giving an exotic appearance Heather had played up more than Meghan did.

"So tell me about yourself, Meghan Edwards. You said you're a photographer. What's your specialty? Babies?"

Meghan groaned inwardly. She could see Cole picturing her at a shopping mall kiosk, arranging squalling toddlers into precious poses for adoring relatives. "I photograph homes. Most of my work ends up in magazines like *Better Homes and Gardens, House Beautiful, Country Living*."

"How commendable." Cole raised his hand to acknowledge yet another person.

Despite his obvious disinterest, Meghan continued. "I've found some interesting homes in Ashton. One house in particular intrigues me. It's near where I'm staying. Tom said you used to live in Ashton, so you might know something about the family who owns it. The Hawkinsons?"

The icy look in Cole's eyes when he turned back to her sent a shiver down Meghan's spine. "I remember it. I can't say I agree with you about its photogenic qualities. It must be a crumbling mess by now, overgrown with weeds."

He apparently hadn't heard about its recent occupancy or improved appearance. "It is, or rather—"

"Damned eyesore should've been razed a long time ago."

His vehemence stunned her. "What about its historic value? The house must be at least half a century old."

"That house hasn't got any value, historic or otherwise." He glanced at his watch. "The band should be warmed up by now. Let's go."

They sat at another reserved table in the lounge and ordered more drinks. Cole was downing Chivas Regal doubles at an alarming rate. The band launched into "Rock Around the Clock," and he reached for Meghan's hand. "Ready to rock and roll?"

They didn't sit for the entire first set. Meghan's cheeks were warm and flushed and her eyes sparkling as they wound their way back to Cole's table. "Whew. That was great. Where did you learn to dance like that?"

He seemed distracted. "On-the-job training. Listen, if you'll excuse me for a few minutes, I've got a couple of things to see to. Can I bring you something from the bar when I return?"

"A tall mineral water would be nice." At his frown, she said, "I don't drink when I drive."

"I could take you home."

She thought of his Chivas doubles. Not for anything would she get into a car with another drunk driver. "Nah. But thanks." She smiled to soften her refusal.

Cole didn't return in the few minutes he'd said he would. Meghan, grateful he'd sent her drink over with a waitress before he'd left the lounge, sat back to watch the dancers just as a man with the dark, fading looks of a former football star slid into the seat next to her.

"Hiya, missy. Looks like Cole got tied up." He shook his head. "Too bad. That's some kinda dancing you two've been doing out there. He's gonna need a new dance floor if you keep it up."

"I'll take that as a compliment, Mr. . . . ?"

"Call me Ralph. Honey, would you bring me and the lady another round?" he called to a passing waitress, waving his beer mug in the air. "Name your poison," he said to Meghan.

"Mineral water, please." She handed the waitress her glass.

The man turned to face her again, almost overwhelming

Meghan with the smell of beer. "Yep, he sure can pick 'em. I haven't seen anything as pretty as you since . . ." He drifted away, then hiccuped and leaned closer, peering into her face. Meghan pulled back instinctively. "My cousin was right. You do look a little like her, especially around the eyes."

"Your cousin? Cole?"

"Hell, no. Cole and I aren't related." Ralph scrutinized her again. "But damned if you don't look like you could be kin to—"

The waitress returned with their drinks.

"You were saying?" Meghan prompted when they were alone again.

"Forget it." Ralph looked out over the dance floor, where couples began slowly swaying in time to "Unchained Melody." "There's no point anyway." He lapsed into a long, moody silence, growing more and more distant as the music swelled around them. "She loved this song," he said to no one in particular, still watching the dancers. "Loved to dance to it, slow and close."

Meghan stared at him, knowing instinctively he was talking about Heather. Heather had loved the Righteous Brothers; anyone who knew her would've discovered that right away, especially in a place like this. But by the end of the song, it was clear to Meghan this man had known her sister beyond acquaintanceship. He acted like a man grieving over the loss of the woman he'd loved. Before she could recover her voice, Cole reappeared.

"Nice of you to keep the lady company for me, Ralph, but I've returned, so you can go back to whatever bottle you crawled out of."

Ralph blinked up at Cole. "What? Oh. Sure, Cole." He got up to leave, seemingly unaware of Cole's insult.

"Tell Ron to send me your tab."

"Uh, yeah," Ralph mumbled. "Thanks, Cole." He swayed across the room.

"I'm sorry about that. I didn't expect to be gone so long. Business," Cole ended, as if that explained everything. But from what Meghan had seen, Coleman Benson had very little to do with the running of The Wharf. His father's holdings seemed more his private playground.

"It's okay. We were having an interesting conversation," she murmured. "In fact, he made a comment similar to yours about my eyes."

"I'm surprised he could see them, he's so drunk."

"Why do you encourage him?"

Cole shrugged. "He works for me. Picking up his tab lets me keep my eye on him. He started drinking a few years ago, but it usually doesn't get this bad. Something must've set him off tonight. Are you ready for more dancing?"

Meghan wasn't. She wanted to ask Cole about Heather, but conversation was impossible with the band now in full swing. So she bided her time and let Cole guide her onto the dance floor. She was so adept at following his lead, she was able to replay her conversation with Ralph while Cole twisted and turned her through a lively jitterbug.

Ralph must've met Heather while working for Cole. But her letter had mentioned only two men. The first Meghan had identified as Nick, the second as Cole. The maudlin alcoholic didn't fit into the picture.

Cole swung her into a deep dip, and Meghan realized they were providing a floor show. The song ended and Cole bent over her, claiming her lips in a congratulatory kiss. Their audience cheered and clapped in earnest. Flushing in embarrassment, Meghan looked around the room as Cole brought her upright.

A lone man leaned against the far wall near an exit, the sole holdout in the applauding crowd. She couldn't make out more than his shape from across the room, but it seemed familiar.

Nick? A hot rush ran through her from head to toe.

Cole chose that moment to ostentatiously bow to her, drawing her attention away from the man behind him. Feeling silly, Meghan waited for her partner to finish. When she again looked at the far wall, the mysterious man was gone, leaving her to wonder if she'd simply been doing a bit of wishful thinking.

*　*　*

Outside, on the dock, Ralph joined his cousin.

"Jesus, you stink," Nick said as they reached the breezeway.

"I know. I've got more beer on me than in me." Ralph grinned. "Your lady friend wasn't too impressed with me either, but at least she had enough manners not to tell me I smell."

"So you met her."

"Yep. And she met Ralph the Lush."

"What did you think?"

"She's gorgeous, sharp as a whip, and moves like a dream. Cole's half-hooked already. Those eyes, Nick, they're incredible. Where the hell did you find her?"

Nick chuckled. He'd told Ralph as little as possible about Meghan so far, wanting him to see her first and form his own opinion as to whether she could be of any use to them. Apparently his cousin's assessment agreed with his own. "She found me."

"Get back. The woman's got more class than you know what to do with. What's her name?"

"Meghan Edwards. Ring any bells?"

"Not a one. Should it?"

Nick hesitated, knowing his next words would cause his friend pain. "I'm pretty sure she's Heather's sister."

Ralph was silent a moment. "Then it's no coincidence she managed to find you." He looked at his cousin, then out over the water. "Is there a reason they don't have the same last name?"

"I suppose they could've been stepsisters, maybe half-sisters." Nick paused. "She also thinks I'm you."

Ralph's head came around. "Run that by me again?"

"She thinks I'm Hawk."

"What gave her that idea?"

"Hell if I know. But don't spill the beans yet, okay?"

Ralph eyed Nick speculatively. "Sure, but what difference does it make?"

Nick looked away, toward the dance lounge. What difference *would* it make? None, other than he wanted to hold Meghan's interest a little longer. Instinct told him she spent time with him because she thought he was Hawk, and once she discovered otherwise, she'd scoot right out of his life. "None, I guess."

"Something tells me there's something going on around here."

Nick shook his head. "Nothing I can't handle."

Ralph looked as if he was about to pursue the subject, but the set of Nick's jaw apparently changed his mind. Instead, he said, "You said on the phone you think she might be able to help us by flushing out Cole."

"No. I've changed my mind about that. All I want from her now is to keep him distracted. I don't want her hurt."

Ralph nodded slowly, studying his cousin carefully. "I see what you mean. If it turns out this woman *is* Heather's sister, and Cole finds out, he's gonna go friggin'—"

"Stow it. Company's coming."

Cole and Meghan had rounded a corner of the dock and were strolling toward Nick and Ralph. Cole was talking. Meghan appeared to be hanging on to his every word. The cousins melted into the shadows on opposite sides of the courtyard.

Cole and Meghan stopped at the railing where Nick and Ralph had stood, no doubt to enjoy the cool air blowing through the breezeway. They talked quietly for a few moments before Cole slowly drew her into his arms. After a kiss that lasted far too long for Nick's taste, Cole whispered something in Meghan's ear, chuckled at her response, then led her away with a possessive arm draped around her shoulders.

"Lucky man," Ralph murmured, his eyes on his cousin's stiff back.

"Not if I have anything to say about it," Nick growled, starting after them.

Ralph scrambled after him and grabbed his arm. "Whoa there, boy. Didn't you just say you wanted the lovely Miss Edwards to distract Cole? Well, it looks to me like she's doing a hell of a job. It also looks to me like she's an adult, and fully capable of making her own decisions on who

she spends her time with." He nudged Nick into the courtyard and toward the parking lot. "So why don't we stick
to the game plan? Those blueprints you asked for are at
my place, and my car's *this* way."

At Ralph's, Nick and his cousin had studied the blueprints to Cole's apartment and two offices: one at Lakeland, one in the town house duplex. Now, as midnight
neared, Nick stood in the shadows outside the condominium sales office, tempted to throw caution to the wind.
The blueprints had shown the duplex had a standard floor
plan. It would be incredibly easy to slip inside through a
back window and look for the information he needed.

But he wouldn't do that until he knew where Cole was.
He'd spent the last fifteen minutes scouting the bar and
the dance lounge, but hadn't seen Cole. Or Meghan. That
bothered him more than he cared to admit.

A soft light came on in an upstairs window of the duplex. One of the bedrooms, Nick recalled from the blueprints. Through the lightweight curtain, he saw two
shadows moving in the room.

Bingo.

He settled back against a large oak tree to wait, a slow
boil starting in his blood. Minutes later, the front door
opened and his nemesis appeared. A pair of slim arms
wrapped around Cole's neck. The sound of a woman's
low voice filled Nick's ears and made him grit his teeth.
Cole allowed her to draw him partially inside the town
house for a long moment. Nick's hands curled into fists
as he ached to yank the kissing couple apart and beat Cole
to a bloody pulp.

Cole ended the kiss and pulled away from the woman.
She obviously didn't want him to leave. He said something
to her, was rewarded by soft, musical laughter, then kissed
her again and sauntered away from the duplex, looking
supremely satisfied with himself.

Anger and a masochistic streak he hadn't known he
possessed compelled Nick to stay where he was, beneath
the shadow of the oak tree, waiting. It wasn't long before

the duplex's front door opened. Every muscle in his body tightened as he braced himself for the sight of her, tousled and flushed by Cole's lovemaking.

A full five seconds passed before his fury faded enough for him to realize the woman wasn't Meghan. The short, buxom brunette in a ridiculous hot pants outfit who languidly made her way back to The Wharf in no manner, shape, or form resembled the woman Nick had assumed was with Cole.

He turned back toward the town house, amazed at the relief surging through him. It took him several minutes to corral his emotions and realize the opportunity he'd waited for was staring him in the face. After scouting the area again to make sure there were no witnesses, he entered the duplex through the back window as planned.

His visit was short and fruitless. It didn't help that thoughts of a certain blond, brown-eyed dancer kept filtering into his mind, distracting him from his mission. Half an hour later, empty-handed, Nick strode onto the pier where he'd left his boat, cast off, and slipped away from the dock. Standing at the helm of his twenty-seven-foot ketch, he lifted his frustrated gaze to Ashton and spotted the speck of light across the water that—had he thought to look for it earlier—would have saved him a ton of aggravation.

A moment later, Mrs. Weaver's bungalow went dark.

SEVEN

Meghan arrived at Nick's midmorning. She rang the bell twice. No answer. Peering through the front windows, she didn't see any movement inside. Maybe he was in the barn or feeding Fred.

In the mud room she saw Fred was alone. His eyes had opened the day before and he peered up at her curiously, nose twitching. She smiled and lightly ran a finger over his fur. "Hey, little fella, where's your housemate?"

He scurried to a corner of his box and burrowed under a pile of newspaper strips. Laughing, Meghan looked through the kitchen window and spied Nick coming through the door from the foyer. Her heart did a somersault against her ribs. He looked like he'd just gotten out of bed. Rumpled and sexy.

She tapped on the window. He looked her way, a less than welcoming expression on his stubbled face. "Good morning," she said cheerfully as he opened the door.

"What's so good about it?"

"Oooh. A bit grouchy this morning, are we? I'm sorry if I woke you. It was me at the front door."

"Persistent, aren't you?"

Something was wrong. According to his body language, Nick was barring her from entering his home. Did he have company? Another woman? An invisible vise squeezed her heart. "I can come back later," she said carefully.

"What for?"

"Well . . . I thought I could help with—"

"I don't need help with the rest of the house, Meghan. I already told you that."

"Yesterday you seemed to think I was pretty handy to have around."

"You were."

"But you can manage by yourself from here on out."

"You got it."

She couldn't mistake the tone of his voice. For some reason, he'd reerected the barriers between them. "All right," she said slowly. "I'll still be around for a while. When you finish the house, give me a call and I'll take those pictures you wanted."

"I've changed my mind about the pictures."

"I see. Any special reason?"

"No."

He might as well have shut the door in her face. To hide her pain, she turned away, and saw Fred had come out of hiding in response to Nick's voice. She approached his box, her anger building. "Take my advice, Fred. Don't do the tall guy any favors. He's got an incredibly short memory and he's not big on appreciation, either."

"Meghan . . ."

Nick's protest became a low groan of misery as the slam of the back door reverberated in his throbbing head. He was paying for the half a fifth of Jim Beam he'd consumed the night before—in spades. On top of his world-class headache, his mouth felt like the National Guard had marched through it.

By the time he'd docked his sailboat in Ashton the night before, he'd been so frustrated and confused, he'd broken out the bourbon in an effort to clear his head. A few stiff shots later, his brain had begun to work overtime and he'd come to some startling conclusions about the intensity of his feelings for one Miss Meghan Edwards.

He'd gotten as far as her front door before he'd realized

the insanity of what he wanted to do. No woman appreciated a drunken lunatic who wanted to stake his claim on her body pounding on her door at four in the morning.

His near-miss had been enough to send him back to the bottle. He'd felt no pain when he'd stumbled to bed as dawn broke over the lake. But now he felt as if he'd spent the night in hell.

Damn the woman! Did she have to slam the door so hard?

"Damned ingrate!"

Meghan stormed through the bungalow, collecting her photography paraphernalia. Obviously Nick's invitation to dinner had been a one-time-only offer. Take it or leave it. She'd left it, and now he'd decided to wash his hands of her.

She looked around the room to make sure she hadn't forgotten anything, and reached for the telephone. Within minutes she was roaring down the highway toward Buffalo. A friend of Jason's had offered to let her use his darkroom during her stay in Ashton.

She returned late that evening with a portfolio full of prints. As soon as she flipped the light switch, she knew something was wrong. Someone had been in the house while she was gone.

Nothing was askew, yet things weren't as she'd left them. She'd left the drapes drawn to keep the house cool, and now they were open six inches. The throw pillows on the couch were no longer precisely centered. It looked as if someone had shoved them aside to sit on the couch and peer out the window and wait.

For her? Good God, were they still in the house?

From the stand next to the door she withdrew an umbrella, one with a hooked handle and a long metal point at the end. The umbrella clenched in her hand, she slowly searched the bungalow, her heart pounding with each cautious step.

She needn't have worried. No one was hiding in the house. Nothing was missing. The only indications that she'd had company were the bedroom closet door, open when she'd left but now closed, and the toe of a pair of panty hose dangling from a shut drawer. She hadn't worn panty hose since she'd arrived in Ashton. It'd been too damn hot.

Someone had rifled through her things but had been careful in doing so. Who? Why? What were they looking for? Had someone discovered she was Heather's sister? Or did they merely suspect her motive for coming to Ashton? Had they canvassed her bungalow hoping to find out who she was and what she was doing there? Having failed, would they come back?

Maybe she should call the police. But what would she say? Someone broke into the house and searched my underwear drawer? Nothing was stolen or vandalized. She checked the door and window locks. None were jimmied, but the window above the kitchen sink was open. No sign of illegal entry showed, unless she counted the dry dirt clod on the floor.

Returning to the bedroom, she propped the umbrella next to her bed and decided going to the police would be about as effective as taking an ad out in the local paper. Wanted: the person who searched my house on Friday. She'd only draw attention to herself. She couldn't risk it.

She'd have to consider the break-in a warning. Someone in town was on to her, or thought they were. After making sure she was locked in, she unpacked the "chicken special" dinner she'd picked up at Kelly's Diner and sat at the kitchen table sorting through the photographs while she ate. Hours later, well after midnight, she headed for bed. On her way she peered past the front curtain. Nick's house was dark, as it'd been all evening.

Despite his rejection, she'd thought about him constantly today, wishing for his comforting presence nearby while she worked, his occasional smile, his rich, deep voice interrupting her thoughts, the sight of his wonderful brown velvet eyes. . . .

How cold those eyes had been this morning. He'd barely been civil. *Why? What had she done?* Did it have something to do with Cole? *Had* Nick been the man she'd seen leaning against the wall last night? If so, what possible difference could her impromptu floor show with Cole have made to him?

Or had he seen Cole kissing her on the dock? She laughed outright at the idea of Nicholas Hawkinson jealous of Coleman Benson. There was no contest between the two. Cole's kiss had been experienced, long, and unsatisfying. She'd let it linger as an experiment. The result? For all his experience, the man had no effect on her.

She hadn't understood it. One look from a man she'd thought *might* be Nick from across a crowded room and she went hot all over. An evening of physical contact with Cole and . . . nothing.

By the time she'd turned out the light and gone to bed last night, she'd come to a simple and frightening conclusion. She wanted more from Nicholas Hawkinson than information about Heather. She wanted to know all there was to know about him.

Saturday was another scorcher. Meghan spent the morning in town beefing up her alibi by passing out photos. In the afternoon she rented a sailboat from The Wharf and spent a few hours on Lake Ashton to escape the heat.

It took a while, but eventually she remembered what she'd learned in the sailing lessons her socially correct mother had insisted all her children take. After dinner at Kelly's—this time she ate in and spent a pleasant hour or so chatting with the locals—she returned to her bungalow.

Darkness settled, and once again, no light came on at Nick's. His truck was gone. By ten o'clock Meghan couldn't stand the watching and waiting any longer. Striding into the bedroom, she pulled out her dancing shoes.

"Meghan!" Cole called from the bar in The Wharf's smoky dance lounge. "Over here!" She spotted him near the bar and began wending her way through the thick Saturday night crowd. He met her midway, taking her arm and shepherding her to his table. "Good to see you again," he said, smiling. "I heard you rented one of our boats today." His eyes traveled over her red and white strapless sundress appreciatively. "I see you came through the experience without mishap."

"Oh?" she shouted over the band. "Are your boats known for getting the best of their passengers?"

His grip on her arm tightened almost painfully for a second before he laughed and released her to pull out her chair. "No, nothing like that. But if you plan to sail again, I'll have one of the better boats set aside for your use. Just give the person at the rental booth your name and they'll take care of you."

"I may take you up on that. Thank you," she said as he seated her and called over a waitress.

"Think nothing of it." He glanced past her shoulder and nodded impatiently at someone behind her. "Listen, I didn't know you were coming or I'd have changed my plans. I've got some business to take care of this evening, so I'll be in and out. But you're welcome to use my table."

"Thank you, but really, I didn't expect you to entertain me. I just wanted to get out of the house."

"Ashton's finally getting to you, huh?" Cole's brief smile was smug. "Glad to hear it. Save me a dance or two."

Watching him leave the room, Meghan wondered if she might be better off shifting the focus of her investigation to Cole. His kisses might not appeal to her, but at least he didn't run hot and cold on her like Nick.

Nick. Why couldn't she get the man out of her mind?

"Hello, Meghan."

Her heart dipped at the familiar deep timbre in the man's voice. But when she turned around, she saw not Nick, but Ralph smiling down at her. He didn't appear to be as far gone as he'd been the last time she'd seen him. "Have a seat, Ralph," she invited. "I'm using Cole's table for the night."

"I wondered about that. I didn't think he'd ask you out

on a Saturday night. Friday and Saturday nights he usually takes care of his . . . business.''

Yes, Ralph seemed much more lucid tonight. Maybe this was her chance to ask *him* a few questions about Heather. ''I'm sorry we didn't get to talk longer the other night.''

''Yeah. Cole's like that. He likes to keep all the beautiful women to himself.''

''Well, tonight I'm on my own. Did you bring someone?''

''Me?'' He gave a snort. ''Who'd want an ugly mug like me?''

''I don't think you're ugly, Ralph.'' She scanned the room. Saturday night was most definitely meat market night. ''Maybe if you didn't spend so much time in here, though, you'd meet someone who'd be good for you.''

He smiled sadly. ''I met a woman like that once. It didn't work out.''

''I'm sorry to hear that.''

''Wanna dance?''

Between dances, they returned to the table to watch the other dancers and exchange small talk. When Cole returned, Ralph excused himself with a ''See ya later, Meghan,'' and slipped away with more unsteadiness than he'd exhibited all evening.

Cole's stay was brief. Afterward, Meghan went for a walk on the pier to escape the smoke and noise. She was leaning her forearms on the railing, missing Nick and studying the moonbeams dancing across the inky, rippling water, when Ralph appeared at her side.

She had the oddest feeling he'd been appointed her bodyguard. ''Did he ask you to keep an eye on me?'' she asked, still looking out over the lake.

''Who? Cole?''

She faced him. ''Who else would think I need a watchdog?''

He shrugged. ''You mind?''

She smiled in friendship. ''No. I enjoy your company.''

He smiled back. ''I aim to please.''

Meghan settled against the railing, her hands braced on

either side of her. "Then would you tell me more about the girl you mentioned the other night? The one my eyes reminded you of?"

He studied her thoughtfully, then looked around as if to make sure they were alone. "I guess it couldn't hurt to talk to you about it. After all, you're . . . new in town."

Meghan hid a frown at his odd reasoning while Ralph looked away, as if pulling his thoughts together. Finally he met her eyes. "Five years ago this woman came to Ashton. Her name was Heather Morgan." He paused, as if waiting for a reaction, but Meghan kept her face a mask of mild interest. Frowning, he continued. "Newcomers in Ashton attract attention, especially if they plan to stay, like she did. She would've been the new English lit teacher at the high school. Prettiest girl you ever saw—dark hair, incredible smile, and a figure that was . . ."

He smiled sheepishly. "Sorry, forgot who I was talking to."

She sent him a reassuring look. Obviously Heather had charmed Ralph as well as Cole and Nick. Par for the course. "That's okay. How did you meet her?"

"She was staying with . . . a family across the lake. She'd come over here every now and then, like you. She caught Cole's eye, and he went after her like he'd never gone after a woman before." He braced his fists on the railing beside Meghan and focused his attention on the lake. "Cole's never had to chase a woman. With his money and looks, they flock to him." He drew a deep breath. "But this one didn't want anything to do with him. That's what made her so different."

Ralph paused, and for the longest time said nothing. Finally he shook his head. "Anyway, not much later, she turned up dead." He looked at Meghan, his haunted eyes searching hers. "Even though it was ruled a suicide, nobody could understand why she'd do a thing like that. She had so much going for her."

Meghan strove to remain politely detached. "Does anyone know for certain it *was* suicide?" She couldn't shake the idea Heather's death had been accidental. Given her history of drug use, she had to have known her limits. Perhaps she'd been upset and misjudged the dose that final time.

Ralph hesitated again, making Meghan uneasy, but she held her tongue, not wanting to say anything to sway his opinion—or prevent him from answering. When he spoke, his voice was dull and flat.

"The dead don't talk."

She exhaled slowly, forcing disappointment from her face. Ralph's eyes narrowed, a clear warning in them. "Nothing like that ever happened in Ashton before, and we sure as hell don't want it to happen again."

Meghan shivered. He knew who she was. Somehow he knew. Was Ralph the person who'd searched her bungalow? Had he played a part in Heather's death? Or was he protecting someone? Cole? Himself? Nick? No, not Nick. Nick was innocent. He had to be.

Ralph took her arm. "We'd better go back inside. You're getting chilled."

Within minutes of their return, Cole reappeared. Ralph again made his slurred excuses and left Meghan wondering why he'd been coherent when alone with her, yet acted the lush when others were nearby. What other subterfuge was he involved in?

She yawned delicately and told Cole she was ready to call it a night. Thankfully, he kept his good-night kiss at her car to a tolerable minimum. Pulling away, he asked, "Would you like to go out on my yacht tomorrow?"

She accepted the invitation, eager not for his company, but for the chance to learn more about his pursuit of Heather. Far from warning her off, Ralph's subversive attitude had renewed her determination to get to the bottom of her sister's death.

"Good. Meet me in front of the sales office around noon. I'll give you a tour of Lakeland before we go out for a spin."

Fifteen minutes later, Meghan fell into bed exhausted, but too wired to sleep. Had Heather committed suicide, or had it been an accidental overdose? Or, God forbid, had she been killed? The prospect of murder chilled Meghan to the bone, but it was time she forced herself to examine the option rationally.

First she needed suspects. It hurt to think Nick might've been involved in Heather's death, but logic forced her to consider all three men who'd fallen under her spell. Nick, the charming lover with a shady past and a possible girl on the side; Cole, the ardent but thwarted pursuer; Ralph, the adoring admirer. Or had more than admiration passed between them?

The night stretched on while she formulated and discarded several theories, each seeming more absurd than the previous one. In the end she gave up. Heather couldn't possibly have been murdered. For murder there had to be a motive. Try as she might, Meghan couldn't think of one. But when her eyelids finally drifted shut, Ralph's words returned to play through her mind like a broken record.

The dead don't talk.

Cole went after her like he'd never gone after a woman before.

She didn't want anything to do with him.

Anyway, not much later, she turns up dead.

Nothing like that ever happened in Ashton before, and we sure as hell don't want it to happen again.

The dead don't talk.

The dead don't talk.

EIGHT

Meghan readjusted the sunglasses hiding her tired eyes and sighed. Everywhere she looked, people were wide-awake, reveling in the glory of a sunny summer day. And rightly so. They hadn't endured a hellish night in which thoughts of murder reigned supreme.

To top it off, strange, garbled images of Carter, Heather, Cole, Ralph, Nick, and a faceless man dressed in cat-burglar black had intruded on her dreams. She'd reached for the umbrella beside her bed at least three times.

Cole emerged from The Wharf carrying a red cooler, looking boyish and energetic in white shorts and a navy blue Izod shirt. Meghan smiled and returned his wave. He caught her arm as he breezed by, pulling her toward the duplex's garage.

"Come on, my car's this way."

Meghan nearly groaned in dismay as the overhead door opened to reveal a baby blue Porsche nestled inside. She'd made a point of avoiding fast cars since her accident. Smiling proudly, Cole ushered her into the gleaming sports car. "It's a great day to be out on the water. Did you bring your swimsuit?"

"Right here." She patted the canvas tote bag in her lap

nervously, remembering another offbeat idea she'd come up with last night while her mind had been working overtime.

He briefly squeezed her thigh and sent her a seductive look that had no doubt sent many a heart fluttering out of control. "Good." As he sped with reckless abandon toward Lakeland, Meghan surreptitiously practiced deep breathing techniques. Her hopes that Cole would drive with less antagonistic zeal than her ex-husband had been dashed before they left the parking lot.

As they zoomed over a rise above a small valley, she spotted four condominiums, surrounded by immaculately kept grounds. An Olympic-size pool, filled with frolicking people, shimmered in the heat, its decking dotted with assorted shades of sun worshipers. Next to it was a circle of sand and a volleyball net where a spirited game progressed.

Eight outdoor tennis courts boasted players dressed in unrelieved white hammering balls across the net. Cole pointed out a large domed building at the edge of the compound. "The racquetball and squash courts are in there."

Security personnel guarded the entrances to the walled community. Cole drove alongside a line of cars waiting to be checked in, passed through an automatic gate, and circled the tall buildings. A lush, verdant golf course stretched off to the left. Cole parked, and they spent over an hour touring the grounds and facilities, Cole talking nonstop, before they returned to the car and he sped past the riding stables to a large marina, where he handed her onto a sixty-foot yacht.

They entered the closed cabin with a fully equipped, if outdated, galley. The appliances were several years old but appeared not to have seen much use. A brown leather couch stretched the length of one glassed-in wall. Matching chairs surrounded a bolted-down table for eight. A leather-padded bar dominated one corner. Another corner housed an equally outdated entertainment center. Oddly enough, the cabin seemed frozen in time.

"It's lovely," she murmured, noticing Cole looking at her expectantly, as he had often during her whirlwind tour. He seemed to feed on her rapidly depleting storehouse of compliments. "Does your family spend much time on the water?"

"My parents do, but they take the cabin cruiser. *Candida*'s pressed into service for their annual Fourth of July bash on the lake, but other than that, she doesn't get out of the marina."

"Ever?"

He shrugged. "I took her out once a few years ago, but other than that . . ."

A few years ago. Five? Had Cole brought Heather here? Was that why he'd invited *her* here? Did he suspect the connection between them? She noticed Cole watching her again and forced a smile. "Somehow I pictured you as an avid yachtsman."

He chuckled. "I hate the water. The only time I have any use for a boat is when I want to be alone with a beautiful lady."

His compliment did little to ease her sudden apprehension. Cole stowed the refreshments, cast off, and with a powerful rumble of engines, they were on their way. Fifteen minutes later, they emerged from a passageway that led from the marina to Lake Ashton. Midway across the lake, he cut the motor.

"There aren't too many places to go on a lake this size. We could've gone the other way and taken the river out to Lake Erie, but then I would've had to check in with my fath . . . staff." He busied himself with the control panel and activated the mechanism to lower the anchor. "They like to know where they can reach me if there's a problem."

Meghan stared at him. She was alone with a man who needed permission from his father to travel beyond certain boundaries?

Cole looked up from the controls. "Why don't you go on deck? I've got a couple of calls to make before I can join you." He flashed an urbane smile. "Unfortunately, business doesn't go away just because the boss takes a day off to play.''

"I understand. Take your time." Meghan slipped through the sliding glass doors at the back of the cabin into bright sunshine, grateful to have time to pull her thoughts together.

Bracing her hands on the bow's steel railing, she inhaled deeply. Why was Cole so determined to play the role of suave businessman? Was he trying to prove something to her? To his father? Was there a reason the elder Benson kept close tabs on his son? Or did he simply have a controlling nature?

She recalled Tom's telling her about the town meeting Donner Benson had called in the aftermath of her sister's overdose. A meeting that had resulted in placing the blame for Heather's death squarely on Nicholas Hawkinson's shoulders. Was it possible Donner Benson had called that meeting with that purpose in mind? That he'd been trying to shift the blame for Heather's death away from someone else? Like his only son?

She took another deep breath, and tangy air filled her lungs as the yacht moved in gentle rhythm with the undulating water. Several minutes of warm wind on her face and clear, azure sky above her helped to put things into perspective. Just because a man had power didn't mean he was crooked. No doubt she was seeing connections where there were none, building scenarios that hadn't happened. Lack of sleep was making her paranoid.

Cole appeared at her side with two icy margaritas. Meghan sipped hers, grateful for the diversion. "I haven't thanked you for inviting me here today. This is wonderful."

"Better than anything Ashton has to offer?"

"You should know. You used to live there."

"Ah, but that was before my father created paradise."

She caught the resentment in his voice and felt sorry for him, a man seemingly trapped in his father's extensive hideaway for the rich, with no real responsibilities of his own. She knew where that could lead. Down the same reckless path Carter had taken.

Reckless. Maybe she wasn't being paranoid. Was Cole reckless enough to kill someone? Unintentionally, perhaps. His driving certainly gave the impression he regarded life lightly.

He settled into a deck chair and closed his eyes. "Why don't you go below and change into your swimsuit?"

Meghan took another sip of her margarita, eyed the sparkling water, and shoved thoughts of death aside. The time had come to implement her unorthodox plan to test a different theory. In the past few days it had inexplicably become important to her to discover if her scars were as repulsive as Carter had claimed. While Cole wasn't the best of choices for her experiment, he was a man. A man who'd made it clear he was interested in her as a woman. His reaction would tell her what she needed to know.

Better him than someone whose opinion mattered. Who that might be, she didn't care to consider. She headed for the stateroom. Once she'd changed into her bright blue maillot, she took a few minutes to admire the richly appointed cabin and screw up her courage.

Suddenly the room lurched and Meghan grabbed the first support within reach, the handle to a teak cabinet above the bed. It popped open, and several sheaves of paper fell out, flying like large pieces of confetti across the room.

"Oh, blast."

The boat began a steady, powerful rocking. Meghan lunged after the scattered papers. Swaying in counterpoint to the yacht's movements, she gathered and stuffed the papers back into the cabinet. Looking around the room to make sure she hadn't missed any, she caught her reflection in a full-length mirror and stopped short. As her scars stared back at her, she realized she needn't bother with her absurd experiment. Mirrors didn't lie. The bumps and indentations pickling her skin would give any man second thoughts.

Impatiently she reached for her skirt, lying on the window seat. She was here to find out what had happened to Heather, not test her feminine appeal. A small notepad

stuck between the wall and window seat caught her eye.
She frowned. She didn't recall seeing anything small and
hard fly past her when the cabinet popped open, only blank
sheets of Lakeland letterhead. She pried the pad loose,
then froze as she recognzied the handwriting on the top
sheet. Heather's.

"Meghan? Are you all right?" Cole called through the
door.

Frantically she searched for somewhere to put the notepad. Shoving it into her skirt pocket, she whirled to face
him, dropping the skirt between them unintentionally. The
notepad slid partially out of the pocket. She prayed he
wouldn't notice what seemed to her a glaring patch of
white on the brown carpet.

"Meghan . . ."

"I'm fine. I—" Her mouth clamped shut. Cole looked
as if he'd seen a ghost. He stared at her face, at her hands
clasped in front of her, at her legs. Taut silence enveloped
them as the rocking boat gentled.

Meghan's heart thudded. Would Cole discover what
she'd found? Her fervent prayers were answered when his
gaze stopped somewhere around her knees. He shook his
head as if to convince himself he'd only imagined what
he'd seen.

"I . . . got worried when the cabin cruiser passed by
so closely. It left a large wake." He didn't meet her eyes.

"It was a bit shaky in here at first, but I managed."
Truth to tell, it was still shaky, and getting shakier by the
minute. Cole was acting unbelievably strange. His eyes
held the glazed look of a man on the edge. He stared at
a point beyond her shoulder, and Meghan stopped breathing. Had she forgotten to shut the cabinet door? Would
he suspect her of snooping?

"I'll wait for you outside," he said quietly.

The door clicked shut and she scooped up her skirt,
stuffed the notepad into her tote bag, then took a deep
breath and slowly surveyed the cabin. She'd left no sign
of the mess she'd made. Wearing her skirt, she left the
stateroom. There was no point in flaunting her disfigure-

ment. Cole's reaction to her scars had left no room for doubt about her feminine appeal.

She found him subdued, unpacking their lunch. "Hungry?" he asked, without looking at her.

"Not really."

"Neither am I, but someone's got to eat all this food." He suddenly stopped, hands in midair, and brought his pained, haunted eyes up to meet hers. "I'm sorry, Heath . . . Meghan. I . . . shouldn't have burst in on you like that."

Meghan's heart dipped. Cole had almost called her Heather. Instinct told her to proceed cautiously. "It's all right, Cole."

The torment in his eyes deepened. "No. It isn't. I shouldn't have brought you here." He turned away, agitated. "I'll take you back now. It's only right."

Meghan wasn't sure whether to be relieved or vexed. Vexation won out. Cole was harmless. A little strange, but harmless. He'd been a perfect gentlemen from the word go. *She'd* been the one to let her imagination run wild, and now, thanks to her half-baked idea to reveal her scars and get a man's opinion of them, she'd lost a perfect opportunity to talk to him about Heather. Never mind she'd decided not to go through with her oddball experiment. He'd seen her scars, and the damage was done.

She could've chewed nails. Cole had withdrawn so far into himself, it would take more than a short ride to the marina to restore a sense of normality to the day. She watched in dismay as he opened a beer and took a long swallow, then wiped the back of his hand across his lips, his gaze falling to her skirt. He stared at it, a touch of remembered horror in his eyes.

"What . . . happened?"

"Car accident. Drunk driver." She didn't feel like offering details.

Cole met her gaze briefly, his eyes blank, then moved to the control panel and started the engines. Meghan went on deck, appalled and humiliated. By the time they reached the marina, Cole had finished two beers and started a third, proving Carter hadn't been wrong in his assessment of her damaged body. Seeing her scars was enough to drive a man to drink.

She hid her pain as she stepped onto the dock and followed Cole to the parking lot. But when he opened the Porsche's passenger door, she stopped cold. The combination of Cole's drinking and reckless approach to driving reminded her too much of Carter to allow her to get in the car a second time. She couldn't do it. Not without losing what remained of her self-respect.

"Thank you for the tour of Lakeland, Cole, and I'm sorry the day on the water didn't turn out as well as we'd hoped, but I'll find my way back to The Wharf from here."

"Don't be silly. I'll drive you back."

"I'd rather you didn't."

He flushed angrily. "Get in the car, Meghan."

She looked pointedly at the beer in his hand. "No."

The baby blue Porsche left the parking lot trailing a shower of gravel. Meghan called a cab from a pay phone and hiked to the nearest gate, proud of herself for not backing down. But by the time she reached her car, she was shaking. By the time she pulled into her driveway, scalding tears streamed down her cheeks.

She hadn't cried since the accident, when she'd realized no amount of tears would change her seemingly hopeless situation. But the sleepless night, her tense afternoon with Cole, the reminders of Carter, and her utter lack of progress in solving the mystery of Heather's death had renewed with a vengeance the feelings of inadequacy she'd felt at the breakup of her marriage.

In frustration and despair, she cried herself to sleep. It wasn't until she awoke around ten o'clock in a dark house, puffy-eyed and ravenous, that she remembered Heather's note. She sat at the kitchen table and munched on a tasteless peanut butter sandwich while she read it.

The note brought her no closer to understanding Heather's death. It appeared to be a list and read:

THINGS TO DO
Call my sister
Ask for blue tweed suit to be sent
Ask Minnie's help in baking a cake
Get Cole's birthday gift
Ask about keeping pets in apartment
Realtor to call me about selling condo in D.C.
Order 20 copies of *Prisoner of Zenda* for class

The first line increased Meghan's melancholy. Heather had never called. The blue tweed suit made no sense. Her flamboyant sister had hated tweed.

The third item was also strange. Heather had been a gourmet cook; she hadn't needed *anyone's* help to bake a cake. And who was Minnie? Meghan hadn't met anyone by that name in Ashton.

Apparently Heather had been fond enough of Cole to want to buy him a birthday gift. Surprising news. The next line was also surprising. Heather was allergic to animals.

The fifth line made no sense, either. Heather had never owned a condo in D.C. or anywhere else. A true free spirit, she'd rented apartments by the month, moving frequently.

The last line was confusing as well. Heather was a notorious procrastinator. Meghan couldn't imagine her pulling herself together enough to order books in advance for a class that wasn't to begin for at least a month.

Thoroughly bewildered, Meghan gave up on the note and turned her thoughts to why Heather might've been on Cole's yacht in the first place. The only logical reason she could come up with was that Heather and Nick must've had a lover's quarrel.

But why would Heather run to Cole if she'd had a quarrel with Nick? According to her letter and Ralph, she'd wanted nothing to do with Cole. *Had* Nick dumped her for the mayor's wife? Or had Nick and Heather fought about their relationship, with Heather running to Cole in an effort to make Nick jealous enough to marry her?

Sorry, baby. I don't jump through those kinds of hoops. It isn't worth it.

Had Heather's attempt to make Nick jealous backfired, sending him into the arms of his former flame? Broken-hearted, had Heather then turned to her old friend cocaine one last time?

Meghan didn't know. But she intended to find out.

NINE

Early Monday morning Tom called to ask Meghan if she'd mind watching the store again. His widowed sister in Buffalo had broken her leg and needed him to pick her up at the hospital, and with Mrs. Weaver gone . . .

Meghan assured him she'd be more than happy to help out. When she arrived at the store, it occurred to her his request was a blessing in disguise. With the number of people who stopped by the store daily, she'd have a chance to regain her investigative footing. Her primary sources of information—Nick and Cole—no longer accessible, she had to branch out. If people didn't like it, too bad. She was determined to find out if Heather's death had been suicide, or accident, or—God help them all—murder, once and for all. Ashton's secret had been kept buried for much too long.

A steady stream of customers and deliveries kept her hopping all morning. Her questions were met with varied degrees of resistance, and she didn't learn anything she didn't already know. During a midafternoon lull, she was stocking fresh produce that had arrived earlier when the bell above the door jingled and Nick walked in.

He spotted her in the corner and gave her a swift, yet thorough assessment that made Meghan, standing amid stacks of empty crates, feel provincial and lacking. She stiffened, her ego still fragile after the fiasco on Cole's yacht.

"Tom around?" Nick asked curtly.

"No."

He moved down the nearest aisle, walking to the back of the store. Meghan added the last tomatoes to the display case before joining him, suddenly not trusting herself to speak. Maybe he'd heard she was asking questions about Heather, thought she suspected him of murder, and had come to set her straight.

"Got any steaks?" he asked over the meat counter.

"Just what you see in the case."

One dark eyebrow arched. "You mean there aren't any more of those special inch-and-a-half-thick ones in the back?"

"I play by the rules now, Nick. I got my hands slapped the last time I tried to do you a favor."

His expression darkened. "By Tom?"

She marveled at his density. "No, by you. Or have you forgotten Friday morning already?"

Nick stared at her, then combed a hand through his hair and exhaled heavily. "You're right. I was a bear. I'm sorry."

Meghan hid her satisfaction. She wasn't about to let him trample her feelings the way he must've trampled Heather's, or fall at his feet after a forced apology. She planted her fists on her hips. "Sorry doesn't cut it, Nick."

A rewarding glimmer of respect entered his eyes, but Meghan soon wished someone else would come into the store or he would make up his mind about the damned steaks and leave. She could maintain her facade of self-righteousness only so long. The frustrating truth was, the more people she spoke to, the harder she found it to believe that this man had played *any* part in her sister's death. She'd also missed him terribly.

"Then how about dinner? Tonight. At The Wharf."

His soft-spoken invitation scrambled her insides. She wanted to refuse to spite him, but knew she couldn't bypass the opportunity. For Heather's sake . . . or her own. "I guess I could. But Tom won't be back until after five. I'm here for the day."

"Pick you up at six-thirty?"

The front door jingled and the sheriff and two deputies sauntered in. From the looks on their faces, Meghan was sure it wasn't for a shopping spree. As they approached the counter, she smiled and asked, "What can I do for you today, gentlemen?"

The sheriff hooked his thumbs in his belt and looked Nick over. "Heard Tom went to Buffalo today. Thought we'd stop by to make sure you weren't having any trouble."

His meaning was clear. Nick hadn't done anything wrong, but if he made one false step, the sheriff would be there. Nick said nothing, but Meghan sensed the anger burning beneath his impassive facade. The injustice of it fired her protective instincts. Hadn't the man been through enough already?

She widened her eyes innocently. "Why, thank you for your concern, Sheriff Taylor, but as you can see, I'm doing just fine. In fact, Mr. Hawkinson and I were discussing our dinner plans when you walked in."

Meghan paced her bedroom and wondered if Nick was still taking her to dinner. After the incident in The Farmer's Market, she half expected him to stand her up. Nick was a proud man, and although he hadn't said a word, she knew it hadn't set well with him that she'd stood up to the sheriff on his behalf.

She needn't have worried. At six-thirty there was a knock on Mrs. Weaver's door. Meghan looked down at her pale blue watered silk sheath and wondered if she'd overdressed. She'd never seen Nick in anything other than a T-shirt and jeans. But she wanted to look her best tonight. Her self-esteem had taken a blow the day before, and she was doing what she could to recover.

Drawing a deep breath, she opened the door. Then forgot to exhale. Nick wore tailored dark blue slacks, a pale blue dress shirt, and discreetly striped tie. His unruly hair was combed back in a conservative style, parted at the side. He looked magnificent. "Wow," she breathed.

He grinned, and her heart flipped over. The look in his brown velvet eyes was one of pure male appreciation. "I'd have to say that goes double for you. You look stunning."

Stunning. He'd said she looked stunning. The words were a soothing balm to her bruised ego. "Thank you," she murmured.

"And about what happened at the store," he added. "Thanks. I appreciate your standing up for me like that."

Meghan beamed. "What are friends for?"

Her response set the tone for the evening. By the time they arrived in the restaurant's foyer, Nick had put on the suit jacket he'd left in the truck, and Meghan was so proud to be seen with him, she thought she'd burst.

She couldn't remember when she'd enjoyed being wined and dined so much. Nick's eyes never seemed to leave her. She, in turn, noticed every move he made. While their conversation was light and full of banter, the undertones conveyed by their eyes and hands bespoke something else entirely. An intercepted and well-met glance here, a caressing movement against the stem or rim of a wineglass there, a smile or two for no apparent reason at all. It was as if their alter egos were enjoying a date of their own.

Meghan smiled contentedly as Nick split the last of their bottle of Dom Perignon between them. The bubbles rising in her fluted glass matched those rising in her heart. Nicholas Hawkinson was no murderer, and anyone who said differently was a liar.

Suddenly an icy voice behind her asked, "Enjoying yourself, Meghan?"

She stilled. Cole. She'd forgotten all about him. Wearing her best cocktail party smile, she turned to face him. "Why, yes, I am." Manners—and more than a little curiosity as to how they'd respond—propelled her into making introductions. "Have you two met? Cole, this is—"

"I know who he is. Frankly, I'm surprised to see you

with him. I wouldn't think you'd want to be associated with him."

Meghan's eyes widened at his rudeness. "Cole, I don't think—"

Nick's hand covered hers. "It's okay, Meghan. Cole and I go back a long way."

"We've known each other for too long, if you ask me."

Nick seemed unperturbed by Cole's naked hostility. "I agree. But I don't think Meghan's interested in our personal problems."

Meghan heard the steel-rimmed warning in his voice, looked from Cole's flushed and angry face to Nick's hand tightening over her own, and suddenly became *very* interested in their personal problems. But she wasn't tactless enough to interrupt and say so, and after several tense seconds, it was Cole who backed down.

"Have a pleasant evening, Meghan," he said tightly, and vanished.

Nick resumed his meal as if it hadn't been interrupted. Meghan was unable to follow his lead. "Would you mind telling me what that was all about?" For a few seconds she'd felt the enmity between the two men so strongly, she would've sworn they would've liked nothing better than to let fly with their fists, right there in the restaurant.

Nick shrugged. "It's an old story. Goes back to high school." With a smile and a wink, he snagged a menu from a passing waitress. "How about dessert? Think they have brownies on the menu?"

Meghan swallowed her frustration with an effort. As usual, she'd get no answers from Nick. Half an hour later, they left the restaurant by a side door that opened onto the pier, having agreed on taking a stroll. As they walked the docks, Nick was pensive, but Meghan found she enjoyed his quiet companionship. She also enjoyed the simple pleasure that radiated from wherever he touched her— her arm, elbow, waist, back. Every nerve in her body became attuned to his touch, and she wished he'd put his arm around her. The thought sent sweet shivers of anticipation down her spine despite the inescapable, sweltering heat.

They returned to the parking lot, and as Nick unlocked his newly washed truck, Meghan admired his hands, so strong, yet capable of heartwarming gentleness, as he'd shown with Fred. Her gaze roved the breadth of his shoulders beneath his tailored dark blue jacket, and she suddenly felt a need to slip her hands inside said jacket and explore the hard planes and contours it hid.

Nick swung the driver's door open. The deep sexual awareness in his eyes when he caught her watching him rocked her.

"If I don't kiss you right now, I think I'll go crazy."

Meghan's breath caught in her throat. "I know the feeling."

He stepped closer, their bodies communicating with a rapport that surprised them both. It was as if they were about to begin a dance, one to which only they knew the music. Meghan's heartbeat soared. She met the dark fires in Nick's eyes with a matching glow in her own. Slowly, ever so slowly, his lips, warm and tasting of mint, descended to hers. His arms slid around her as though they'd been custom-made to hold her.

Meghan moaned as his tongue slipped past her parted lips. A lean hunger pulsed through her as he kissed her with a thoroughness that sent her senses reeling. Her arms encircled his neck, her fingers rejoicing at the opportunity to ruffle through his hair, now windswept, just the way she liked it.

Nick groaned, and she felt the full heat and hardness of his arousal against her stomach. She arched and moved against him, feeling pressure build in her body like water against a dam. His tongue plunged deeper in bold imitation of another, far more intimate act. Desire exploded in her brain.

Meghan forgot all else. She forgot she was in the middle of a public parking lot. Forgot how angry Nick made her at times. Forgot about Heather. Forgot about the possibility of murder and the enmity she'd seen between Coleman

Benson and Nicholas Hawkinson as Nick's callused hands drew her against him and moved over her back in urgent, spine-tingling caresses.

"You haven't changed a bit, Hawkinson. You still like to get your rocks off in my parking lot."

Meghan blinked as the icy voice pierced the haze of passion clouding her brain. She started to pull away from Nick, but he kept his arm around her, drawing her to his side.

Cole stood a few feet away, his pale blue eyes hard as diamonds. "I don't think Meghan's going to appreciate your lack of discretion, Hawkinson. You've attracted an audience."

As Cole and Nick's eyes engaged in silent war, Meghan looked around. Sure enough, people had stopped to stare. Heat flushed her cheeks, but she kept her head held high. She might have gotten carried away, but she'd done nothing to be ashamed of.

"Why don't you let me escort you home, Meghan? I'm sure this lowlife had done enough damage to your reputation already."

Nick's hand tensed on her waist, and Meghan knew she had to get him away from Cole, fast. Her eyes met Cole's. "I'm afraid that's not possible."

"That's right. I forgot. You always leave with the man you came with, don't you?" Cole sneered. "Have it your way. But don't say I didn't warn you."

She turned away. Nick helped her into the pickup and swung into the seat beside her. "See you around, Cole," he said, his voice calm, yet cold with fury. Meghan shivered involuntarily, then studied him through lowered lashes as they crossed the bridge over Lake Ashton. Nick was cool and remote, an entirely different man from the one she'd spent the last few hours with.

She didn't like his growing silence. On the dock it had been companionable. Now it unsettled her. "Tell me what's going on between the two of you, Nick. Please."

To her great disappointment, his only response was a bleak smile. He drove through Ashton's quiet streets without speaking, then parked in her driveway and looked across the seat at her.

For the longest time, neither of them moved. Meghan sensed a strong debate taking place inside Nick, and wondered who would win. The dark, dangerous, passionate man who'd kissed her senseless in a public parking lot? Or the composed, controlled, self-assured gentleman with whom she'd spent most of the evening?

In the end it was a disappointing combination of both. "You're one hell of a woman, Meghan Edwards," he said finally, his eyes dark and dangerous, his manner composed and controlled. "You deserve a hell of a lot better than me."

He hardly touched her as he helped her alight from the truck. At her doorstep their eyes locked again. Hers held confusion; his, a cool distance she didn't care for at all.

"Go home, Meghan. Now. Before you get hurt."

With that, he left her standing on her doorstep, swung into his truck, and drove away.

TEN

Early the next morning, Meghan stalked over to Nick's. To her immense displeasure, he wasn't there. A quick check in the barn confirmed his truck was gone. Fists on her hips, she glared at the sky. The morning was cloudlessly beautiful, despite the muggy heat and her foul mood. Returning to her bungalow, she collected her camera and headed into the woods behind Nick's house. After last night, she'd trespass anywhere she damn well pleased.

The first thing she saw when she emerged from the peaceful forest well after noon was Nick's truck, backed against the barn. The loft doors were open, and she heard someone moving inside.

She entered the barn, depositing her camera bag at the foot of the narrow wood steps. Poking her head into the loft, she found Nick, shirtless, shoveling a small mountain of decayed hay into a pile near an open door to toss into the truck bed below.

Sweat glistened on the bronzed muscles rippling across his back and in his arms as he rhythmically forked the hay. Meghan felt an unwelcome jolt of sexual electricity, and her mouth thinned into a grim, determined line.

She climbed into the loft. "I want to talk to you."

Nick stilled, straightened, then slowly turned to face

her, his hands resting on the pitchfork's handle. "About what?"

"About that charade you played at The Wharf last night."

"Oh?" He propped his pitchfork against the wall, leaned casually against the weathered wood, and crossed the powerful arms that had held her so tightly the night before. Meghan felt an unwanted yearning to be enclosed in their warmth again.

"I'm listening."

"It was you I saw standing near the back exit at The Wharf Thursday night, wasn't it?"

Nick nodded once.

"The next morning you told me to get lost."

"Get to the point, Meghan."

She ignored him, needing to establish the sequence of events before she leveled her accusation. "On Monday you showed up at The Farmer's Market and apologized. To give it that special touch of sincerity, you asked me out."

Nick didn't flicker so much as an eyelash. With a sinking heart, Meghan realized her assumptions were true. She paced, while Nick remained motionless. If she hadn't been so upset, she might've recognized the warning signal.

"Given the obvious enmity between Cole and yourself, I was surprised you would take me to The Wharf. You had to have known we'd run into him."

Still no response. Meghan fumed. Couldn't he have at least denied it? Attempted to explain?

"But you did. While we were there, you plied me with the most expensive food and wine they offer, made a big show of walking me around the pier, and then, when you *knew* you had Cole's attention, kissed the hell out of me."

He lowered his arms. "So? What's wrong with that?"

"*What's wrong with that?* You used me! After I made you brownies and helped you clean your house, somehow you got the idea Cole was interested in me and you deliberately *used* me to score a point against him in some ancient rivalry between you two."

Nick shifted almost imperceptibly. "I see. When did you figure this out?"

"I was up for *hours* trying to sort out what happened last night. I want to know who in hell you think you are to use me like that to get even with Coleman Benson for . . . for some no doubt idiotic male reason known only to yourselves." She closed the distance between them and pushed a finger into his chest. "I want to know what makes you think you have the right to—"

Meghan gasped in surprise as iron hands manacled her wrists and her back suddenly collided with the rough boards Nick had been leaning against. For the longest time the only sound in the loft's sweltering stillness was that of her impotent fury. Pinned against the wall, she quelled the urge to struggle, knowing he only meant to subdue her temper with his intimidation tactics, not hurt her. Raising her chin, she met his hostile gaze without flinching.

"It occurred to me you might try something primitive like this, but I chose to give you the benefit of the doubt."

Nick glared down at her. "Your mistake. But since you asked so nicely . . . I'll tell you what gives me the right. First you show up on my doorstep all sweetness and light, acting like you'd rather eat *me* than your brownies. Next you come around to help me fix up my house and strut your stuff all over my living room. When I make a move, you practically go up in flames, but suddenly turn cold, stick up your nose like I'm not good enough to touch you, and say, 'I don't want to. I want to go home.' "

Meghan squirmed, but Nick tightened his grip on her wrists, forcing her to meet his anger. "The next thing I know, you've put me on ice and gone panting after Benson." She opened her mouth to deliver a heated denial, but Nick shook his head. "Equal time, Meghan. You gave your opinion, now I'm giving mine. If you had a problem with my choice of restaurants, you should've said something. But you didn't, and when we met up with Benson last night, *you* were the one who acted like you had something to prove, not me. So who's using whom?"

His brown eyes, gone black with fury, glittered dangerously. "What's the matter, Meghan? Cat got your tongue?" He smiled coldly. "Good. Now that I've finally got you speechless, we can use that mouth of yours for what it was meant for."

Meghan saw his intent and turned her head, but Nick captured her jaw in his hand. "Don't fight me on this, Meghan. Please."

She kept her mouth clamped shut as his lips covered hers. The pressure of Nick's fingers on her jaw increased until her mouth opened to let his tongue surge inside. Meghan moaned, rendered helpless by the maelstrom of desire engulfing her.

Heat flooded her body as Nick parted her legs with his thigh. She melted against him, and a groan rumbled from deep within him. His powerful chest teased her sensitized breasts, and his hold on her slackened. His hand slid to her waist, his palm tormenting taut, aching nipples as it passed slowly over her breasts. Her hands came to rest on his broad shoulders as her tongue shot out to challenge his in a battle of wills.

When it became apparent neither would allow the other declared the winner, Nick pulled his lips from hers to burn a fiery trail of kisses from her temple to her throat. Meghan gasped for breath and flexed her hands on his shoulders, absorbing the satiny texture of his smooth, dark skin. His hands slid to her buttocks and fitted her to him like glove to hand.

"That's it, baby. Now tell me it's me you want, not Benson."

His impassioned directive filtered through the cloud of desire enveloping Meghan, and she suddenly realized what was happening. Nick's overwhelming demonstration of sexual prowess, which she was wantonly enjoying, was simply a means of scoring another point against Coleman Benson!

She brought her knee up as hard as she could. "You bastard."

Nick yelped and stumbled backward, his eyes registering shock, then pain. His breath came in ragged gasps as he struggled not to hold on to the spot where her knee had struck home. He felt excruciating pain; of that, Meghan had no doubt. A lesser man would've been rolling on the floor. She hoped he burned as if he'd been stung by a man-of-war.

"Don't . . . ever . . . touch . . . me . . . again." Nick's pain-glazed eyes fused with hers, but she didn't back off. "What may or may not have happened between us has nothing to do with Coleman Benson, and you know it. I haven't done *anything* to warrant your inexcusable behavior toward me. Nor did I deserve to be used as a pawn in some childish feud between you and Cole. If you even think of trying something like that again, I'll find a way to make your life so miserable, this thing between you and Cole will seem like a playground squabble. Do I make myself clear?"

Heart pumping, injured manhood throbbing, Nick watched her sail from the loft without a backward glance. Leaning his back against the wall, he slowly slid to the floor. Crossing his arms across his bent knees, he rested his forehead against them and drew several deep, agonizing breaths.

She was right. He'd used her. Badly. What had begun as a plan to distract Cole by romancing Meghan in front of him, while Ralph raided Cole's Lakeland office in secrecy, had backfired with a bang that could be heard clear across Lake Ashton.

"Oh, Meghan, I'm sorry."

Nick knew he'd committed two monumental errors. The first was, he'd underestimated Meghan Edwards.

The second was, he'd fallen in love with her.

He'd forgotten his plan to distract Cole the moment he'd seen her in that bewitching creation of a dress the night before. When he could contain his need no longer, he'd taken her in his arms. Her sweetness and uninhibited response under his hands had, instead of satisfying his desire, increased the fever raging through his blood. Without stopping to think, he'd acted on the elemental need to feel her silk-sheathed softness against his hot, hard body. Christ, he'd almost jumped her in the parking lot!

Then, when any other woman of her caliber would've given him an icy dressing down for his exhibition of un-controlled lust, she'd stood by him in front of Benson and God knew who else.

Again.

He'd known right then and there he had to back off. If he'd taken her to bed as he'd ached to the night before, by this morning Meghan would've been a target for mur-der. So he'd tried to get rid of her. Told her to go home. But Meghan Edwards had a will and tenacity that matched his own. She wasn't going anywhere until she had her answers about Heather. Answers he wasn't willing to give until he could prove his innocence—and Cole's guilt.

The sound of Meghan's car roaring to life pulled Nick out of his frustrated misery. He looked out the door to see her back her dark blue Mustang convertible out of Mrs. Weaver's driveway and gun down the street, hell-bent for leather.

Meghan barreled down the highway to The Wharf, de-termined to forget about Nick and his games by going sailing. Coleman Benson might not care for the company she kept, but he was a businessman above all. He wouldn't refuse to rent her one of his sailboats.

"I'd like to rent a sailboat, please," she said to the young man at the rental booth.

"Sure." The high-school-age youth in shorts and a rugby shirt reluctantly pulled his nose out of the latest issue of *Sailing*. While he went to prepare a boat, Meghan completed the liability release form he'd scooted her way. When he read her name, he said, "Oh, I didn't know it was you, Miss Edwards. Mr. Benson stopped by the other day and said we're supposed to take good care of you. I'll have your boat ready in another minute."

He returned the small sailboat and untied a newer, cleaner, larger boat. It looked about fourteen feet long. "Here you go, Miss Edwards." He handed her onto the boat. "Anything you need, just ask. You can keep it as long as you want. No charge."

Meghan smiled and thanked him. Apparently Cole hadn't gotten around to rescinding his offer. She paddled into the lake and hoisted the sails. A stiff breeze blew, and she was thankful for the respite from the oppressive heat. Looking into the sky, she saw it turn gray but didn't give the possibility of rain a second thought. They'd had too many false alarms in the past week when the sky had gone dark and . . . nothing. The clouds had simply blown over. These would no doubt do the same.

For over an hour she sailed the lake, waving at other boaters as she glided by on increasingly strong breezes. It wasn't until her third lap that she noticed the number of craft on the water had dropped substantially. Boats were heading for the marina in droves. She glanced at the sky again. To the west loomed an ominous thundercloud.

Gauging the distance to The Wharf, she realized she wouldn't be able to beat the rain. She decided to sail to Ashton instead, pop into Kelly's Diner for a bite to eat, and wait out the storm. Halfway there, it hit with a blinding flash of lightning and an instantaneous clap of thunder. The heavens opened, and the rain descended in torrents.

Meghan couldn't keep the boat on course. The high winds and churning water sent her rolling everywhere but the direction she wanted to go. The storm's increasing force swept her farther into the lake. She shortened sail to get the boat moving faster.

Wind and rain pelted her in steady sheets as another fierce bolt of lightning struck near enough to crackle the air around her. The chilly rain plastered her hair to her face, her clothes to her body. The boat rocked dangerously, and she felt like a rubber duck in a whirlpool. Thunder crashed, and her heart reverberated in her head. A powerful gust of wind pushed her from behind. She jibbed with all her might.

Something was wrong. Terribly wrong. One moment she was meeting resistance in the lines, and the next she was clawing at thin air. A loud splintering sound penetrated her brain, and she looked up in horror to see the top of the mainmast had broken off. Another gust of wind swept across the boat, and the deck rose to meet her, clipping her behind the knees.

She pitched backward, her head striking the boat's hull as she fell overboard. Pain ripped through her skull as she slid into Lake Ashton's roiling waters. Then everything went black.

ELEVEN

Twenty yards away, Nick sunk anchor and hit the water. With a strength he hadn't known he possessed, he triumphed over the swirling crosscurrents threatening to pull him under and reached Meghan's capsized boat.

"*Meghan!*"

He couldn't see her anywhere over the trailing mainsheet being swept away by the storm. Icy tentacles of fear gripped his vitals. If she'd been knocked unconscious, she was as good as dead. Shoving aside the splintered end of the mainmast, he called her name several more times, but the howling wind slammed his cries back into his face.

Another bolt of lightning ripped through the charcoal sky, and Nick spotted a bright flash of orange. *Her life preserver.* He dived in that direction, but when he surfaced, the patch of orange was gone. Off to his left it popped up again.

It was Meghan, all right. The lake's unnaturally high waves were tossing her around like a rag doll. She went under, and Nick lunged. He sliced through the water, lashing out blindly until his forearm connected sharply with a slender limb.

He shot to the surface, his lungs burning, hauling Meghan behind him by the ankle. As soon as he'd gulped enough air to sustain him, he reached down to turn her upright. Pulling her limp torso against his side, he struck out for his own boat.

An eternity later, he painfully climbed aboard, dragging Meghan's deadweight body. With as much gentleness as the storm would allow, he laid her on the deck, then began CPR. He checked for a pulse. Either she had none or the storm's fury rendered him unable to find it. He prayed it was the latter. He examined her mouth for foreign objects, pinched her nose, and blew into her mouth. Nothing. He pumped her chest and forced breath into her again.

"Damn you, Meghan! You're too strong to die!" He tried again. Nothing. "Fight with me, baby, *fight!*"

On the sixth attempt, she jerked spasmodically. Nick swiped a drenched hand across his sweat-and-rain covered face and watched, his muscles bunching with anxiety. "Come on, Meghan. *You can do it. Breathe, dammit, breathe.*"

He breathed into her and pumped once more. Slender arms lifted as if to ward him off, but barely cleared the deck. A spasm of coughing racked her body so intensely, it wrenched Nick's insides. She turned her head, and what looked like a gallon of water spewed from her mouth. She groaned and hacked, curling into a fetal position.

Nick checked for broken bones, found none, and lifted her against his chest, cradling her tenderly against him as he double- and triple-checked for injuries. Satisfied she would live, he lifted his head to the driving rain and offered a silent prayer of thanks.

But they weren't out of danger yet. "Meghan, I've got to get us out of here," he shouted. "Can you understand me?"

She opened her eyes. "Nick?" she croaked.

It was the sweetest sound he'd ever heard. "I'm here, Meghan. I'm going to take you home."

"My boat."

"The boat capsized, love. You're on my boat. You're safe."

"My boat, Nick. Something wrong," she rasped, and slumped against him.

Was the woman insane? The storm had nearly swallowed them whole, and she was worried about Benson's rental boat? No, not worried. What was it she'd said?

Something wrong. Something was wrong with the boat?

Nick scanned the lake. Her wrecked sailboat floated nearby. The storm showed signs of abating. He looked down at Meghan in his arms, and a surge of emotion more powerful than any he'd ever felt flowed through his veins. If someone had tried to hurt her by sabotaging her boat . . .

There was only one way to find out. Carefully Nick lowered her to the deck and yanked dry blankets from below to cover her. Resolutely he hoisted anchor and maneuvered his ketch alongside Meghan's half-submerged sailboat. He fastened a grappling hook to the end of his towline and tossed it out. It connected. He dived into the water, secured the smaller boat to his, clambered back into his boat, and powered up the motor. The operation took all of five minutes. They headed for the Ashton dock.

Meghan came to as Nick lowered her drenched and battered body onto a bed at Mrs. Weaver's. Her eyes fluttered open, and it took a full ten seconds before she grasped the situation.

Nick was undressing her. He'd pulled off her shoes and socks and unfastened her pants. She struggled to sit, but pain slashed behind her temples.

At Meghan's feeble attempt at movement, Nick paused. "Lie still. I'm going to get you out of these wet clothes and into bed. I've called Dr. Wilmot. He'll be here any minute."

Nick looked as sodden and cold as she felt. His shiny black hair was pasted to his skull, and water ran off him in rivulets, making puddles on the floor. He didn't seem to notice. Instead, concern filled his deep brown eyes.

Gentle hands began to ease her cotton trousers from her. In less than a minute he'd see her scars. She couldn't let that happen. She couldn't bear to see his expression change to pity or revulsion. Her shaky hands covered his, stilling them.

"No. I'll do . . . it," she whispered, her raw throat burning.

"Meghan, you almost drowned. All I want to do is get you into some dry clothes."

"No," she repeated, desperately.

His temper exploded, showering her with angry sparks. "For Christ's sake, woman! This is no time for misplaced modesty!"

"Please?" she whimpered, her eyes echoing her painful plea.

If she'd asked any other way, he would've overruled her. But the thought of Meghan begging him for anything cut him like a knife. Nick backed off, his mouth tightening. If she didn't want him to touch her, so be it.

"All right. I'll get you something to change into and leave you alone for five minutes. If you're not changed by then, I'll undress you myself whether you like it or not." He strode across the room, pulled open a few drawers, yanked out a long, baggy T-shirt that looked familiar and some underwear. Tossing them onto the bed, he left.

Meghan leaned her head back against the pillow and tried to gather her nonexistent strength. Precious seconds later, she sat up and peeled her clammy clothes from her ice-cold body. Inching one of the towels on the bed toward her, she dried herself as best she could and slipped into her T-shirt and panties, her every muscle wailing in strenuous protest at her slow movements.

With a determined effort to keep the black dots dancing behind her eyes from growing larger and overwhelming her, she stumbled over to the second twin bed, where Nick had already turned back the bedcovers. She climbed between the sheets as the bedroom door swung open to reveal an impatient and scowling Nick.

"Satisfied? Or are you aiming for a relapse? Dammit, Meghan, you're the most stubborn woman I've ever met."

"Thank you," she squeaked, sending him a weak smile.

His expression immediately softened. He entered the room and gently rearranged the covers, tucking her in. Picking up a dry towel, he perched on the edge of her bed to pat droplets of water from her hair. "You scared me half out of my mind."

"I'm sorry. I didn't mean to."

Time suddenly stood still. Nick blinked back the emotion in his eyes at the utter sincerity in Meghan's. Smoothing a rebellious strand of hair away from her face, he caressed her soft, cool cheek with his knuckles. "No, I'm sorry. About what happened in the barn, Meghan—I didn't mean the things I said."

"I know."

"I behaved like a complete jerk."

"I goaded you into it."

In spite of what he'd done to her, she'd forgiven him. Lord, how he loved her. He placed his hands on either side of her head, feeling as nervous as a teenager on his first date. He wanted to lose himself in her soul, so full of gentle forgiveness. Fearing rejection, he moved cautiously. She'd been so adamant about his not touching her earlier.

Her eyes softened and her pink tongue flicked out to lick her bottom lip. An almost painful stab of desire knifed through him in response. Twining his fingers in her damp hair, he closed the remaining inches between them, whispering her name.

Her lips were as sweet as he'd remembered. But cold. So damned cold. He warmed them with his own, wishing he could crawl in beside her and warm her entire body. His was on fire. She smiled against his mouth and moved her arms as if to reach for him, but the thick layer of blankets between them prevented the longed-for embrace.

The sound of someone in the room clearing his throat startled them both. Meghan's eyes flew open wide. With a last lingering look at her parted lips, Nick pulled away and turned to find a portly man with a silver handlebar moustache standing in the doorway. He held a familiar black bag in his left hand.

"Dr Wilmot. Thank you for coming so soon," Nick said, rising from his seat on the bed.

"No trouble at all, my boy. If you'll let me take a look at the little lady, I'll meet you outside in a few minutes."

Half an hour later, Nick was still pacing the living room. Why was Dr. Wilmot taking so long? Was Meghan going to be all right? Had he missed something? Somehow mangled her in his hurry to get her to safety? Muttering curses, he strode to the bedroom. His hand was on the doorknob when the door opened. He strained to catch a glimpse of Meghan over the doctor's shoulder.

"Would you mind?" Dr. Wilmot asked gently.

"What? Oh, sorry." Chastened, Nick stepped back. Casting an anxious glance over his shoulder, he followed the rotund man into the living room, where Dr. Wilmot turned to face him.

"She's sleeping. Just plain exhausted."

Relief flooded Nick's aching body. The doctor smiled and answered Nick's unasked questions. "She'll be fine. She's a little bruised and battered, but there are no broken bones or internal damage, nor does she show signs of fever. She does have a rather large lump on the back of her head, though."

"She must've hit it when she fell overboard."

The doctor nodded. "Someone will need to keep an eye on that bump. Would you mind staying with her?"

"Not if it's what she needs."

"She'll need to be awakened hourly. When you wake her, check to see if her pupils are dilated. If they aren't, ask her some simple questions—what's your name, where are you, and so forth. If her pupils are dilated or she gives you any strange answers, call me immediately. If she answers correctly, let her go back to sleep until the next time. I've left her something for the pain, but she can't have it for the next twelve hours. Not until we see what's going on with that bump. I want her as coherent as possible."

"I understand."

The older man eyed Nick thoughtfully. "Are you sure

you don't want me to call someone to come over here and take care of her? You've been through a lot yourself, young man. You need to take off those wet clothes and get some rest, too."

Nick became uncomfortably aware of his sodden state and regretted not having sprinted across the street for dry clothes when he'd had the chance. He shook his head. "I'll take care of her. I can change while she's sleeping."

The doctor hesitated. "She said you saved her life."

Saved her life? She'd almost lost it because of him. Nick was positive she would've recognized the danger she was in sooner if she hadn't been so upset about their argument.

"I did what I had to."

Dr. Wilmot held out his hand. "I'm glad you were there for her, Nick. By the way, welcome back to Ashton."

Nick couldn't hide his startled expression at the first sign of welcome he'd had since his homecoming. He returned the man's firm handshake. "Thank you, Dr. Wilmot."

The doctor placed his hat on his head. "One last thing. Don't let her out of bed for twenty-four hours, no matter how good she says she feels."

Nick swallowed and nodded. He'd like nothing better than to keep Meghan in bed for twenty-four hours—at least—but he didn't think that was what Dr. Wilmot had in mind.

Dr. Wilmot left, and Nick slipped into Meghan's room. His eyes lingered on her pale features, then lowered to her chest to find her breathing soft and steady. Satisfied, he went into the bathroom to get out of his soaked clothes.

Dressed in a towel, he pulled the wet bedding off the second bed, mopped up the floor, and replaced the sheets. He scanned the bedroom curtains and decided Miss Peabody would have a field day with this latest episode in her neighbors' lives. In the kitchen he tossed the bedding and his clothes into the dryer, then returned to the bedroom and pulled a wicker chair from a corner. Moving it to Meghan's bedside, he settled in to wait.

As he watched her sleep, his mind filled with images of this woman who'd touched his bitter heart in so many ways. Meghan on her delectable derriere in the loft. Meghan with a plate of brownies in her slender hands. Meghan wallpapering, filling his bathroom with her essence. Meghan bopping around his living room to the tune of the Supremes. Meghan silent in thought, doing dishes. Meghan with her silky hair down.

Meghan, her aristocratic nose in the air. Meghan, her luscious mouth telling him to go to hell in a variety of ladylike ways. Meghan madder than a hornet, her eyes snapping with fury.

Meghan cold, lifeless, and as gray as the sea.

Just like Heather.

An hour later, Nick, dressed in dry clothes, eased into the wicker chair and touched Megan's shoulder lightly. "Meghan." When she didn't move, he shook her a little harder. "Meghan, honey, wake up."

She blinked sleepily. "Huh? What is it, Jason?" she mumbled. "Did I fall asleep on you again?"

Nick recovered from his surprise enough to say tightly, "It's not Jason."

Her eyes focused on him blearily. "Nick? What are you doing in my bedroom?"

He kept the sharpness from his voice with an effort. "You had an accident. Do you remember?"

She thought for a moment. "I fell into the lake."

"That's right. Dr. Wilmot wants me to ask you some questions because you hit your head when you fell. Ready?"

She nodded once.

"What town are you in?"

"Ashton, New York."

"What day is this?"

"Tuesday, the fifteenth."

"What kind of car do you drive?"

"A 1966 Mustang convertible. Dark blue."

"Good. Now go back to sleep," he said gently, but needn't have bothered. Her eyes were closed before he finished his sentence. Nick heaved a sigh of relief and closed his own eyes. They immediately flew open again, narrowing.

Who the hell was Jason? And why would Meghan expect to find him in her bedroom?

Who's Jason? "Whose house is this?"
"Mrs. Weaver's."
What is he to you? "What month is this?"
"June."
Do you sleep with him? "What do you do for a living?"
"I'm a photographer."
Is he the reason you wouldn't make love with me? "Good. Go back to sleep."

Meghan awoke to the sound of snoring. A pale pink early morning glow suffused the room through the lightweight curtains. She turned her head to find Nick slumped in what had to be an uncomfortable position in Mrs. Weaver's wicker chair. He sat, one long leg draped over an arm of the chair, the other stretched out before him. His arms were crossed, his head thrown back, his mouth open. Another snore ripped through the air, and she stifled the urge to laugh. Her throat hurt too much for that. Nick shifted, scratched his nose, and closed his mouth.

Meghan grinned. She'd wondered what it would be like to wake up beside Nick, but this hadn't exactly been what she'd had in mind. She cleared her sore throat. "What year is this?"

Nick awoke instantly, his eyes alert. His crooked smile warmed her. "That's supposed to be my question."

"You've been sleeping on the job. It's my turn. Answer the question."

"You're a heartless woman, Meghan Edwards," he grumbled.

"I owe you a few. A girl can't get a decent night's sleep with you around."

Nick laughed, then looked at his watch. "How do you feel?"

"The truth? Like a school of porpoises used me for a game of volleyball."

"Dr. Wilmot left some pain pills. It's safe for you to take some now."

"No, thanks." She'd had enough painkillers to last a lifetime. She was grateful when he didn't press. Instead, he stood and stretched. The unabashed show of muscle and sinew he displayed through his snug T-shirt went a long way toward making Meghan forget about her aches and pains.

"I think I'll make coffee." He looked down at her and smiled. "You've got to be hungry by now. How does scrambled eggs and sausage sound?"

"Wonderful. I'm starving. But I'll get it. You've done more than enough already." She started to flip the covers back, but Nick's hand on her wrist stopped her.

"Doctor says you have to stay in bed for twenty-four hours. You have another twelve to go."

He couldn't be serious. "Nick, I'm all right."

"He said you'd try that one on me. The answer is no. You'll stay in that bed if I have to sit on you to keep you there."

Meghan didn't doubt him.

TWELVE

Nick returned bearing a tray laden with a delicious-smelling breakfast that made Meghan's stomach rumble. She fed her eyes on the sight of his broad back as he placed the tray on the dresser. He turned, caught her admiring him, and smiled.

Pulling the pillows from the second bed, he helped her sit up, then placed the pillows behind her with the efficiency of a well-trained nurse. Meghan didn't mind his coddling at all. Any excuse to feel those strong, capable hands on her would do.

"Comfortable?"

She nodded, and he brought the tray over to set it across her lap. A mountain of fluffy eggs and what had to be half a pound of sage sausage stared back at her. "Aren't you having any?"

"Mine's in the kitchen."

The thought of eating alone suddenly dulled Meghan's appetite. "Why don't you bring it in here? There's plenty of room on the tray."

He smiled again and her toes curled. "I'll be right back."

Watching him leave, Meghan knew she was falling in love with Nicholas Hawkinson. Bittersweet pain accompanied the knowledge. Would she ever be able to forget he'd been Heather's first? Heather. Heather and Nick. What exactly had happened between them?

Her mood brightened as they ate. There was something irresistibly cozy about sharing breakfast in bed. Something warm and sunny and wonderful. She nibbled her food, savoring each moment, putting off the questions burning in her brain until she was strong enough to withstand the answers. A few minutes later, Nick had cleaned his plate, while she'd barely touched hers.

She didn't want him to have an excuse to leave. "These are delicious, but I can't eat them all. Here." She lifted a hefty portion of her eggs onto his plate and gave him all but two of her sausages. He smiled his thanks, and sunshine filled her heart; followed by a stab of guilt. After he'd risked his life to save hers, how could she broach the topic of murder?

Their breakfast over, Nick put the tray aside and picked up a napkin. "You've got eggs on the corner of your mouth." He reached out to wipe the speck from her lips, but stopped short, leaving Meghan's pulse skittering wildly. Placing the napkin in her hand, he curled her fingers around it. "It's on the left."

Disappointed, she wiped her own lips. Nick watched her every movement, seeming utterly fascinated. When she'd finished, his eyes met hers with an uncertainty that mirrored her own.

Did he wonder how much she knew? Had he sensed her reluctant suspicions? Was he waiting for her to make the first move? Ask the first question?

Or was something else happening between them? Was he feeling the same pull toward her she was feeling toward him? The desire to reach out and haul him into the bed with her was strong, her scars and sexual inadequacies be damned. They'd work something out.

"I'll get the dishes. You go back to sleep," he said gruffly, and stood. She noticed he couldn't leave the room fast enough.

* * *

Meghan awoke several hours later to find Nick resting on his side, one arm stretched over his head, watching her. Her first thought was that he was too far away. She wanted to touch him, to have him touch her. "Did you get any sleep?" she asked quietly.

"Some," he answered, just as quietly. "I've been awake about twenty minutes."

Meghan flushed at the idea of Nick watching her sleep. It seemed so intimate. "I, uh, need permission to get up."

"No problem. I'll help you." He rolled to a sitting position and came off the bed with an easy masculine grace that set butterflies aflight in her stomach. She couldn't wait for him to touch her, so she didn't protest.

Flipping back the covers, she had her legs over the side of the bed by the time he reached her. Earlier, after breakfast, she'd claimed she was cold and asked Nick to bring her a pair of footless tights. The effort of pulling them on had nearly done her in, but at least her scars were covered.

As he helped her stand, she noted her dizziness was gone. She almost wished it weren't. She wanted a reason to lean on Nick's solid strength, a reason to postpone their inevitable confrontation.

She emerged from the bathroom to find him straightening her bedcovers. "Good. I don't want to go back to bed anyway."

"Meghan," he warned.

"Nick," she parroted. He tried, but couldn't suppress his grin. "How about a compromise? I'll get in bed if you let me show you my pictures of Ashton. They're in my portfolio on the couch in the living room."

Nick settled her in—propped against the pillows—and went after the photographs, then helped to identify them from the wicker chair. An hour later, picturesque scenes of Ashton and candid shots of its inhabitants littered her bedspread.

He picked up a shot of the sunrise over Ashton. "You're good." His smile was both appreciative and teasing. "But I can think of a spot in Ashton you've missed."

She didn't believe him. "Where?"

"I'll show you tomorrow afternoon if you have some time."

They spent the rest of the afternoon playing cards. When they got hungry, they ate peanut butter sandwiches Meghan insisted she loved after Nick offered to go out and buy food. She didn't want him away from her side for a minute. Early evening they spent watching an old John Wayne western on the ancient black-and-white TV Nick rolled into the room on a cart.

What they didn't do was talk about themselves. Or Heather. Or Cole. Or Meghan's accident. Or any other topic that might mar the day's tranquility. Nor did they touch, except when Meghan made a trip to the bathroom.

At nightfall Dr. Wilmot came by and pronounced Meghan stiff and sore but healthy. To celebrate, Meghan suggested they order Chinese carry-out and eat it on the deck. She showered and changed while Nick went home to do the same.

But, to Meghan's dismay, a large cold front had settled in Ashton after the storm, dropping the temperature a dramatic thirty degrees. After a few minutes of exposure to the brisk, chilly air, she set their plates on the coffee table in the living room instead. Nick returned, steam rising from the bag of Chinese food he'd picked up.

"Hurry, or you'll let in the cold," she said as she held open the door for him.

He frowned. "Are you still cold?"

"A little. I tried to turn on the heat, but Mrs. Weaver must've shut the furnace off for the summer. So I thought maybe we could build a fire?"

He hesitated briefly, then nodded. "I've got some seasoned wood stockpiled in the barn. I'll go get it."

Smiling contentedly, Meghan turned on the radio and hummed along with the Platters as she emptied the bag's contents. Sweet and sour soup, egg rolls, fried wontons, rice, two entrées, and last but not least, two fortune cookies. She took two candles from the mantel, placed them on the coffee table, and lit them. A couple of large throw pillows on the floor would do for chairs.

She looked around the room in satisfaction. A fire in the hearth, Chinese food, soft music, candlelight, and Nick. What more could a girl ask for? The seductive implications of the scene stopped her in her tracks. What was she thinking? She and Nick needed to talk, not . . .

She hurried forward. This would never do. They needed distance, not intimacy. But before she could snuff out the candles and put them back on the mantel, Nick returned. He took in the cozy sight of dinner ready and waiting, candles glowing softly on the table. "Looks nice," he murmured, and Meghan's heart rejoiced, overriding all thoughts of distance.

"I can reheat the food in the microwave while you make a fire. Or would you rather eat now?"

"Let's get you some heat first."

Heat was suddenly the furthest thing from Meghan's mind. Nick's eyes reminded her of a banked campfire and warmed her from within. "I'll get the door while you bring in the wood."

Minutes later, they settled side by side at the coffee table, sitting cross-legged on pillows, their backs to the couch. The fire caught quickly and the room lost its chill as dinner evolved into a playful affair, with Meghan—who, as a diplomat's daughter, had spent several years in the Orient—teaching Nick how to use chopsticks.

Meanwhile, Nick was quietly going insane. Every time Meghan touched him, positioning his fingers just so, he felt a nearly overwhelming need to push her down onto the pillows and make slow, delicious love to her. All day long she'd tormented him in a hundred subtle ways— smiling at him impishly, beating him at poker . . . asking him to take her to the bathroom more times than he could count.

Not that he'd minded. He'd welcomed the excuse to touch her. Especially when he was trying so damned hard not to, when all he could think about was Meghan a few feet away with a mouth that was made to be kissed.

When she'd suggested the fire and he'd returned with the wood to see candles burning and hear her favorite music playing, he'd begun to hope. Now, after a tantaliz-ing lesson on the use of chopsticks, his hormones were raging. Looking up from his plate, he noticed her watching him, and her soft smile of approval made him forget all about food.

Making up his mind, he slowly set his chopsticks aside. Meghan's eyes widened, then darkened with desire as she caught the need in his. Unable to stop himself, he leaned toward her. She didn't say a word. Instead, her warm, pliant lips met his more than halfway.

He didn't try to gain entry into her mouth. He only wanted to taste the sweetness that was Meghan. Any more than that and he was afraid he *would* take her right there on the floor. He forced his hands to stay in his lap. When he pulled away, the light in her eyes was both knowing and mischievous.

"Why, Nick. Does Chinese food always put you in such an amorous mood?"

He threw back his head and laughed. She made him feel so damn good. With Meghan he could lower his barriers a little, and it made him feel alive again. But he couldn't afford to pursue their relationship any further. Not until the issue of Heather's death was resolved.

He sobered at the reminder of why Meghan was in Ashton. They needed to talk. About Heather, about the danger Meghan was putting herself in by dredging up the past. Ralph had told him about the questions she was asking around town. Somehow he had to convince her to leave Ashton, to go home. He didn't want her to leave. With her would go the only happiness he'd known in years. But her safety was more important than his happiness.

He decided he'd give her one more day to recover from her near drowning, tell her the truth about Heather, then send her back to the city. Smiling to hide his pain, he winked and said, "Finish your dinner and we'll see."

She laughed, and they settled back into the easygoing, companionable mood they'd shared all day. When they'd finished their meal, Meghan cleared their plates while Nick added logs to the fire. They moved to the couch to open their fortune cookies.

Meghan went first. "It says . . . 'Success comes through hard work.'" She smiled expectantly. "Your turn."

Nick opened his cookie and read the message inside silently. *Open your heart and you will find love.*

"Well?"

He sent her a sly sideways look. "It says a hard-working woman will succeed in teaching me how to use chopsticks."

"It does not." She reached for the fortune, but he shook his head and pushed it into his pocket, then grinned at her indignant disbelief.

"A man's got to have some secrets."

"Seems to me you have more than your share."

The minute she said it, Meghan knew she'd spoiled the mood. Nick's grin vanished and his face closed up tight. But, dammit, she couldn't keep backing down. There'd never be a good time to talk to him about Heather. She just wished she knew how to begin.

"You've got to admit I don't know much about you, Nick."

The fire crackled and a log fell. Nick regarded her silently, his expression inscrutable. Frustrated and miserable, Meghan looked away, into the fire. A Peter, Paul, and Mary ballad filtered across the room. The answer was blowin' in the wind.

Nick got up to rearrange the logs. He didn't add more wood. Returning to the couch, he said, "What do you want to know?"

Meghan felt as if she were standing at the edge of a minefield, with the explosive topic of murder waiting on the other side. She shrugged. "Oh, the usual things."

"You dig into men's pasts often, do you?"

She let his tense comment slide. Curling her legs under her, she turned toward him, settling in. At the opposite end of the couch, he shifted into a reclining position, his long legs stretched out before him. Clasping his hands over his middle, he leaned his head against the back of the couch. The impression he gave was one of relaxation after a good meal, but Meghan knew better. Nick was as wary as a jungle cat.

"How about . . . what do you do for a living?"

"I remodel houses. I'm a professional building contractor."

"In Texas?"

"Houston."

"Do you like it there?"

He shrugged noncommittally.

"Is that where you've lived since . . . leaving Ashton?"

The silence in the room was deafening. Midnight had arrived, and the radio station had gone off the air. The last log crumbled into the fire with a shower of sparks. Meghan shifted, then quietly changed the subject. "You once mentioned your father was a carpenter. Did you learn the trade from him?"

"Some of it." She waited for more, but to her chagrin, he said, "Listen, Meghan, could we stop the questions for now? It's been a long day."

Nick suddenly looked inescapably weary. Meghan winced inside. The poor man had sat up half the night with her, and in return, she grilled him. "I'm sorry. I didn't mean to pry."

He attempted a smile. "It's all right. I'm just not used to talking about myself."

Meghan damned her suspicious mind. The man was innocent. He desperately needed someone to believe in him. Why couldn't she come right out and say she did, no questions asked?

Because trust was a two-way street.

Nick came to his feet, and she felt as if her life force were being drawn from her. She didn't want him to leave, but couldn't ask him to stay. Not with things so unsettled between them. Uncurling her legs, she reluctantly accompanied him to the door.

"You know, I never did thank you for rescuing me, or—"

Nick's fingers against her lips silenced her. "Forget it.

It's over." He paused, frowning. "Or is it? How do you feel?"

She smiled tiredly. "Like I'm running out of gas, actually. A good night's sleep ought to take care of it."

"Will you be all right alone here tonight?"

She wanted to lie and say no. But what would be the point of it? Even if Heather's death weren't standing between them, she couldn't settle for a summertime fling with Nick. Not when she knew she was in love with him. "I'll be fine."

With a lingering caress Meghan felt to her toes, he gently tucked her hair behind her ear. His dark eyes held a longing that made her ache to reach out to him, but she met his gaze steadily and held firm. Without mutual trust, they had nothing.

"Good night, Meghan," he said quietly. "Sleep well." Halfway out the door, he turned and added, "Don't forget to wear your hiking shoes tomorrow. I'll be by around noon."

THIRTEEN

Meghan slept in late and felt renewed when she awoke. The weather had returned to normal for late June in western New York, so she dressed to suit her mood in light green pants and a green and white striped cotton blouse. Humming, she dotted perfume behind her ears, on her wrists, inner elbows, and ankles.

The doorbell rang. Meghan grinned. A last impulsive dab between her breasts and she went to meet Nick. He wore the same jeans and black T-shirt he'd worn the day they'd met. The thought of how far they'd come since then expanded her smile. "I'm all ready." She patted her camera bag. "I've got my extra film and special lenses right here."

"We'll have to stop at my place first." At the house he sprinted up the steps to the mud room and returned with, of all things, a wicker picnic basket.

Meghan was thrilled. And embarrassed. Packing a lunch hadn't entered her mind. How could she think of food when the idea of spending time with Nick had her insides all aflutter?

At least one of them was thinking rationally, she mused as Nick tacked a folded note to the door. They walked in the woods behind his house until a few rays of dappled sunlight filtered through the tall oaks, maples, and pines. Meghan reveled in the cool air on her skin and the smell of fecund soil they kicked up. In time, she gathered her courage to ask the question that had been on her mind most of the night.

"Nick? How did you know I was caught in the storm?"

The sudden stillness in his face told her he'd rather not discuss her accident. She recalled his shushing her when she'd tried to thank him for rescuing her. Good grief. He didn't think they could avoid talking about it forever, did he? She was about to repeat the question when he spoke quietly.

"To tell the truth, I didn't know it was you at first. I saw the storm brewing, so I went down to the dock to check on my boat. I noticed you bobbing around on the lake, and when I saw you were trying to make it to Ashton, I motored out to see if I could help bring you in." He faced her, his eyes dark and solemn. "I recognized you just as the storm hit."

A chill crept across Meghan's soul as she realized how lucky she'd been. "Then if it weren't for you, I'd be—"

His features hardened. "Don't say it. You're here now. That's all that matters."

He was right. There was no point in dwelling on what might have happened. Especially if it was going to cause tension between them. She resumed walking. "I didn't know you had a boat. What kind is it?"

He fell into step beside her. "A twenty-seven-foot ketch. I brought her up from Texas to have something to do when I wasn't working on the house. I've been taking her night-sailing."

So he'd expected to spend his evenings in Ashton alone. The knowledge tugged at her heartstrings. She sighed wistfully. "If I owned a sailboat, I'd take her out for days on end. Explore coastlines. Leave the world behind and get deliberately lost."

He grinned. "Would you like to get lost on mine sometime?"

"Are you serious? I'd love to. But with my luck, I'd sink us before we left the marina."

His humor vanished. "I doubt that. From what I saw, you were doing a hell of a job keeping the boat under control, considering."

Considering she was as inexperienced as they came. A vignette of the accident flashed across her mind. She'd been tugging on the lines and then . . . nothing. She recalled thinking something was wrong. Very wrong.

She stopped short as an unpalatable thought struck her. Maybe it hadn't been her inexperience that had sunk the boat. "Nick. . . ?"

His fingers touched her cheek. The caress was soothing, but his smile didn't reach his eyes as he smoothed back her hair. "Trust me. You did everything you could."

"But—"

"Meghan, anybody could have trouble in a storm."

He was trying too hard. He knew something. "You didn't."

"I was raised on Lake Ashton. I've been out there in every kind of weather. I know every dip and swell." He draped his arm across her shoulders, urging her forward. "C'mon. We didn't come here to discuss our failings, imaginary or otherwise."

Meghan acquiesced reluctantly. Even if she let her mind run wild and assumed the boat had been tampered with, the issue was dead anyway. The boat was gone. Lost at the bottom of the lake.

They emerged into a grassy clearing and decided to break for lunch. Nick smiled apologetically as they settled on the ground. "Sorry, I didn't think to bring a blanket."

Actually, he'd considered it at length, but decided against it. It could lead to all sorts of complications if he ended up with Meghan on a blanket in the great outdoors. He was having trouble keeping his hands off her as it was. Her perfume was driving him crazy. He wanted to explore every inch of her and discover where she wore the scent that made her smell like sweet summer roses.

"No outdoorsman badge for you," she quipped, snapping a few pictures.

What he wanted to do with her, they didn't give out

badges for. Lord. What had made him think he could spend another day with her without taking her in his arms and showing her how badly he wanted her? Dammit, he should have sent her home last night.

He opened the picnic basket and handed her a napkin and a piece of chicken. "We'll have to take this one course at a time. I must've left the plates on the counter." Along with your common sense, Hawkinson.

Meghan nodded and bit into her chicken breast. She closed her eyes, and he had the feeling she would savor every mouthful. She seemed to find enjoyment in the smallest things. He'd bet his sailboat she'd carry that enthusiasm with her to bed. He shifted uncomfortably at his body's response to the image of Meghan in bed, her long, long legs wrapped around him.

"I have to tell you, Nick. You make the best fried chicken I've ever tasted."

He nearly groaned. Here he was thinking of them locked together in lust, and she was praising his domestic talents. One of these days he'd have to show her his experience wasn't limited to kitchen duty—but not today. There were too many lies between them, too many uncertainties ahead of them.

"It's my mother's recipe. It won her an album full of blue ribbons at the county fair." He smiled in bittersweet remembrance. "People for miles around would come when Minnie Hawkinson brought her fried chicken to a picnic."

Meghan looked as if she'd arrived at a sailing regatta half a day late. "Minnie?"

He nodded, unable to hide the sadness and regret that always came when he thought of his mother. He'd disappointed her so badly. "Her given name was Minerva. She died while I was away."

Meghan's eyes suddenly reminded him of the rich chocolate his mother had used to make her award-winning fudge. Her hand came to rest gently on his forearm. "Oh, Nick. I'm so sorry."

The feelings her touch elicited in him were anything but

comforting. Forcing himself to break contact, Nick reached into the basket for the second course. "Ready for some fruit salad?"

A flash of hurt entered her eyes before anger overtook it. "Dammit, Nick. Why do you keep doing that? Shutting me out."

He spoke tersely. "I don't need you to feel sorry for me, Meghan."

"Seems to me you don't need me for much else, either. Certainly not to talk to, or cook, or clean, or to offer moral support. You're a regular one-man show."

Hell. He'd done it again. Why couldn't he get through a single day without hurting her? He lifted a hand to her still-flushed cheek. "Come here and I'll show you what I need."

Meghan blinked, then shook her head and pulled away. "Oh, no, you don't, Nicholas. I want to know exactly what it is you expect from me."

Her response startled him. "I don't 'expect' anything."

"All right then. "What do you *want* from me?"

Christ. What kind of question was that? He looked away, into a nearby copse of trees. No wonder he'd never been any good at conversations with women, if this was the kind of stuff they got into. He looked back at her and saw she wasn't going to be put off by some flippant answer. Taking a deep breath, he said, "Okay. I'll tell you what I want. I want . . . your friendship." Coward.

She crossed her arms. "That's a start. Anything else?"

Stubborn little witch, wasn't she? Strangely enough, it was her stubbornness that appealed to him the most. Or was it the way she wasn't afraid to stand up for what she believed in? "And I enjoy watching you take my side against the good citizens of Ashton so much, I have to stop myself from deliberately provoking you into doing it. Satisfied?"

How was he supposed to think straight when her eyes went all soft and dewy on him like that? It was all he could do not to yank her into his arms and cover her with his body. Instead, he dug in to his fruit salad.

Meghan quietly followed suit, her emotions suddenly too close to the surface for her to speak. When she finally did, she kept it light, asking him to tell her more about his sailboat and the trips he had taken. He seemed relieved by the change of subject, and the rest of the meal passed pleasantly. Afterward, she took pictures of the clearing and Nick.

Returning to the woods, she directed him to sit on a fallen oak. "Straddle it."

He sent her a funny look. "What for?"

She knew he wasn't keen on posed shots, but couldn't resist trying this one. "For fun. I'm going to set the timer. If you straddle the log, there'll be room for me in the picture."

He grinned, then complied with her order while she placed the camera on a nearby stump, focused, and set the timer. Racing across the ground, she leapt onto the fallen tree.

Strong arms circled her from behind. Steely thighs cradled her bottom snugly. Too snugly. Something hard and male poked her in the rear. Meghan's eyes widened. The camera clicked.

"Wait. I wasn't ready. We have to do it again."

"Can't you set that thing so it takes more than one shot?"

"Only if I use the hand control." Rummaging through her bag, she found the cord. For the pleasure of it, she focused on Nick again, then tossed him the control and hopped onto the log again, fanny first. She overshot her mark and started to slide. With one smooth movement, Nick caught and kissed her.

Click. Before she could recover, he shifted her to face the camera and rested his chin on her head, his arms sliding around her middle to hold her tight.

Click. Nick shifted again, nuzzled her hair, and brushed a feather-light kiss on the side of her neck.

Click. He lifted his head, and Meghan leaned back to encounter smoldering eyes. "Have you got enough pictures now?"

She nodded, mesmerized. She wasn't sure how she'd managed to end up exactly where she wanted to be, and she didn't want to say anything to spoil the moment.

"Good." Nick dropped the hand control, and his lips came down on hers in a kiss that was anything but playful. Fireworks exploded behind her eyelids. She twined her arms around his neck, and the passion that had been building between them for the last three days erupted in a shower of color.

One arm held her fast while his free hand roamed, branding her with an intimate urgency that left her breathless. His hand burned through her hair and down her arm until their fingers entwined. He seemed to be forcibly holding himself back. Meghan squeezed his hand, offering silent encouragement, before placing it on her thigh, her scars forgotten.

With a groan, Nick released her lips and buried his face against her neck. Meghan threw her head back as he rained kisses on her throat and kneaded her thigh, sending swirling currents of desire on a direct course to the core of her womanhood. Her fingers jubilantly tunneled through his hair.

Nick pulled away and looked deep into her eyes. The passion she saw burning there dazzled her. "I want you so damn much."

His eyes flamed with a need that begged her not to refuse. Meghan's heart felt as if it could reach the top of the trees. She framed his face, brought her lips up to his, and slipped her tongue past his teeth. Nick immediately resumed command, plundering her mouth with a hunger that would've frightened her if he'd been anyone else.

They shifted on the log, and she felt the stone-hard evidence of his desire against her leg. His hand spanned her rib cage, holding her prisoner. When his fingers grazed her breast, Meghan pressed closer and molded her fullness against his palm, moaning as he kneaded gently.

"I've needed this for so long," he rasped. "To touch you, to have you touch me. Touch me, Meghan. Please."

Her hands drifted lower, obliging him. His unsteady

fingers unbuttoned her blouse. Their tongues teased and tormented. He pulled her shirt from her pants. She returned the favor. With the heated urgency of teenagers in the first throes of passion, flesh met flesh.

The combination of hard calluses against her back and hot skin against her stomach electrified Meghan. She moaned as his work-roughened hand unfastened her bra and reclaimed a breast. Mindlessly she fumbled with his belt buckle as his tongue delved deeply into her mouth, pitching her senses into glorious chaos. His hand moved to capture her other breast, rolling her nipple between his thumb and forefinger. Gasping her pleasure, Meghan arched against him . . . and lost her balance.

Together they toppled, landing on the hard ground with matching grunts. Stillness enveloped them as they stared at each other in astonishment, Meghan sprawled atop Nick, her hands braced on his chest, her blouse open to expose her breasts and lacy white bra.

A nearby twig snapped, and two heads jerked around.

"Oops. Sorry folks."

"Dammit, Ralph, what the hell are you doing here?" Nick thundered, drawing Meghan closer to shield her from Ralph's eyes.

"Enjoying nature, same as you are," he replied with a grin. "I also read your note." He recognized Meghan from behind, and sobered. "Think I better make myself scarce."

A stunned Meghan looked from Ralph's retreating back into Nick's scowl. "You two are friends?"

"Cousins," Nick replied dryly.

Meghan buried her face in his chest. When he saw her shoulders shake with laughter, Nick released a wry chuckle of his own. "Let me up, minx. These pine needles are poking the devil out of me."

She got up and buttoned her blouse. Nick stood and yanked down the bottom half of his T-shirt. Throwing each other wary glances neither caught, they tucked in their clothes. Nick dusted the seat of his pants and carefully looked Meghan over.

"You all right?"

She grinned. "As all right as anyone caught doing what we were just doing can be."

A slow smile spread across Nick's face. Placing both hands on her shoulders, he kissed her nose. "Don't worry about Ralph. I once caught *him* out here with . . . with someone almost as beautiful as you are," he ended quietly.

Smiling, Meghan went to retrieve her camera. As she bent to pick up her bag, Nick said, "I was taking Meghan up to Burnham Hill so she could take some pictures. You want to come along?"

Ralph stepped from behind a tree. "Sure you don't mind?"

Meghan blinked in surprise, then glanced at Nick, who'd turned away to pick up the picnic basket. Apparently he now felt they needed a chaperone. "Oh, no. We'd love to have you," she said, and surprised herself by meaning it.

In friendly camaraderie they charted an uphill course, to emerge in a meadow with a bird's-eye view of Lake Ashton. Meghan was enchanted. The lake sparkled below like a huge diamond in the afternoon sun. She wandered away from the men to take pictures, and when she was finished, focused her zoom lens on them across the meadow. Ralph was speaking, and Nick didn't look at all happy with what he was hearing. His stance was rigid, his hands clenched at his sides.

Frowning, Meghan made her way back to the men. By the time she joined them, they were talking sports, and all outward signs of Nick's agitation were gone, save one. He turned to her, his dark eyes guarded. "Ready to head back?"

Dammit. He'd shut her out again. "Sure."

They moved in single file along the path, each absorbed in thought. The jocular atmosphere that had accompanied them up the hill was noticeably absent on the way down. When they reached the bottom of the hill, Nick plunged ahead, leaving Meghan feeling cut adrift. She didn't like the feeling. Not a bit.

She turned to Ralph, annoyed. "What did you say to him?"

He studied her for a moment. "Don't get me wrong, Meghan. I like you. A lot. But I'm not about to tell you anything that puts me on the bad side of Nick. It isn't worth it. So if you have any questions, I suggest you take them to him."

Meghan knew a dismissal when she heard one, but was tired of politely letting people sidestep her. "It had something to do with Coleman Benson, didn't it?"

He said nothing, but his eyes gave him away.

"Dammit, Ralph! All I want to know is what's going on between those two! Is that too much to ask? If it's such a big secret, why does everyone in town know about it but me? And why did you have to come running after him with the latest development? For God's sake, couldn't it have *waited*?"

Mortified, she turned away, blinking back tears. "I'm sorry. That was uncalled-for."

"You're in love with him, aren't you?" he asked quietly.

She said nothing, refusing to look at him.

"I take it he doesn't know?"

"There's no reason to tell him. I'm leaving in a few days. Maybe sooner. I don't belong here. If anything, these past few days have shown me that. No one will talk to me. . . ."

"If you're referring to Nick, he never was much of a talker. But don't hold that against him. He needs time, Meghan. Time to put the past behind him and come to terms with his life. He's determined to settle this thing with Benson once and for all."

"Will you at least tell me what started their . . . feud?"

Ralph smiled enigmatically. "Sure. I've got a feeling it's something you're gonna hear about sooner or later anyway." Taking her elbow, he started walking. "Cole's family moved to town when we were high school sophomoies. He and Nick rubbed each other wrong from the first. Cole had been some sort of hotshot at the school he'd left. Star quarterback and all that. Nick was Ashton's quarterback and—''

Meghan stopped and stared. ''Nick was involved in sports?''

Ralph laughed and resumed walking. ''I know what you mean. He was a loner then, too. I'm the one who talked him into going out for football. Took me months.'' He paused, remembering. ''Cole tried every trick he could to get Nick off the team. No dice, though. Then, during an intense game with our arch-rivals, we lost one too many to injuries, and Coach had to send Cole in as an offensive guard.'' He shook his head in disgust. ''It was tough to tell whose side Cole was on that night. He kept letting Nick get sacked.''

''Didn't anyone see what was happening?''

''Of course. But tensions were running high. We were behind. Winning would mean we'd go to the state championship.''

''But what about Nick?''

Ralph smiled at her concern. ''The man's no quitter. Broke a few ribs and his nose, but he won the game.''

''You mean Cole got away with it?''

''Nah. Coach kicked him off the team just before the game ended. That was our junior year. Cole didn't play again. Then Cole's girlfriend, Mary Lou Brighton, dropped him and took a liking to Nick that wouldn't quit. Pissed Cole off to no end.''

Mary Lou. The mayor's wandering wife. Jealousy tightened her stomach muscles, and Meghan swallowed. ''What did Nick do?''

''The usual things. It was hot and heavy there for a while, until he started getting into trouble. After high school he started hanging out with some guys whose best years were behind them.'' Ralph sighed. ''Nick should've gone to college. He had the brains for it. If he'd gone away, none of this . . .''

Nick had discovered they weren't keeping up with him.

Ralph appeared to consider his next words. "I meant what I said earlier, about Nick needing time. He might have his quirks, but he deserves a shot at happiness, and I'd like to see him get it."

"Moving in on Meghan?" Nick asked lightly as he returned to them, his expression anything but teasing.

"Nope," Ralph answered blithely. "Just making sure her intentions toward you are honorable, cousin."

Nick looked at Meghan, an odd light in his eyes. "Are they?"

Feeling heat blossom in her cheeks, she ducked her head and busied herself with putting her camera back into its bag.

"Nice weather we're having," Ralph commented idly. "Weatherman says we might be in for another storm, though."

Storm. Boat. Rental boat. Meghan remembered her responsibility to Cole. "Then I guess I'd better make arrangements to find what's left of Cole's boat before it hits."

Both men looked at Meghan strangely.

"You know, the rental boat I left at the bottom of the lake? I'll have to tell Cole what happened and offer to pay for it."

"The hell you will."

"Nick. Be reasonable. I can't just leave it in the lake."

"You didn't. I brought it up from the dock this morning."

Meghan was astonished. "You saved Cole's boat?"

"What's going on here?" Ralph interjected.

Nick ignored him, still looking at Meghan. "It's in the barn. What's left of it, that is." He placed his hands on her shoulders, and she felt a cold sense of foreboding. "Dammit, I didn't want to have to tell you this, but your accident wasn't caused by any sailing mistakes you made."

It was one thing to have nebulous suspicions, quite another to hear them voiced with conviction. "What do you mean?"

"Someone tampered with the boat."

"Hell." This from Ralph. "Are you sure?"

"How can you tell?" Meghan asked.

Nick took her hand in his. Its strength bolstered her own. "Come on, I'll show you." In the barn he picked up the frayed end of a shroud, one of four wires that supported the mast laterally. "The shroud's been cut part-way through. My guess is, it was done with a hacksaw. Whoever did this cut just enough to weaken the wire. The storm did the rest."

Meghan found it hard to accept that someone actually wanted her hurt. "Are you sure the storm didn't do it all? Couldn't the shroud have been weak to start with? I mean, a hacksaw seems awfully dramatic."

"Meghan, all four shrouds were cut."

"Oh."

"It was only a matter of which one of them went first. The results would've been the same. The mast would've snapped and the boat would've capsized. Do you want to see the others?"

She nodded. Nick peeled back the electrical tape covering the junctures of the remaining shrouds to expose the damage.

Ralph whistled, low. "It's not unusual to use electrical tape to protect the rigging from the elements. A perfect way to hide the hacksaw's damage."

Both men looked at Meghan expectantly. "What do you think we should do about it?" she asked.

"Do about it?" Nick gave a short, harsh laugh. "There's not a damn thing we *can* do about it without a witness to say they saw someone cut these wires."

"Why would someone want to sabotage your boat?" Ralph asked.

Meghan hedged. "I don't think it's a case of someone wanting to hurt me, specifically. The Wharf has a fleet of rental boats. I happened to get this one. Maybe someone has a grudge against The Wharf, a disgruntled employee—"

"That's hogwash and you know it," Nick snapped.

She glared at him. "Are you calling me a liar?"

"No. Just blind. If you can't see Benson's hand in this—"

"You think Cole did this?"

"Not think. Know. It reeks of his handiwork."

"Oh, for— When are you going to stop blaming Coleman Benson for everything that goes wrong around here?"

Ralph swore. Nick opened his mouth to say something, then apparently thought better of it. Raking a hand through his hair, he sighed. "All right. I'll tow the boat back to The Wharf for you tomorrow."

"No." She didn't want Nick confronting Cole. If there was any confronting to be done, she'd do it. "I'll take the boat back. I'm the one who signed for it, I'm the one who sank it. It's my responsibility to return it, not yours."

Nick crossed his arms. "And just how do you propose to get it back to The Wharf?"

Meghan felt her cheeks pinking. "I'll rent a trailer."

"Over my dead body."

With that, Nick and Ralph grudgingly hitched the trailer holding what remained of the rental boat to Nick's truck. Ralph excused himself to go inside and use the telephone. With Meghan's guidance, Nick backed the truck onto the street. He jumped out and faced her, leaving the motor running.

"You know how to drive a stick shift?" he grumbled.

"I have one in the Mustang." Which reminded her. She needed to retrieve her car from the marina.

"I can't talk you out of this?" he persisted.

Meghan smiled and placed a hand on his cheek. "I'll be fine. Please don't worry."

His expression softened and he slipped his arms around her. "I can't help but . . . Oh, hell. Listen, Meghan. We need to talk."

Her brows lifted. "About. . . ?"

"About a lot of things, but I don't have time right now. Ralph and I have to . . . ." He paused. "Tell you what. Why don't you come over at sunset and we'll go up to the loft. The view of the lake is great that time of day."

Suddenly he smiled. "You don't even have to bring your camera if you don't want to."

His thighs brushed hers as his deep brown eyes issued an invitation she couldn't mistake. Her heart catapulated into her throat. Maybe it was time to let the past go. Nick wanted her. She wanted him. Life was too short to worry about ghosts. Whatever had happened between Nick and Heather, it was over now.

Placing her hands on Nick's chest, she stepped on tiptoe and gave him a quick kiss on the lips. "For you, I'll leave my camera home."

She started to move away, but Nick tightened his arms around her. His kiss was long, lingering, and filled with promise. Her knees went weak, and the hours until sunset stretched before her like years. He smiled and helped her into the driver's seat.

"Until tonight."

Spirits soaring, she drove through Ashton, trailing Coleman Benson's wrecked rental boat like a victory banner.

FOURTEEN

"I understand one of our boats is missing, Fedders," Cole announced imperiously, eyeing the youth at the boat rental booth. "What do you know about it?"

The young man swallowed. "I loaned the boat to Miss Edwards, Mr. Benson . . . like you said to, sir . . . two days ago."

"Two days ago? Where is it now?" Cole scanned the docked boats, masking a grim smile. The one he'd designated for Meghan's use was indeed missing.

"I . . . I don't know, sir."

"What do you mean, you don't know?"

Meghan approached the rental booth from behind Cole. "What he means is, I haven't returned the boat yet."

Cole turned. "Meghan."

Was it her imagination, or did he seem surprised to see her? She eyed him shrewdly, supposing he would be—if he'd sabotaged the boat. "I understood you'd given your approval for me to keep the boat as long as I liked. As it happens, I'm afraid I have bad news for you, Cole." She chafed at ignoring the issue of sabotage, but Nick was right. They had no proof it was Cole.

Still, nothing prevented her from seeing if she could make him squirm. "I got caught in the storm. The mainmast snapped when the boom came in contact with a shroud—which I might add was in suspect shape to start with—and the mainsheet came loose from the force of the storm. I would've been here to tell you about it sooner, but I had a small accident myself."

"I trust you're all right?"

Meghan forced a smile. "I'm fine, thank you. But I don't believe the boat is salvageable. Here's my card." She placed it on the counter. "If you bill me for the damages, I'll see you're reimbursed. Now, where would you like me to leave the boat?"

Cole's tan faded a shade. Meghan wished she had her camera. "It's here?"

"In the parking lot." She pointed to Nick's truck with the pitiful sailboat in tow.

After a long moment, Cole spoke. "Give him your keys. He'll see it's unloaded." He turned to the youth. "Run up to the main building and get someone to help you. Now!"

"Yes, sir!" The young man raced away.

"There's no need to take it out on the boy. It wasn't his fault the boat was unsafe to start with. He only did what you—"

Cole rounded on her. "Don't tell me how to treat my staff!"

"I see your mood hasn't improved since we last met."

"And I see your taste in associates hasn't improved."

"Nick loaned me his truck so I could bring back *your* boat."

"I'm sure it wasn't willingly."

"It's here, isn't it?"

An evil light came into Cole's eyes. He leaned against the counter and crossed his arms. "Tell me, just what kind of thrill does it give a woman like you to spend your time with a convicted criminal?"

"Excuse me?"

He smiled smugly. "Obviously you're not aware of the man's police record."

"Nick was arrested, Cole. And released without being charged."

"Five years ago, yes. But before that . . ." He shrugged.

A sudden uneasiness gripped her as she vaguely remembered Tom saying something about Nick having had some sort of drug trouble. She'd forgotten about it until now, not once having considered Nick the type to use drugs. He cared too much for his body. Heather's letter had also said he was straight.

"What's your point, Cole?"

"That you obviously know very little about the man. He was in trouble with the law long before being arrested for Heather Morgan's murder, and now that he's back, it's only a matter of time before he gets into trouble again. If you're not careful, you're going to find yourself right in the middle of it."

"Is that a threat?"

"Of course not, merely a statement of fact. You can't think the amount of time the two of you have spent together has gone unnoticed. Ashton's buzzing with speculation. Naturally I'd hear about it since half the town works for me. Would you like to know what they're saying? They're wondering why you've decided to become so chummy with a man who killed one woman and destroyed another's marriage to hide his guilt."

Meghan flushed. "Nick didn't—"

"Defend him until you turn blue if you want to, Meghan, but it won't do any good. I intend to see to it no one *ever* forgets what he's done." His voice vibrated with such hatred, it gave Meghan chills. "You know, Meghan, I expected better from you. But then again, Hawkinson's always had the devil's own luck when it comes to the ladies. Take the way he rooked Mary Lou into being his alibi. And how did he repay her? By disappearing without a word to anyone, leaving her to face her humiliated husband and the town's censure alone." Cole's eyes narrowed into pale chips of ice. "But I suppose you knew all that, seeing as how you and Hawkinson are such good friends.''

Meghan said nothing, unwilling to admit how sketchy her knowledge of Nick's past was. Refusing to admit that each time she'd come close to asking him about it, he'd either withdrawn or found a way to distract her.

"But that was nothing compared to what he did to Heather.'' Cole looked away, and Meghan followed his gaze to where two youths were returning Nick's truck and trailer to the parking lot, minus the sailboat.

"His jealousy killed her, you know,'' Cole said suddenly.

Meghan's eyes jerked to his. What was he talking about?

"Yes, jealousy,'' he repeated with a smooth conviction that jangled her nerves. "Her killer couldn't stand the idea of her wanting another man over him.''

Confused, she studied Cole's smirking face, then played a sudden hunch. "Tell me, Cole, since you know so much about it—who was this other man Heather was involved with?''

He sent her a pitying look, mistaking her motive for asking. "Stop looking for excuses, Meghan. The man's guilty. If you don't believe me, ask him.'' He paused. "Then again, that might not be a wise idea. His temper is legendary, you know. If you push him too far, you might end up the same way Heather did.'' He smiled unpleasantly. "Wouldn't that open those exotic eyes of yours?''

Meghan tensed at the malice in his voice. "Don't be ridiculous,'' she snapped. "Nick wouldn't hurt me.''

Cole's eyes glittered. "Don't be a fool. He doesn't care for you, any more than he cared for the others. He's only using you to annoy me.''

The boy returned, preempting her response. "It's all taken care of, Mr. Benson, sir.''

Cole held out his hand for the keys, his hard eyes not leaving Meghan. Taking her elbow, he escorted her to Nick's truck. "Don't tell me you didn't notice how quickly he latched on to you once he got wind of my interest in you. It's a habit with him. He's always wanted what I have. The sooner you understand that, the better off you'll be.''

He smiled coldly as he shut the door and handed her keys through the window. Meghan started the engine and threw the truck into gear, not trusting herself to speak. Cole glanced at the empty trailer, then back at Meghan.

''You needn't have bothered you know. The boat is insured.''

Whistling, he sauntered away. Meghan rolled out of the parking lot and made her way back to Ashton, her mind spinning. Pulling into Nick's driveway, she cut the engine, then crossed her arms on the steering wheel and stared at the barn, trying to piece together what had just happened.

Cole had accused Nick of murdering her sister. Or had he? He hadn't come right out and said the words ''Nick killed Heather,'' but he'd come damned close. Setting her emotions aside, she analyzed their conversation. Cole had said Nick's jealousy had killed Heather. She found it difficult to believe, given his supposed involvement with Mary Lou Brighton, but assuming for argument's sake Cole's statement was true . . . the question was . . . jealousy over Heather's association with whom? Cole?

Why not? It made sense. But if Cole was to be believed, Nick's jealousy had little to do with the woman involved. His jealousy was directed at Cole, the enmity between the two men so strong, any woman would do. Correction. Any woman who divided her time between Nicholas Hawkinson and Coleman Benson would do.

As Mary Lou Brighton had. As Heather had.

As she had.

Meghan swore and jumped out of the truck. She'd had enough of secrets, lies, and this endless finger pointing. It was time to bring things to a head. Returning to her bungalow, she called Jason, the only member of her family who knew she'd come to Ashton. He'd done his best to talk her out of it, to convince her to let the past be, or to at least wait until he could go with her, but she'd been adamant about leaving immediately once she'd discovered Heather's letter. In the end, he'd let her go after extracting a promise she'd call him if she needed him.

She needed him now. If only to talk to someone whose every word wasn't suspect.

He wasn't home. With a resigned sigh, she left a message on their machine and settled in to stew and wait. She returned to Nick's only minutes before sundown, having waited until the last possible moment in hopes Jason would call. She also didn't like the questions running through her mind, and liked the prospect of asking them of Nick even less. But she didn't see any alternative. Until he confirmed his innocence, she would be vulnerable to vicious attacks like Cole's.

Her hand was in midair, preparing to knock on the kitchen door, when Nick opened it, smiling. "Hi." Wineglasses in hand, he gave her a friendly kiss, startling her. "Glad you could make it. Another five minutes and you'd have missed the show."

Breezing past her, he scooped up a bottle of Valpolicella and went out into the yard. Meghan gritted her teeth and followed, wondering what the devil he was so happy about. In the barn she noticed Nick had put everything in its place. No more clutter, no more musty smell, no more corners filled with spiderwebs and dirt. The loft was also clean. The hay was gone, the floorboards scrubbed, the cobwebs and hornets' nests cleared from the rafters. The doors were thrown open, and a subdued orange light filled the room.

Nick unfolded a red and black checkered blanket, spreading it on the floor in front of one of the open doors. "I didn't forget the blanket this time," he said with a slow smile.

"So I see," she mumbled, still put off by his sunny mood when hers was so dark.

They settled on the blanket to watch the sunset. The fiery red sun eased downward, while Meghan's thoughts churned. Minutes later, the sun dipped below the horizon, leaving the lake a tranquil shade of blue. The opening act was over. It was time for the real show to begin.

Sipping her wine, Meghan looked over at Nick. He seemed lost in thought. A cool breeze ruffled his black hair as she absorbed the strength in his profile, his tanned skin, the lines that crinkled around his eyes when he smiled. She recalled his smile of welcome tonight, his affectionate kiss, and her fingers tightened on her glass.

Damn Cole for putting her in this position. Damn them both. She didn't for a minute believe Nick was guilty, but he hadn't offered her any evidence to the contrary. Why? Didn't he trust her? The thought stabbed her like a serrated knife.

He turned to her with a gentle smile, and the knife twisted. "You're awfully quiet tonight. How'd it go with the boat? Any problems?"

This was her opening. Slowly she set her wine aside, then met Nick's eyes, her own quietly watchful. "I left my card and offered to pay for damages, but Cole said they were insured."

Nick tensed. "You saw Cole?"

"Yes. We talked for quite a while." Nick broke eye contact first, to stare out over the water. Meghan recognized his withdrawal and became more determined not to let him elude her this time. "Will you tell me why you left Ashton, Nick?"

He turned, his dark eyes searching hers. Her heartbeat accelerated, but she kept her face impassive. Cole might have been lying through his teeth, but he was right about one thing. Nick owed her some answers.

"Let me guess," he said slowly. "Cole had a fit when he saw you driving my truck and decided to fill you in on a few unpleasant aspects of my past."

Meghan held firm. "Was he lying to me?"

Nick looked into his wine for a moment, then at the lake, then back at her. "Depends on what he said. If he said I left because of Heather's murder, it's true enough." His voice hardened. "I would've gotten life if it hadn't been for Mary Lou." He paused, noting the sudden tightness in her face, then smiled bitterly. "So you know about that, do you?" He looked away, his jaw clenched. "I thought so."

Meghan didn't speak. She couldn't. The pain she felt at the idea there might be even a kernel of truth in Cole's words was too strong. Nick finished his wine, then met her eyes again.

"Cole enjoys telling people what an unscrupulous bastard I am. I'm sure he got a special kick out of telling *you*."

"Why is that?" she whispered.

He gave a harsh laugh. "Because I've so obviously snookered you into believing I'm innocent of adultery and murder."

She shivered. This wasn't what she'd expected. What she'd wanted. But it was too late to turn back now. "Have you?"

He stiffened and his eyes went flat. "What do you think?"

"It doesn't matter what I think."

"Surely you must have some opinion."

Her heart thundered in her ears. "Answer me, Nick. Did you kill Heather Morgan, as Cole claims, or not?"

A muscle twitched in his cheek. "What difference would it make if I said I didn't? You've obviously made up your mind."

"I want to hear you say the words."

Nick simply looked out over the lake.

"Damn you, I have a right to know!"

He turned on her, his eyes blazing. "Jesus. You and your damn rights. What gives you the right to dig up my past? A few shared meals and a couple of kisses? I've been with a lot of women in my time, but not one of them has ever claimed they had any rights over me, and I did a hell of a lot more with them than I did with you. What makes you so damn special?"

Meghan's heart cracked. Cole had called that one right. Nick didn't care for her. She was nothing to him but a pawn in some warped game of one-upmanship. Knowing her feelings meant nothing to him and refusing to show how the knowledge devastated her, she lashed out with the only weapon she had.

"Heather Morgan was my sister. My *sister*, Nick. I think that gives me a considerable right to know who killed her!"

His face registered satisfaction before it became a blank mask. "I've been wondering if you were going to tell me."

Meghan froze. "You knew?"

"Since the beginning."

"Is that why you've spent so much time with me?"

"Among other reasons," he offered coolly. "One of them was to keep you out of Benson's clutches."

The last shred of hope in her heart died. "Then you're no better than he is."

Nick stared. *"What?"*

"The pair of you are worse than two dogs with a bone. Cozying up to me was nothing more than part of a calculated plan to see who would win the girl this time, wasn't it? What are you playing? Two out of three?"

"What are you talking about?"

"Mary Lou Brighton. Heather Morgan. Meghan Edwards. One. Two. Three. The first lost her husband, the second her life, and the third is going to find out which of you two bastards is responsible before the week is out." She scrambled to her feet and started for the exit, knocking her wine over as she rose.

"Meghan, wait!"

She kept moving. Now that the sun had disappeared over the horizon, she could barely see her feet in the barn's dim light. Her eyes were also moist, but she refused to shed a tear. There was no way in hell she was going to let Nick see how his game playing had hurt her.

"Meghan!" he repeated, his voice suddenly sharp.

She picked up speed and didn't see the coil of thick rope in her path before it was too late. Stumbling, she flailed for something to hold on to to break her fall. She caught a portion of the rope wrapped around a hook on the wall. Searing her palm, it slid from her grasp and slithered into the rafters.

She jumped backward, her legs tangling in the uncoiling rope, and lost her balance, falling onto her back. Iron arms encircled her calves as Nick tackled her and jerked her downward and beneath him. Her backside burned at the roughness and speed with which he dragged her across the floor.

She kicked and clawed as panic engulfed her. "Let me go, you slimy son of a—!"

What happened next, Meghan would remember for the rest of her life as if it had happened in slow motion. She squirmed free of Nick's hold, scooted a foot upward, and yanked her arms out from between them. One arm flew over her head, and she saw the last of the rope snake toward the ceiling. The hanging pitchfork she'd seen that first day bore down on her as smoothly as a guillotine.

She screamed.

The pitchfork buried its gleaming tines in the floor with a loud thunk. Meghan lay perfectly still, feeling as if she'd shattered into a million pieces. Her eyelids fluttered open at the sound of labored breathing echoing in the loft. She and Nick were tangled together as if they'd been locked in mortal combat. His face was buried in her neck, his arms covering her head. A low moan of pain escaped her clenched teeth.

Nick raised his head. He looked forward and his face went white. "Don't move. Your jacket's caught by the pitchfork."

Move? Meghan didn't think she'd be capable of movement ever again. The shock of what had almost happened to her held her paralyzed. She could've been skewered to death by a giant pitchfork. If it hadn't been for Nick . . .

She closed her eyes and tried to will away the horror, while Nick disengaged their legs and crawled above her to remove the pitchfork that had her jacket sleeve pinned to the floor. "Hold still and I'll ease it away from you. I don't want to hurt you."

Meghan didn't tell him she was already hurt. Her heart

was rent asunder, her palm burned, her backside felt battered, and a series of sharp pains was ricocheting through her wrenched leg. He pulled the pitchfork from the planking and gently lowered her arm to her side. She groaned involuntarily.

"Where does it hurt?"

"My . . . leg," she gasped. "It's twisted."

Gently he straightened it, and the pain subsided to a dull throb. Meghan closed her eyes and breathed deeply, then opened them again to find Nick looking down at her, his face filled with remorse.

"I'm going to carry you into the house."

She braced herself for more pain, but needn't have. Nick lifted her into his arms and descended the narrow stairs without allowing any part of her to bump against the wall. Entering the house, he carried her upstairs and gently laid her on his bed. He left, and Meghan heard running water as she tried to focus on her surroundings in an effort to regain her wits. All she could absorb was that his bed seemed to stretch clear across the room.

Nick returned and lightly pressed a cool washcloth against her forehead. In his eyes she saw deep apology. Silently he smoothed salve on her rope-burned palm. Meghan grimaced.

"What is it?"

"My thigh. I must've pulled a muscle."

Nick finished bandaging her hand. "I'll take a look." He began a gentle probe of her upper thigh, stopping when she winced. "Sorry."

"It's all right. I'll recover." He started to undo her pleated trousers. "Nick! I said it would be okay."

"It can't hurt to have a look."

She glared at him. "I don't want you to."

He sighed in exasperation. "Meghan, I won't be seeing anything I haven't seen before."

"How gentlemanly of you to point that out."

"I meant you. I've seen you naked before."

She gaped. "When?"

"I'll tell you after I've checked that thigh. Now, lift up so I can get these pants down."

Meghan obeyed, her thoughts swirling. Nick ran his fingers over her thigh, and she nodded when he touched the tender spots. He didn't seem to notice the scars crisscrossing her upper thighs and abdomen. Or if he did, he chose to ignore them politely. As soon as he finished the examination, he pulled a blanket up to cover her from the waist down.

"There, that wasn't so bad, was it?" he asked gently.

"When did you see me naked?"

"First, are you comfortable?"

Meghan nodded, wanting to get on with her questioning.

"I'm not. I could use a stiff drink. I'm going to go downstairs and make you some tea. But first I want you to take a couple of aspirin." He left the room and returned with a glass of water and aspirin. He sat behind Meghan, holding her against his chest as she took the medication. With his arms around her, she realized she'd never felt so safe, secure . . . or loved.

Loved? By Nick?

Meghan choked, but recovered and spoke quickly to avoid a slap on the back. "I'll be fine in a minute." She patted her chest, her eyes watering.

"What was that all about?"

"Some water went down the wrong way. I'm okay."

"Are you sure?" He tilted her chin upward with a knuckle. She met his eyes and trembled. Love. Good God. Was it possible Nick returned her feelings?

His concerned gaze searched her face, then came to rest on her mouth. He drew a callused thumb across her lower lip, the friction against her skin echoing in her womb.

"Meghan . . ."

His head descended slowly but stopped, their lips a hairsbreadth apart. "No." He pulled away, his eyes dark with regret. "When we make love, I don't want any unanswered questions between us." Sliding out from behind her, he settled her back against the pillows. "I'll be back in ten minutes. Have your questions ready."

_____ FIFTEEN _____

Nick paused outside the doorway, Meghan's tea, a bottle of dark rum, and a highball glass in his hands. Meghan sat in bed, her back against the pillows, looking deceptively fragile. His body filled with need as he took in the curve of her cheek, the gentle rise and fall of her breasts, the delicate hands clasped in her lap. He wanted to touch her, to love her, to let actions speak louder than words . . . but the words were needed.

He stepped into the room. "Ready for your tea?"

Her smile as she accepted her mug made him ache even more.

"I brought some rum."

She held out her mug. "Please." He poured her a shot and refilled his own glass. Switching on the bedside lamp, he settled on the bed, taking care not to crowd her. The soft light spilling across the calico quilt encapsulated them in a world far removed from the darkness descending outside.

Meghan remained silent, and Nick sensed she was waiting for him to make the first move. He drained his glass and cleared his throat. This was proving harder than he'd thought. "I mean what I said earlier," he said quietly. "I'll answer any questions. Tell you anything you want to know. We can talk all night if you want to. About Heather, about me, about . . .''

Meghan took a long draft of tea and reached over to put her mug on the nightstand. The quilt covering her hips followed her movement, and Nick caught a tantalizing glimpse of her thigh. His throat tightened. It was going to be a hell of a long night.

She leaned forward and eased his glass from his clenched fingers. Placing his glass next to her mug, she took his hand and looked him in the eye. He started to panic, thinking it might be better to cut his losses and run.

''You didn't kill Heather any more than I did.''

Her firm declaration hit him squarely in the solar plexus. For a long moment he couldn't breathe. ''How do you know that?''

''I know you.'' She squeezed his fingers reassuringly.

''No, you don't. Meghan, you don't know anything about me.''

She placed her free hand on his chest. ''I know what's in here—in your heart. You could never end another person's life.''

His heart thudded against her palm. The feelings her touch ignited were far too intense for quiet conversation. ''You're wrong.'' He'd kill anyone who tried to take her away from him.

Her hand lifted to his cheek. Nick almost groaned. ''Nicholas,'' she whispered, ''don't do this to yourself. I know you mean well, but you don't want to talk any more than I do.''

Christ. Was he that transparent? ''Meghan . . .''

''Make love with me, Nick. Please. Now. No questions asked. I know you want me. I can feel your heart beating. Here . . .'' She caressed his neck. ''Here . . .'' Her hand slid to his heart, trailing fire. ''And here.'' Her fingers dipped lower.

He captured her hand and stilled it against his thigh. ''Meghan, no. It wouldn't be right.'' His soul filled with a dark desperation. ''Don't you see what's happening?

You've had a shock. You only want me because you're feeling vulnerable.''

She withdrew her hand. "That's not true."

Anger. That was the key. He had to make her angry enough to keep distance between them. "Face it, Meghan. You wouldn't be here if that pitchfork hadn't scared the hell out of you."

A clock ticked slowly in the silence that followed.

"I would've returned."

His resistance was crumbling. He forced himself to try to make her see reason. "If we made love now, in the morning you'd regret this . . . this impulse. I don't want that to happen."

Meghan looked down and fingered the calico quilt. Nick felt cold without her touch to warm him. "How about a compromise?" she asked quietly. "Would you lie next to me while we talk?"

Nick could no more have refused than turned back the tide. He helped to rearrange Meghan and her pillows and stretched out beside her, propped on one elbow. "How's this?"

"You're still too far away."

She hadn't given up. Her persistence was tearing him apart. He touched her hair with a trembling hand. "I'm sorry. We can't make love. Not unless we talk about Heather first."

Meghan rolled onto her side to face him. "Dammit, Nick, you've picked the worst possible time to get talkative on me."

"I know, sweetheart, but the answer is still no. If you can't accept that, I'll have to leave."

"All right. As long as you insist, I do have one question."

He braced himself. "Anything."

"When did you see me naked?"

"Meghan, that's not what we need to—"

"You said 'anything,' Nick."

He looked into her eyes, no longer filled with emotions that threatened to undo him, but cool determination, and sighed resignedly. "That first night, when you told me to call you if you weren't back in an hour. I didn't call at first I came over. When you didn't answer my knock, I peeked through the back window and saw you sound asleep, stark naked. Deciding I'd embarrass you if I woke you, I went back home and called you."

Meghan stared at him in disbelief, then closed her eyes, groaning. Nick grinned at the memory of what he'd seen. "I remember thinking what I wouldn't give to be able to put that expression on your face. What were you dreaming about, anyway?"

She opened one eye. "Guess."

"*Us?* As in . . . you and me?"

She only smiled.

"Did we . . . have our clothes on?"

"Nope."

He digested this information slowly. "Would you mind if I asked how long you've been having these fantasies about us?"

She grinned. "Since we met."

Nick sent her a slow smile. He would lose this battle, willingly. "You still want to put the questions on hold?" At her single nod, his smile broadened. "So, Miss Edwards, whose fantasies would you like to start with? Yours or mine?"

Meghan's smile lit the room. Nick leaned forward and kissed her. Her uninhibited response chased the last of his doubts away and nearly destroyed his control. Long moments later, he reluctantly pulled back. At her murmur of protest, he smiled and said, "I'll be just a minute, love."

He rose and shed his clothes, then suddenly felt paralyzed. Paralyzed by his awareness of her and the intensity with which he wanted her. She sat up, her eyes making a slow, sweeping survey of his nudity. Lord, what she could do to him with just a look. A wildfire raged in his body, and he had yet to touch her. She began to unbutton her blouse, and his throat went dry.

"I might need a little help with this," she whispered.

He went to her then, and gathered her in his arms. "Maybe we should wait. Your hand . . . your thigh . . ."

She captured his hand and brought it to her lips. "No. We've waited too long already."

Nick's heart swelled with love. Slowly he slid her shirt from her shoulders, kissing each inch of bared skin along the way. She tasted of roses and sultry summer nights. With painstaking care he drew her silk panties down the soft smoothness of her legs. At the foot of the bed he paused to drink in the sight of Meghan, naked in his bed . . . wanting him.

Her arms opened and he fell into them, his need for her pulsing inside him like a raging river. But he held himself back. As though he had all the time in the world, he worshiped her with his hands and mouth, exploring every curve, every dip, every swell. He blessed each tiny ridge of scar tissue he found with a kiss, a lover's testimonial to her strength and courage.

Slowly he learned what she liked, what tickled her, what made her smile. His spine rippled as she ran her hand over his back in long, sensual strokes, tangling in his hair, urging him on. He kissed her for what seemed like hours, loving the taste of her, the feel of her, the essence of her. Moaning her pleasure, she came alive beneath his questing hands and mouth.

"Nick," she gasped, as his fingers dipped into the hot, sweet center of her.

"Shh, love. Everything's going to be all right."

Soon the tension ebbed from her body, while her growing heat trailed up his arms. He nuzzled and nipped her breasts, her stomach, her hips, her downy curls. Reverently he touched his mouth to where his fingers had been.

Meghan was too far gone to protest. As his tongue delved into her deepest secrets, her breath came in shallow, ragged gasps. Her stomach muscles knotted and her body went still as she cried out his name. Seconds later, he felt the shudders that rippled though her like undulating waves on the sea at sunset.

"God, you're beautiful. So soft, so warm, so responsive.'' He trailed kisses across her quivering abdomen, her rib cage, her breasts. He measured the strong pulse in her throat with his lips, then reclaimed her mouth with a hunger too long denied.

Her skin felt so good against his. Supple, yielding, yearning, welcoming. His hardness pressed against her hips as he drew sustenance and strength from her mouth's sweet nectar. Her arms wrapped around him, and the ache that consumed him went beyond the stiff, driving need in his loins. He wanted her to hold him forever.

"Please, Nick. I need to feel you inside me. Now.''

Reluctantly he eased away.

"Nick? Where are you. . . ?''

He captured her hands and kissed each palm. "I'll be inside you before you know it. Just give me a minute.'' He kissed her once more before reaching for the nightstand drawer. Returning to her, he enfolded her in his arms, nudging his thigh between legs that parted in welcome like a flower opening to the sun, and entered her velvet softness with one smooth motion.

Her startled gasp echoed his own. She was so tight, so tense, almost as if she were a . . .

"Meghan?''

She smiled and moved against him. "I'm fine, Nicholas, fine. It's just that you're slightly more than I imagined.''

A low chuckle rumbled deep in his chest. "Only with you angel, only with you.''

Dropping kisses onto her eyes, nose, hair, and lips, he committed to memory her passion-drugged beauty. Her softness closed around him, drew him back again and again. Soon he was lost in sensation, his blood roaring in his ears, his skin heating to the level of an inferno, his whole being surrounded by the scent, taste, and touch of Meghan. She was an oasis of sensuality in the desert of his life.

He'd wanted to take it slow, to be gentle, but her hands clasped his hips, urging him on, higher and harder. Sweat met and mingled between them as he felt her hips arch to meet his, the press of her mouth against his shoulder, the tremors that shook her body. Her legs ensnared him and she pulled him even deeper within her, trapping him in a tidal wave of desire.

With superhuman effort he tried to regain control, but it was too late. Muscles straining, he lifted himself above her, and with a hoarse cry surrendered to his fierce, consuming need for what only Meghan could give him. Buried inside her, he became a part of her, she an inexorable part of him.

An eternity later, he braced himself on elbows weak with the aftershocks of their union. He found her eyes closed, and traces of tears on her cheeks. Guilt grabbed his heart.

"Oh, no. I hurt you, didn't I?"

Her delicate lashes lifted, exposing eyes filled with a deep inner glow—and a touch of wonder. She slowly shook her head and lifted a hand to his face. "No. I'm just savoring the feeling. I never knew it could be like this, Nick. Never."

Tenderness and love for this woman who had so unselfishly given herself to him filled him to overflowing. He brushed her tears away with a smile and kissed her gently. "Neither did I."

Easing away, he rolled onto his back and pulled her with him. She nestled against him, drawing one leg over his thighs as if she'd been doing it for years. Her toes explored his calf, her hand his chest and side. His savored the silken curves of her hip, her back, her shoulder. He couldn't stop touching her. Nor she him. For the longest time neither of them spoke. No words were necessary. Their souls were in absolute harmony.

It wasn't long before he wanted her again.

"Nick?"

"Yes?"

"It's my turn."

"Your turn for what?"

She found him with her hand. "Paybacks are hell,

Hawkinson, but I'm going to do my damnedest to see you get yours.''

Nick grinned broadly. He couldn't have been more pleased. Her gentle hands and soft lips traveled the length of him, matching his earlier exploration of her, move for move. The lady, he discovered, was not shy. He found himself wanting—no, *needing*—to feel her imprint on every inch of his body, and vowed to make sure she didn't miss a single spot.

She didn't. Meghan brought him to the brink of release once, twice, and yet a third time, only to pull her hands and lips away, then begin to work her special magic anew. He finally understood what sweet torture he'd inflicted on her with his endless probing, teasing, tasting, taunting. When he groaned he could take no more, she smiled wickedly, dipped her hand into his nightstand drawer, then sheathed him. Rolling her over, he lost himself inside her once more.

Someone was knocking on the front door. Nick lay in the dark and listened, hoping whoever it was would go away. To his annoyance, the knocking was repeated, this time louder. Slipping out of bed before the noise woke Meghan, he bent to brush a kiss on her forehead, then snatched up his jeans and went downstairs, flipping lights on along the way. It was well past ten.

His visitor was a tall, ruddy-complexioned law officer who introduced himself as Deputy O'Reilly.

''What can I do for you, Deputy?''

''I've come to investigate a complaint. Someone reported an argument. Shortly thereafter, you were allegedly seen carrying an injured woman into your home. Mind if I look around?''

Nick swore silently. It had to have been Miss Peabody. Didn't the woman have a life of her own? ''As a matter of fact, I do mind.''

''I'm afraid that's going to be a problem, then,'' the man returned curtly. ''Because I'm not leaving until I do.''

Nick's muscles went taut. "If you've got something to accuse me of, Deputy, do it now."

"I'm not accusing you of anything. Just doing my job." O'Reilly opened the door. "Now, if you'll excuse me—"

Nick moved to block the officer's path. "I'm sorry, but if you plan to go any further with this, you'd better have a search warrant. Otherwise, you're wasting both your time and mine."

The man looked at Nick's clenched fists, then his face. "Mr. Hawkinson, it wouldn't make me happy to haul you in for assaulting an officer, but I'll do it if you don't back off."

Scenes from his past raced through Nick's mind. His hands lifted to stop the advancing deputy. There was no way in hell he'd allow Meghan to become the hot topic of conversation at the local police station.

"Nick, I can't find the—"

He whipped around to see her standing on the landing, dressed in one of his long-sleeved shirts. The shirt's hem reached almost to her knees, covering her scars. She'd rolled up one sleeve past her forearm. The other was loosely rolled and looked askew, as if it had just fallen down. Consequently, it hid her bandaged hand.

She smiled guilelessly and stepped forward. "Oh, I didn't know we had company. Hello, Seamus," she said with the aplomb of the lady of the house greeting an invited guest, stunning Nick. She moved to stand beside him, keeping her injured hand behind him. "Has something happened?"

The screen door snapped closed. "No . . . Miss Edwards," O'Reilly stammered, removing his hat as he tore his eyes from her long, shapely, bare legs. Nick wanted to rip the man's awed expression right off his face. "We got a call at the station and thought you might . . ." He trailed off as the situation he'd stumbled onto became obvious. "Someone heard a scream."

Meghan laughed lightly, her laughter sounding to Nick like wind chimes stirred by a summer breeze. "Oh, that. A mouse ran over my toes in the barn. I . . . overreacted.'' She smiled in apology. ''I'm sorry you had to come out here for nothing.''

O'Reilly jammed his hat back on his head. ''No trouble at all, ma'am. Just checking things out. I'll be on my way.''

''Tell Becky hello for me. I'll bring some pictures by as soon as I get a chance. I've got an especially cute one of the baby.''

''Uh, yes, ma'am.'' The deputy reddened, then turned away, thoroughly flustered. ''Have a . . . Have a good evening.''

Staring at Meghan, Nick slowly shut the door. ''What the hell was that all about?'' he asked, just as slowly.

''I thought it was pretty clear-cut,'' she answered, the picture of innocence. ''Someone heard me scream and sent the police to investigate.''

''And you came downstairs wearing nothing but my *shirt*.''

For an instant she looked hurt. ''Are you ashamed of me?''

''Hell, no! But, Meghan, this is a small town, and you just lied to an—''

''Fibbed, Nick. I fibbed. There's a difference. And I thought it better to fib than let you do whatever it was you were planning to do when I showed up. If I hadn't come downstairs, I probably would've had to bail you out of jail, and then we really would've had some questions to answer.''

She lightly placed her fingers on his compressed lips. ''So before you say any more, would you mind helping me back to bed?'' She winced delicately. ''I think I over-exerted myself trying to get down here in time to keep you out of trouble.''

The idea of Meghan in pain closed off every other thought. With a muttered curse, Nick scooped her into his arms and carried her upstairs. By the time they got to his room, he was so attuned to the feel of her fingers in his hair, her nose nuzzling his neck, her soft breasts pressing against his chest, and the sight of her long legs spilling over his arm, he no longer cared why she'd sacrificed her reputation for him.

He lowered her onto the bed. "Where does it hurt?"

She smiled mischievously, her eyes sparkling. "Nowhere, Dr. Hawkinson, now that you're back where you belong and in a proper frame of mind." She began to undo the buttons of his shirt, which looked a hell of a lot better on her than it ever had on him. "But you might want to check me over again, just in case."

Nick grinned. "Would you like some help with that?"

Nick lay in silence, absorbing the sounds of midmorning, his arm curled around Meghan as she slept peacefully at his side. Her cheek rested on his chest, her bandaged hand on his waist. Never had he felt so at home, so at peace.

Throughout the night he'd made love to her with gentleness and hard urgency, and in each case she'd understood and met his need without reserve. What they'd found in each other's arms was indescribably wonderful. But could it last? Could Meghan be happy with him? Could she live with the stigma of his past? Day after day? Year after year? Some people would never forget.

She shifted against him, and he kissed her hair. "Morning."

She tilted her head and sent him a smile whose sweetness rippled through him. "Good morning. You've been up a while. I could almost hear wheels turning. What's up?"

From the start, he'd felt as if she could read his mind. It had frightened him at first. Now it made him feel closer to her, as if they were a team. "We need to talk."

"I agree."

"You do?"

"Just because I know you're innocent doesn't mean I'm not interested in what happened. Heather was my sister." His arm tightened around her, and she smiled. "I should've told you that first night. I wanted to, but was afraid you'd send me packing."

"Only because I'm here to do the same thing you are."

"You are?" How could that be? she thought. She'd come to Ashton looking for Hawk. And Nick was Hawk. Wasn't he?

Nick frowned. "What's the matter?"

"Uh . . . I think I'm getting a crick in my neck." To cover her confusion, she scooted upward, wrapped the sheet around her, and curled her legs under her.

Nick sat up and readjusted the pillows. "Do you want to tell me your story first?"

"No. I'd rather you did. Start with high school. I understand that's when the trouble began between you and Cole."

Nick shook his head. "High school was minor compared to what happened after. Still, I had a grace period of about two years. I got a job at Lakeland, in the supply warehouse. The work was steady, the money good, the hours great, and best of all, Cole was out of my hair."

"How so?"

"He went off to some fancy upstate college. His big chance to get away from here, and he blew it. Got thrown out of three colleges before he came back."

"Then what happened?"

"Drugs began showing up at The Wharf. No one knew where they came from, but I figured Cole had something to do with it."

"How did that affect you?"

"Indirectly, at first. Some of the guys I worked with got involved. One night about a year later, I was coming home from The Wharf and got stopped by Sheriff Taylor. Broken taillight or something. I was alone. I didn't know it, but someone had left a stash on the backseat. The sheriff spotted it, and that was that."

"But it wasn't yours!"

Nick smiled, touched by her automatic defense of him. "It was my car, so it was my pot. That's the way the law works. It could've belonged to any one of the guys I'd had in the car with me earlier. Or it could've been put there by someone else. Either way, it didn't matter. I was busted."

"Did you ever use drugs?"

"Hell, no. I'm not stupid." He paused. "Anyway, while I was awaiting trial, some boys from DEA tried to recruit me as a narc. I turned them down, just wanting to be left alone. Since it was my first offense and I had no record, I had my car impounded and got three years probation. That was before they started cracking down on drug offenses. Today I'd be looking at mandatory jail time."

"Did you ever find out whose drugs were in your car?"

"No, but after my brush with 'the law,' the guys I worked with began telling me more and more about what was going down. I couldn't understand their eagerness to get involved. Maybe it was the money. Maybe it was the free drugs. I don't know.

"I knew they were being used, but there wasn't anything I could do about it. One day a guy I worked with died of an overdose. He wasn't a close friend, but it didn't make his senseless death any easier to take. I called one of the men from DEA and told him what I knew. About two weeks later, they raided and cleaned up the place, but not for long. They couldn't get near the source."

"By the time I was twenty-five, I'd called DEA with information for two more raids, with the same results. I'd also worked my way up to assistant supervisor of shipping and receiving, and Cole was getting to be a real pain in the ass. He kept trying to get me fired."

"That shouldn't have been too hard for him. After all, his family owned the place."

"Yes, but there's something you have to understand. When Cole bombed out of college, his father laid down the law. Cole might've walked around like he owned the place, but he couldn't even sign for a delivery."

"It must've been rough for you."

Nick shrugged indifferently. "I'd been living with Cole's stunts for years." He ran a thumb over her knuckles. "Then your sister came to town."

She stiffened. "I don't know if I want to hear this part."

Nick's expression grew puzzled, then filled with understanding. "Honey, I might've messed around with a lot of girls back then, but I never even kissed your sister."

Meghan was more than surprised. "What?"

"Never. Old Ralph would've beat me to a pulp if I had. He came over the second day she was here, took her for a ride on his Harley, and that was that. I got moved to big-brother status, pronto."

"You mean *Ralph* is Hawk?"

Nick rubbed his bristly chin. "I wondered where you'd heard the name. I should've guessed you got it from Heather. It threw me for a loop when you asked me if I was him that day in the barn. I know I wasn't too convincing when I said no, but at the time I didn't much care what you thought." He frowned. "Oh, no. Are you telling me that all this time you thought Heather and I were lovers?"

Meghan's flush gave her away. "Oh, babe, no wonder you didn't want anything to do with me." Nick smiled and kissed her nose. "For the record, Heather wasn't my type. I prefer tall, sexy blondes, who make the cutest little sounds when they—"

"Enough. I get the picture," she grumbled, embarrassed.

Nick laughed. "Ralph got the nickname during football. He could pick passes out of the air like he had talons and fly across the field with the speed of a hawk. Nobody's called him that since Heather died."

"He loved her?"

"He wanted to marry her. She was crazy about him, too. She'd go over to The Wharf and wait for him to get off work. He was a bartender in the dance lounge. Now he works in security at Lakeland."

"So while she was waiting for Ralph, she met Cole."

Nick grunted. "Cole kept pestering her to go out with him. She didn't want anything to do with him. But she didn't want to get Ralph in trouble with his boss, so she danced with Cole now and then." He looked away. "That was her biggest mistake."

"Are you saying Cole . . . is responsible for her death?"

"Not publicly. Not yet. One day I hope I can. In the meantime, I don't want you to have anything to do with him."

Meghan wasn't about to make a promise she couldn't keep. If Cole had killed her sister, she'd see to it he paid dearly. "Where was Cole when she disappeared?"

"In and out. He didn't do anything unusual."

"And Ralph?"

"Was frantic. He thought she'd left town without telling him. He didn't know how to get in touch with her. She'd never said much about her family."

Meghan could understand that.

"I tried to convince Ralph she'd gone away for a few days to think things over. It happened so fast between them."

She could understand that, too; Meghan guessed it had taken her all of ten minutes to fall for Nick.

"Three nights after she disappeared, I found Heather in the loft, dead of a drug overdose."

"The loft? Why was she in there?"

"Someone put her there—to implicate me in her death. Nobody, but nobody, was allowed up there but me. It was a fact of life in Ashton. The loft was my hideaway, the place I went when I wanted to be alone." He brought her hand to his lips and kissed her fingertips. "You were my first guest."

A warm glow suffused her at his quiet admission, but was snuffed out by his next words.

"Five minutes after I entered the barn that night, the yard filled with flashing lights. The police found me standing over Heather's body and arrested me. A bag of cocaine was in her pocket. The police took one look at my record and started pushing to call it murder."

"Tell me about your alibi."

Nick shrugged. "Not much to tell. It's true Mary Lou

was with me that night. But by then she was Mary Lou Watkins and having problems with her marriage. She'd been coming around, trying to pick up where we'd left off."

"I see."

"I said trying, Meghan. She didn't succeed. Once she got engaged to Sam, it was over for me. I won't mess with another man's woman. I'm also a selfish man. When I get involved with a woman, I like to know I'm the only man in her life."

Meghan wished she had the courage to ask if Nick considered them involved. Instead she asked, "If you rejected Mary Lou, why did she come forward to help you?"

Nick's smile was bleak. "To score a point against Sam. She'd found out he was cheating on her with some woman he'd met over at Lakeland." He sighed wearily, then stared into middle distance, remembering. "It got me out of jail, but by then I'd lost my job, and no one in town would have anything to do with me. After all, I was an accused murderer and supposedly having an affair with a married woman, to boot. It filled me with so much bitterness, I became a walking bomb, just waiting to explode. Sheriff Taylor watched every move I made. People I'd known all my life crossed the street when they saw me coming."

He looked out the window, where the afternoon sun beat brightly over the town and lake. "It was worse on my mother, though. That's part of the reason I left. I couldn't stand to see the pain in her eyes. She stood by me all the way, but it cost her." A dark, deep sadness etched his profile. "I figured if I left town, maybe her friends would start coming around again and she'd be able to put her life back together. I think it worked, but she died two years later. Passed away in her sleep." He was quiet for a moment. "I didn't even know she was sick. She never told me."

Meghan's heart ached for him. "Where were you when she died?"

"Still drifting. I didn't find out she'd died until her lawyer's letter caught up with me. But by then the funeral was over, so there didn't seem to be any reason to come back. Finally I ended up in Texas, working day to day as a laborer on short-handed construction jobs. That's where I met Ed Michaels."

"A friend of yours?"

Nick nodded, warm respect entering his eyes. "He's a general contractor in Houston. Got his start in the fifties as a carpenter, like Dad. I guess he saw something in me that reminded him of himself. He noticed I was good with tools and offered me a full-time job. I worked long hours, saved my money, took some night courses. Within a year Ed and I became partners and the business just sort of took off. We got into remodeling old houses in borderline neighborhoods. Bought them for next to nothing, renovated them ourselves, then sold them at a tidy profit to up-and-coming professionals."

"What made you decide to come back to Ashton?"

"Ed. He told me it was time to either fish or cut bait. Every time we'd start on a new house, I'd think of this one, and he saw it was getting to me. I figured what the hell. I finally had the time and the money, so here I am." He smiled and lifted his brows. "Your turn. Anybody in Ashton know who you are?"

"Nope. I was afraid if people knew who I was, they wouldn't open up to me."

"What took you so long to get here?"

"I never suspected foul play, for one thing. Between the coroner's report and my mother, I was convinced Heather's death was a suicide. My parents refuse to talk about her. They pretend she never existed. Heather was what Mother called her 'problem child.' " Meghan sighed. "All Heather wanted to do was live her own life, not be forced into some mold that was created for her before she was even born. After she died, Mother got rid of every reminder of her. But by then I'd—" she hesitated, feeling a guilty flush creep into her cheeks, and wished she'd told Nick about Carter sooner "—gotten married."

Nick studied her thoughtfully for a moment, feeling something inside him die as he realized Meghan had been in love before, and quite possibly still was. He remembered the night she'd called him Jason, and wondered just how involved her relationship with the man was, despite the fact her tanned fingers showed no signs of having recently worn a wedding band.

"I've wondered why you and Heather had different last names," he said, then hesitated, not sure he wanted to hear the answer to his next question. "I take it you're divorced?"

Meghan smiled wryly. "Don't worry. Your record remains unblemished."

"Meghan, that's not what I—"

She held up a hand. "I know, I know. I'm sorry. Bad joke." Sighing, she looked away, toward the window, then startled him by saying, "The whole marriage was one, actually."

Nick couldn't help himself. "What do you mean?"

She continued looking out the window. "He wanted Heather. He got me instead. In the end, he left me." Her eyes met his, and in them he saw the pain she couldn't hide. "End of story."

Nick felt a sudden need to pummel the bastard for hurting her. "The man was a fool."

She smiled softly, her eyes softening as well. "Thank you."

He tried, but couldn't quell his curiosity. "How old were you when you married him?"

"Twenty-two. The marriage lasted all of a year." Meghan looked away, suddenly embarrassed. "Looking back, I think I did it mostly to get away from my mother. She tends to be overly ambitious—in other words, a social climber to the tips of her pedicured toes." Her fingers toyed with the calico quilt. "I guess I was tired of being manipulated, being told what to do."

She smiled dryly. "Unfortunately, it didn't stop once I was married. My ex-father-in-law is a U.S. senator, so suddenly I had an entire staff of people telling me what I could and couldn't do.'' She looked up, saw the growing distance in Nick's eyes, and realized she was probably boring him to death.

"But to answer your original question about why it took me so long to get here, between the senator and Mother, I had become totally convinced that suicide was the cause of Heather's death.''

He was silent a moment before asking, "What happened to change your mind?''

"About a month ago I found a letter from Heather addressed to me in my mother's nightstand drawer. She'd asked me to get her Valium for her.'' She hesitated, then met Nick's gaze steadily. "My mother's hooked on prescription drugs. Which is why I try to avoid using them. Especially since the accident, when I learned how easily one can come to depend on painkillers.''

"Tell me about the accident.''

"Some other time, all right?'' She didn't want to talk about the past anymore.

He hesitated a beat, then nodded. "Okay. How about the letter you found, then? What was so special about it?''

"It was postmarked in Ashton. Mailed a few days before Heather died. Most of it was about Ralph, and how much she . . .'' Meghan trailed off as a jarring thought came to mind. She placed her hand on his thigh to ground herself. "Nick . . . is it possible whoever killed Heather thought it was you she was involved with?''

He considered the idea thoughtfully. "Ralph and I used to look a lot alike back then. The three of us spent a lot of time together—and she did live here—so people *could've* thought it was me she was out with after Ralph got off work. We both worked the three-to-eleven shift.'' He frowned. "Why?''

"She'd been missing for three days before you found her?''

Nick nodded, still frowning. "Nobody knows where she went.''

"Then is it possible her killer suspected you of being

an informant and kidnapped her? To find out what she knew about your dealings with the DEA?''

''She didn't know anything! No one did. Not even the DEA, which is why they left me to rot when Heather was killed. My calls were anonymous, made from a pay phone in Buffalo.'' He paused, eyes narrowing. ''Then again, Cole's mind works in mysterious ways. He knew I suspected he was behind the drugs. I suppose he could've kidnapped her, hoping she would confirm it.''

''And when she couldn't tell him anything . . .'' She trailed off at the cold fury in Nick's face.

''Do you still have the letter?''

''Of course.''

''I want to see it.''

SIXTEEN

"It's gone!"

Nick looked up from the local area real estate listings booklet he was reading at the kitchen counter as Meghan burst back into the house. "Are you sure you brought it to Ashton?"

"Of course I'm sure! I had it right in this pocket." She thrust her camera bag at him. "I've spent the last half hour looking for that letter. I can't find it anywhere."

Nick took the bag and set it on the table. His eyes narrowed as he placed steadying hands on her shoulders. "Was anything different when you went back to the house? Anything not where you left it?"

"Oh, no. Not again."

His fingers clenched. "What do you mean, not again?"

"Someone broke into the bungalow once before and—"

"You didn't think it was important enough to tell me?"

"You weren't even speaking to me at the time! How was I to know you'd give a damn if—"

"Let's go." He was out the door before she could blink.

Meghan searched the bungalow while Nick checked the windows and doors. She entered the living room to find him standing by a small, south-facing window. "Do you use this window?" he asked.

"I haven't touched it."

"Then it's safe to say someone paid you a visit last night."

Once again, there were no visible signs of forced entry. The window was closed and the screen was in place, but outside, the grass beneath it was scuffed. "There's nothing missing but the letter," Meghan said quietly.

Nick shook his head. "All I can say is, it's damn lucky you weren't home last night."

He was right. Who knew what might've happened if she'd been there alone? The intruder couldn't have known about the letter, and the sailboat sabotage made it obvious whoever wanted her out of the way was serious. "What do you think we should do now?"

He opened his arms, and she stepped into them willingly, needing the security they offered. "Will you admit the incident with the sailboat wasn't an accident?" She burrowed her nose in his chest and nodded. He hugged her hard and said, "Then I think you should leave town. Go home."

His words, in direct conflict with the message his body was sending, stunned her. She pulled back, but he didn't release her.

"What did you say?"

"Think about it. Someone knows who you are and why you're here. It would be safer for you and better for me if you left. Then Ralph and I could solve this mystery without having to worry about something happening to you, too." His eyes darkened. "Go back to Washington, Meghan. It's where you belong."

This time she did break away from him. "You think I should leave? Just because Heather's letter is missing?"

"If you need a specific reason, yes."

Meghan heard the reluctance in his voice. Something wasn't quite right. His expression told her nothing, but he held himself as if braced for bad news. "Do you *want* me to leave?"

"You asked my opinion. The decision's yours."

"Then I'm not going anywhere until I find out who killed Heather and why."

Nick closed his eyes and exhaled slowly. Whether it was in relief or exasperation, she couldn't tell. "I was afraid of that. All right. Stay. But not here. Stay with me."

"You're kidding."

He shook his head. "Why not? I've got plenty of room."

"Don't you think it's going to look a little strange?"

His expression dissolved into amusement. "You're worried about appearances after you paraded in front of a deputy sheriff wearing nothing but my shirt? Between O'Reilly and Miss Peabody, by now the whole town knows what we were doing last night."

"That's not what I meant! I meant people might wonder why I suddenly packed my bags and moved in with you."

"Then we'll just have to convince them it's because you're crazy about me and can't keep your hands off of me," he said, approaching her. She opened her mouth to protest, and he kissed it shut, then swatted her on the behind. "Go pack."

Meghan considered herself independent, not stupid. She didn't want to be there if the intruder came back. She packed.

They locked the bungalow and returned to Nick's, where he ushered her into the bathroom, turned on the claw-footed tub's spigots, and adjusted the water temperature. "Take a nice, long bath. It'll relax you and clear your head. When you come downstairs, we'll compare notes."

Meghan entered the kitchen to find Nick flipping a pancake out of a cast-iron frying pan and adding it to a plate holding two others. With a smile and a flourish, he handed her the plate. "A little late for breakfast, so we'll call it brunch."

Ravenous, she accepted the plate and set it on the table, then went in search of silverware in the drawer near the sink.

"Somehow I get the feeling if I depend on you to feed me, I'll be a thin man before long," Nick said over his shoulder.

"Sorry, I'm hopeless in the kitchen. Frozen entrées and boil-in-the-bag dinners are my specialties."

He turned and looked at her in amusement. "What about the brownies?"

Meghan grinned. "A fluke. It's a minor miracle they turned out as well as they did."

Nick stilled. "You went to all that trouble just for me?"

She nodded, dazzled by the deep brown in his eyes.

"Why?"

"If you have to ask, I've been giving you more credit than you deserve."

Grinning, Nick pointed with his spatula to the pancakes on the table. "Eat up, before they get cold."

Meghan dug in with alacrity. Nick joined her shortly, his own plate piled high. "Those were great," she said a few minutes later, pushing her empty plate away in satisfaction and reaching for her coffee. "Your mother's recipe again?"

"Yep." He continued eating. "Now, talk while I finish."

Meghan did, telling him of her unsuccessful attempts to uncover information and the brick wall she'd come up against in dealing with the townspeople. The only person who'd given her any information was Ralph, and Nick already knew Ralph's feelings on the subject.

They cleared the dishes together. Nick wiped the counter and flipped the dish towel into the sink. "Since you're going to be staying a few days, would you like an official tour of the rest of the house? Or have you already seen it?"

She smiled, stifling a pang of disappointment at the reminder his invitation extended only to the remainder of her stay. "No. Since the doors were shut, I resisted temptation. I didn't think you'd appreciate catching me snooping, especially after the way we met."

It was true. Despite her overwhelming curiosity at

times, she'd never ventured past the bathroom or Nick's room to peer behind the three closed doors farther down the upstairs hall.

The first room he showed her had wallpaper dotted with small red and blue sailboats. A matching spread adorned the twin bed. Framed pictures of clipper ships decorated the walls. Meghan smiled with delight. "Let me guess. This was your room."

"Yep. I moved into the basement when I was fifteen. I'll show you that some other time. It's not fit for human habitation, but it has a shower and a door to the outside—a definite plus for a male adolescent on the prowl." Draping an arm around her shoulders, he gazed into his former room. "My mother was big on tradition. She kept hoping I'd settle down, so she could show my children the room where their dad used to sleep."

Meghan looked up at his profile and wanted to ask if he'd ever met anyone he'd thought might help him fulfill his mother's hopes, but was suddenly afraid of his answer.

"Which room's next?" she asked instead.

Nick dropped his arm to his side, and she wondered if she'd said something wrong. They moved on to a sunny sewing room overlooking the backyard and woods beyond. With the exception of a thick layer of dust, it seemed as though Minerva Hawkinson had stepped out only for a moment. Squares for a patchwork quilt much like the one covering Nick's bed littered the floor. Two half-finished crewelwork pillowcases draped the couch.

"I take it cooking was only one of many talents your mother had," she said.

Nick's smile was wistful. "She loved to sew. She made gifts for weddings, anniversaries, housewarmings, graduations, confirmations, you name it." He pointed to a set of double doors across the room. "That closet's full of things she made. She'd sit in here for hours, humming and sewing. She only stopped for canning season. My father kept the big garden in the backyard."

Meghan envied the loving relationship Nick and his parents had shared. It showed in the way their home had been cared for, despite its recent neglect. His father had built the house and much of the furniture. His mother had made the decorations that had turned the house into a home. Her parents' houses overflowed with exotic, expensive furnishings gathered during their world travels. Jason's apartment was a functional, easy-to-maintain mixture of beige, white, chrome, and glass.

"They must've loved each other very much."

"They were inseparable until the day my father died."

"Is it . . . painful living with so many memories of your parents?" she asked, wondering if that was why he was so determined to sell the house. She'd seen the booklet of real estate listings he'd left on the kitchen counter.

"It was at first." He smiled softly. "But that's changing."

Meghan didn't delude herself into thinking she had any part in the change. Turning away, she preceded him into the last bedroom, decorated in lavender and white. Antique white furniture with gold trim included a four-poster bed and a dainty desk. A quilt in light and dark shades of purple stretched diagonally over a white eyelet spread that matched the curtains on the single window. A door led to the sun porch that ran the length of the front of the house.

"This is where Heather stayed," Nick said from behind her.

"I can see why she was so happy here. It's beautiful." She stepped around the bed, spotted her suitcases on the floor, and glanced back at Nick.

"I thought you might be more comfortable in here." Meghan looked away to hide her disappointment. Nick approached her and placed his hands on her shoulders. "Was I wrong? Will it bother you, sleeping in Heather's room?"

"No," she said dully.

"Would you rather sleep with me?"

Her cheeks warmed, but she nodded yes. Nick turned her in to his embrace and smiled. "Last night was very special to me, Meghan, but I invited you to stay here for safety reasons. I couldn't assume you'd want to share my bed. I'm glad you do."

Meghan slipped her arms around his neck and leaned back. "With you is the safest place for me to stay, don't you think?"

"I don't know about that. It could turn into a pretty dangerous proposition. I might not want to let you go home."

He might also decide he didn't want her around when this mess was over. Heather's death bound them together now. Once they solved it, he would be free to start his life anew, without Meghan as an unpleasant reminder of why he'd left Ashton.

She forced a smile. "I'll take my chances."

Nick carried her bags into his room. Meghan followed as far as the connecting sun porch. Gingerbread trim and a dark screen allowed for privacy and kept the enclosure cool. She looked down at Mrs. Weaver's bungalow and shivered at the thought of her nocturnal visitor. Nick returned and wrapped his arms around her, pulling her back against his chest. Meghan placed her arms over his and basked in the warm comfort and security she felt.

"I like to sit up here and listen to the sounds of the town and lake. Sometimes on a clear night I can hear the music from The Wharf," he said, resting his chin on her head. A long moment later, he asked, "How'd you get to be such a good dancer?"

"Years of practice." She didn't want to talk about dancing, or how she'd been determined to dance again after Carter had left her. Turning, she combed her fingers through Nick's silky black hair. "How'd you get to be such a good kisser?"

He smiled roguishly. "Oh, I'm not nearly as good as I'd like to be. Care to practice with me?"

"I've got all afternoon."

"And then?"

She brought her lips to his. "I've got all night."

Nick returned her kiss, then took her hand and led her to bed, consoling himself with the thought it was the most he could ask for or expect. Meghan Edwards was the damnedest woman he'd ever known. She gave her all when they made love, but outside of bed, there was a part of her he simply couldn't reach.

He'd never been good at subtle word games, but he didn't want to come right out and ask how she felt about him. He wasn't sure what her answer would be. So he'd tried hinting—about having children, about the way she'd changed his life, about staying in Ashton. He'd either failed miserably or she'd purposely ignored his hints. He hoped to hell he could solve Heather's murder soon. He didn't feel right about asking Meghan to share his life when he had such a dark cloud hanging over his head—especially after what she'd told him about her family.

Meghan was overwhelmed by the consuming and fierce, yet undeniably tender way Nick made love to her that afternoon. He left no part of her untouched, inside or out. Their interlude had begun languorously, and ended in a mindless frenzy that still surprised her, two hours later. She'd never imagined herself capable of responding to a man's touch with such wild abandon. She couldn't wait to feel that wild abandon again.

Snuggled against Nick's side, their legs entwined, Meghan felt replete. She dreaded the prospect of leaving him and returning to her sterile existence in D.C. But she couldn't stay forever without an invitation, and for all his whispered promises in bed, Nick hadn't extended one.

Maybe he considered her fickle; didn't trust her after that business with Cole. It certainly hadn't gone a long way toward making him feel as if he was the only man in her life. She hazarded an upward glance. His eyes were closed, but his hand was lazily stroking her hip. "Nick?"

"Hmmmm?" he answered with a deeply contended murmur.

"I want you to know . . . nothing happened between Cole and me."

His eyes opened and an amused expression crossed his face. "I know."

"What do you mean, you *know*?" He rumbled with suppressed laughter, and she started to push away. "What's so funny?"

He let her put half an arm's length between them before he resisted. "I saw you on Cole's yacht last Sunday. I was working in the loft and saw *Candida* come out onto the lake."

"How did you know it was me?"

He gave her bottom a proprietary squeeze. "I'd recognize this delectable tush anywhere."

Meghan rolled her eyes. "First you spy on me while I'm asleep, and now this. Are you sure you're not a Peeping Tom?"

He smiled rakishly. "Only when it comes to you."

"Were you using binoculars?"

He nodded. "Superman, I'm not. I saw you come out on deck. You talked awhile, had something to drink. When you went below, Cole waved one of his buddies over and apparently asked him to circle the boat a few times. The boat started rocking, and Cole went down to check on you or rescue you or whatever. Ten minutes later, you were on deck alone and Cole was motoring the boat home." He grinned. "Did you hit him where it hurts, too?"

Meghan burst into laughter. "No."

"Then what put such an abrupt end to Cole's amorous plans?"

"I was in the stateroom, changing into my swimsuit. When the boat started rocking, I accidentally yanked open a cabinet. A bunch of papers fell out and went flying. I'd just finished stuffing them back inside when Cole opened the door and scared the devil out of me."

"How?"

"I must've looked guilty as sin, because Cole got the strangest look on his face. He stared at me for the longest time. It made me nervous, because all I had on was my bathing suit, and . . ." She closed her eyes and shuddered.

Nick tensed. "What did he do to you?"

"Nothing. He turned around and left."

"Maybe he noticed the resemblance between you and Heather. What happened then?"

"I put on my skirt and went into the cabin. Cole started pounding down beers. He took me back to shore, where we argued when I refused to get in his car because he'd been drinking."

Nick searched her face, his expression thoughtful. "I thought you looked upset when you came home. I wanted to come over and ask if you were all right, but figured I was the last person you'd want to see."

She brushed a lock of hair away from his forehead. "I needed you so badly that night."

He folded her into his arms. "I'm here now."

"I thought he was horrified by my scars," she whispered.

"Tell me how you got them."

Meghan hesitated, torn between the past and the present, then decided Nick deserved to know. "Four years ago I was in a car accident. My husband was driving. He'd also been drinking. We were arguing, and the car went over an embankment. Luckily I had my seat belt on. My pelvis was shattered and I broke a few ribs. I also got a pretty bad knock on the head. I was in a coma for a month. When I woke up, I was paralyzed from the waist down.

"My husband walked away without a scratch. Six months later, he left me. He never stopped drinking, never even tried. He's still at it, from what I hear. He's also on his third marriage, and a constant embarrassment to his father."

"I can see why. The man's worse than a fool. He's a contemptible, self-centered bastard."

Meghan smiled. "Jason's words exactly."

"Jason?"

"My brother and roommate. You know, the photojournalist I told you about?"

Nick offered an oddly relieved-sounding "Ah." When he offered no explanation, Meghan continued. "Anyway, if it hadn't been for Jason, I'd still be in a wheelchair.

The rest of my family was content to let me remain a pampered paraplegic—Mother was in her glory with the drama of it—but not Jason. He came home from Kenya and became my own personal shadow.

"He coached me and bullied me and drummed into me that wasting my life because of a bastard like Carter would be stupid and self-destructive. He saw me through two years of therapy, and moved me into his apartment. He bought me my first professional camera—I'd always been interested in photography, but both Mother and Carter convinced me my talent was at best mediocre—and took me on assignments with him. I watched, I learned, I practiced, and when I was ready, broke out on my own."

Nick studied her in thoughtful silence. When he spoke, his voice and eyes held admiration, respect, and a confusing touch of sadness. "So your brother took a docile, dutiful wife and daughter, and turned her into an independent, self-sufficient career woman."

"That's about it."

"Do you have much contact with your parents?"

Meghan looked away, feeling as if she were failing some kind of test. "We meet for dinner once a month," she said, trying to keep the guilt from her voice. "It's usually a strained affair."

"So you haven't cut the strings completely."

Meghan smiled sadly. "I guess I keep hoping that one day Mother will stop trying to interfere in my life and simply accept me as I am."

"And your father?"

She shook her head. "He decided a long time ago the best way to keep his sanity was to do things Mother's way."

"Then I'm glad you have your brother."

Meghan nodded. "I owe him a lot. In fact . . ." She looked at her watch, remembering the message she'd left on his machine the day before. He'd be worried if he couldn't reach her. "I need to call him." She glanced at the bedside phone. "Would you mind if I used your phone?"

"Not at all. I'll go downstairs and leave you to it."
He rolled off the bed and grabbed his jeans. "You want
something to eat? I could rustle up a sandwich or two."

Meghan was already dialing. "Sure. I'll be down in a
few minutes."

In the kitchen, Nick stared out at his barn and told
himself it was time to stop deluding himself. Knowing
what he now knew about her, it was plain as day that
Meghan could never be happy living in Ashton. She'd
worked damned hard to get where she was today, and he'd
be chasing rainbows to think she'd give up the career she
loved to settle down with him in some obscure little town
that didn't even have a movie theater to its name.

Scrubbing his hands over his face, he pushed back the
pain, and got to work making their sandwiches. Ten minutes later, Meghan still hadn't come downstairs. He listened to make sure she was off the phone, then returned
to the bedroom to find her dressed and sitting on the bed,
staring at a notepad in her hands.

"Everything okay?"

She looked up and shook her head. "I found this when
I was getting dressed. I'd forgotten it was in my suitcase."

Concerned and curious, he joined her on the bed.
"What is it?"

She handed it over. "A list of sorts. I found it on Cole's
yacht, when I was changing into my swimsuit. Heather
wrote it."

"Heather?" Nick looked at the list, then back at
Meghan, an uneasy feeling curling up his spine. "What
was she doing on Cole's yacht?"

"I have no idea."

He read the list again. "This make any sense to you?"

"No. I've gone over every line." Briefly she explained
the confusing discrepancies in the note.

Nick frowned and rubbed his chin. "Did you and
Heather use codes when you were kids?"

"Codes? No . . ." Her eyes widened. "Wait. There
was one. We used it in high school. We . . . took the

first word of the first sentence, the second of the second, and so on. Try it.''

"Let's get some paper and pencil first. I'll copy the note and work from the copy. I have a feeling we might be needing the original." Meghan fished a pencil and paper out of her camera bag, and Nick got to work. When he'd underlined the key words on the copy he'd made, the message read, "Call . . . for . . . help . . . gift . . . in . . . selling . . . Zenda.''

Nick frowned at Meghan. "Are you sure there isn't more to this code?"

She closed her eyes and rubbed her temples. "Okay, now I remember. The check mark is like a period. It means to start a new sentence. Then, starting with the second sentence, you underline the second word and go from there, until you hit another check mark. With the third sentence, you start with the third word and so on. Try it again.''

Instead, Nick flipped on the bedside lamp and held the original note to the light. "Look, there's something else. In this blank space at the top are indentations. It looks like Heather wrote on the sheet before this one and threw it away." He lightly shaded the blank spots. The indentations formed a date—August 15, five years earlier. The day before her death.

Nick rewrote the list and underlined the key words again. The decoded note read, "Call for help. Cole's keeping me prisoner.''

"Oh, my God," Meghan whispered, horrified. She looked at Nick, then scrambled for the phone. Her hand was on the receiver when he stopped her, his dark eyes grave.

"Who are you calling?"

"The police. They need to know about this so they can bring Cole in.''

"You can't tell anyone about this. Not yet.''

"He kidnapped and killed my sister.''

Nick tugged at her arm, bringing her back onto the bed.

"I know, sweetheart, and I'm sorry. But this isn't enough to put him away."

She stared up at him, her eyes awash in pain and confusion. "Don't you think he did it?"

Nick ached to take her in his arms, but needed to keep his mind clear. "I wouldn't put it past him. But he's also been known to hire men to do his dirty work." He sat back, paper and pencil in hand. "You found the note in the stateroom, so he must've kept her prisoner there. Let's work from your earlier theory and assume Cole thought it was me she was seeing instead of Ralph. If so, he could've seen her as another way to get to me, or to find out if I was up to anything with the DEA. It makes sense now, his interest in shipping and receiving. That must've been where he stored the drugs. He's still at it, from what Ralph says, but he's more careful now, his clientele more exclusive. Cocaine's apparently the drug of choice at Lakeland these days."

"How does Ralph know Cole's still involved with drugs?"

"Cole meets with a string of respectable-looking men, sometimes women, in the duplex on Saturday nights. Claims it's condominium sales meetings. Ralph got a line on who the regulars were and had a buddy of his in Buffalo check them out. That's why he came looking for me yesterday. The report came in."

"But there wasn't anything in it you could use against Cole," Meghan surmised, remembering watching Nick's tense discussion with Ralph and the way he'd gone off by himself afterward.

"Not without turning a whole lot of lives upside down. Turned out most of Cole's visitors were tenants at Lakeland. Legitimate professionals and businesspeople enjoying their summer vacations."

"With a little recreational boost from Cole, the candy man."

"Ralph thinks we should turn the whole lot of them in, then sit back and watch the fireworks, but I want to solve Heather's murder first. I think we owe her that much. We also owe it to ourselves to find out what really happened between her and Cole.''

Meghan shivered at the thought. ''Why does Cole keep Ralph around? He has to know you're cousins.''

''To keep his eye on him. He's convinced Ralph is a harmless drunk, but can't be sure of what Ralph knows about him.''

''Is Ralph really an alcoholic?''

''No. He took up drinking for a while after Heather died, but I haven't seen him drunk since I've been back.'' Nick set the deciphered note aside and held out his arms. ''C'mere. I want to thank you for being so stubborn. If you'd left town, we wouldn't have this new lead.''

Meghan stayed put. ''Why *did* you tell me to go home?''

''I wanted you somewhere safe. I still think it's the best alternative.''

She opened her mouth to argue, then changed her mind. ''When are you meeting Ralph again?''

With a resigned sigh, Nick sank back against the pillows. ''Tonight. At Lakeland.''

''I want to go with you.''

''Not this time. We're going to search Cole's apartment. I'm tired of waiting for the information I need to fall into my lap.'' Nick's watch alarm went off. ''Lord, is it that late already? I've got to get going.'' He rummaged in the closet for a shirt, kissed her once, hard, then headed for the door.

''Nick, wait. How long will you be gone?''

''As long as it takes.'' His eyes grew dangerously cold and dark. ''We'll nail him for you Meghan, I promise you.''

She heard the dead bolt click at the back door as he left.

''Not if I get to him first,'' she vowed.

SEVENTEEN

Meghan waited fifteen minutes before leaving the house. Coleman Benson had the answers she and Nick needed, and she was determined to get them from him. Especially since Nick's methods might very well land him back in jail. If he and Ralph were caught casing Cole's apartment . . .

Tucking Nick's spare key into her pocket, she marched into the Ashton police station. The sheriff, who was just on his way home for the night, was reluctant at first to agree to her demands, but when she pulled out the big guns—namely her family connections and the prospect of a full, very public investigation into Heather's death—he changed his mind. Ninety minutes later, she left, the first phase of her mission completed.

Back at Nick's, she put on her makeup, deliberately emphasizing her eyes. No point in concealing her identity now. She'd use her similarities to Heather to her advantage. Emerging from the bathroom, she crossed the hall to the bedroom to call the police and tell them she was on her way. Her hand was on the receiver when she heard footsteps on the staircase.

"Damn." She'd hoped to be gone before Nick returned. She braced herself for a confrontation. Nothing would stop

207

her from doing what had to be done. Her breath left her lungs when not Nick, but Coleman Benson, appeared in the doorway.

He wore tight-fitting black clothes, reminding her of the faceless cat burglar in her dream, and made a striking contrast against the white wall behind him. Something metallic glinted in his hand. Meghan's heart jumped into her throat as she found herself staring into the barrel of a gun.

"How did you get in?" she managed to ask.

He shrugged. "I used a key."

Cole had a key to Nick's house? He must've pirated it from someone. Her eyes rounded. "Heather," she whispered.

Cole chuckled. "You're smart, Meghan. Too smart for your own good." Now, walk toward me, slowly."

Meghan didn't move. "What are you doing here?"

"Don't waste my time with questions you already know the answers to." He jerked the gun. "Now, move."

Her heart hammering, she obeyed, while Cole backed into the hallway. Noting the strange, unnerving light in his eyes, she made her way downstairs with painstaking care. The man was either on something or bordering on madness. When they reached the foyer, Cole opened a closet door and yanked out one of Nick's jackets to cover the gun, still trained on Meghan.

"We're going for a drive, with you behind the wheel. There's a brown sedan parked two blocks down the street. Now, open the door, and remember, I'm right behind you."

Struggling to hold on to her wits, Meghan fumbled with the dead bolt. Stepping into the descending darkness, she drew deep, calming gulps of cool night air. Cole placed an arm around her shoulders, leveling the weapon against her side, and she went rigid. "Act like we're enjoying an evening stroll. And loosen up. I don't want to attract attention."

Meghan took a last deep breath and tried to relax, but her skin crawled at Cole's nearness. She suppressed a shudder as, whistling tunelessly, he shepherded her down the street. Passing Miss Peabody's, Meghan searched the lace-covered windows in vain. They reached the car without encountering a soul.

Cole opened the passenger door, and she slid across the cracked vinyl seat, Cole right behind her. "Take us to Lakeland, and stay under the speed limit. No fancy driving, either."

As they drove through Ashton, Meghan recognized several faces, but had no opportunity to signal she was in danger. When they left the town limits, her spirits nosedived and her thoughts turned to Nick. Was he all right? Cole seemed especially cocky tonight. Had he caught Nick and Ralph in his apartment and done something to them? Was that why he'd so brazenly walked into Nick's house tonight? She wanted to ask, but refused to give Cole that weapon against her.

Dammit, why hadn't Nick come home?

"Meghan! I found what we need. Cole kept records and—" Suddenly Nick noticed the house seemed strangely still—and contained the same cloying smell of men's cologne that Cole's apartment had held. *"Meghan!"* He raced upstairs, panic clawing his heart. Wild-eyed, he took in the clothes strewn across the bed, the assorted bottles and tubes littering the bathroom sink.

Where the hell was she? What the hell was going on?

The telephone rang, and he sprang across the room to snatch it up, praying it was Meghan. The raspy breathing on the other end sent a chill down his spine until he recognized the equally raspy voice. "I thought you should know, Nicholas. That Benson boy came and took her away."

"Miss Peabody?" Nick's fingers clenched on the receiver, raw fear surging through him. "Are you sure?" he asked, hoping it was someone else she'd seen, anyone other than Coleman Benson.

"Of course I'm sure. I've got eyes. He was skulking around the house the same way he skulked around the house the night you were arrested for killing that Morgan girl. It was too dark to make out who he was that night, but this time I saw his face.''

Nick didn't stop to think what his former English lit teacher's words meant for him. His mind was on Meghan, alone with Cole. ''Where did they go?''

''I don't know. They got into a brown sedan and went west.''

''Thank you, Miss Peabody.'' He was out the door in a flash.

''You're being quiet for a change,'' Cole said as they approached the Lakeland exit. ''I hear you've been asking questions all over town about Heather. Why didn't you simply ask me? I could've told you what you needed to know, and saved us both a lot of time and trouble. Now maybe you know too much.''

Traffic was heavy. Meghan kept her eyes on the road, searching in vain for a patrol car. ''I didn't think you even knew her that well until . . . now,'' she lied, deciding against telling him about Heather's note. It might set him off.

Cole chuckled. ''No, I guess you didn't. Heather's letter didn't say much about me.''

Meghan's mind raced. Cole had the stolen letter. Maybe she could get him to confess to more. He seemed in a talkative mood. She glanced over at him. ''Why did you take it?''

''I hadn't planned on it. I didn't even know it existed. I'd hoped to have a little talk with you instead. But you weren't home, to my disappointment. You were across the street rutting with that Hawkinson bastard.'' He sneered. ''I hope you enjoyed yourselves, because the two of you are going to pay for what you've done to me.''

Meghan's composure slipped. ''*Done to you?* You killed my sister and put an innocent man through hell, and you think *you're* the one who's been wronged?''

''Temper, temper, Meghan,'' he chided calmly. ''Have you forgotten who's in charge here?'' He poked the gun into her ribs, sending her into seething silence. She pulled onto the access road to Lakeland. A delivery van exited the highway behind them, giving her a measure of hope until it turned down a side road.

"Take the left back gate. I sent the guard on an errand." As they pulled up to the gate, Cole handed her a card to open it. "Head for the marina. We're going for a boat ride, unless you do something stupid first."

Meghan had no intention of being used for target practice. She pulled into the deserted parking lot and killed the engine, staring dead ahead.

"Now get out very slowly and walk toward the dock."

"Which one?" she asked, stalling, hoping someone would drive by and notice them sitting there.

"The one where *Candida*'s berthed. I'm sure you remember."

She opened the door and got out, Cole again right behind her. But at the edge of the dock, her feet refused to cooperate anymore. Once she got on the yacht, her chances for escape or rescue were slim to none.

"What's the matter, Meghan? Having trouble comprehending my instructions?"

"No. Just the reasoning behind them. Why are you going to so much trouble to get rid of me, Cole? Nobody in Ashton wants to dredge up a five-year-old crime. Believe me. I tried and got nowhere."

"I'm surprised at you, Meghan. Maybe you don't know as much as I thought you did. Your amateur investigation has made things somewhat uncomfortable for me. Take tonight, for example. Keeping my eye on you is keeping me away from business."

She turned to face him slowly. "Drug trafficking?"

He shrugged. "Among other things."

She knew then that Cole intended to kill her and she had nothing to lose. "Why did you kill Heather?"

He hesitated, then smiled sadly. "Because she wouldn't tell me what I wanted to hear."

"She couldn't, Cole. She didn't know anything."

He gave an unsettling laugh. "You've got your facts mixed up. What was she supposed to know?"

She realized Cole wasn't aware of Nick's connection to the DEA. Relief coursed through her. Maybe Nick was safe after all. "I thought it had something to do with the drugs," she hedged.

Cole shook his head. "Wrong. She'd never even seen cocaine until I introduced her to it."

Meghan knew better. "Then what was it you wanted her to tell you?"

His eyes met hers. "That she loved me."

The admission stunned her. Cole had loved Heather? Meghan's mind began working double-time. Maybe she still had a chance of getting through this alive. "You were in love with Heather?"

Cole nodded, his eyes clouding over, apparently unconcerned that they were no longer moving. "She wouldn't have anything to do with me. So I had some friends pick her up and bring her onto *Candida*. We were going to go away together—leave this miserable place behind."

His voice grew bitter. "I hate it here. I've hated it since day one. But she didn't want to go. I kept her on *Candida*, hoping she'd change her mind. I did everything I could to convince her to come with me. I wined her, dined her, gave her gifts. She wouldn't budge. I didn't even lay a hand on her—until the end. I couldn't take it anymore. All she wanted to do was go back to *him*." His voice broke.

"Who?" Meghan asked softly.

Fresh rage welled in Cole. He spat. "That mongrel you've been spreading your legs for, who do you think?" His eyes glazed over with hatred. "He stole Heather from me, and now I'm going to have my revenge."

Mention of Nick seemed to make Cole lose control. Meghan groped for a way to change the subject. A sudden inspiration hit her. "What if I told you I could help you leave Ashton?"

His eyes refocused. "How?"

"You know as well as I do, money talks. I've got plenty of it. Enough for you to disappear for the rest of your life. You can travel the world, live in any city you choose.''

Cole was silent, considering. Meghan prayed.

"I can't do that," he said, dashing her hopes. "How do I know you won't tell my father where I've gone? He'll come after me, you know. He knows what I did. That's why he called that town meeting after she died. He wanted to know what everyone else knew so he could cover my tracks. He's very good at that sort of thing. He's had a lot of practice.''

His hand came up to touch her face. Meghan tried not to flinch. "He knows about you, too. I had to tell him when you brought the sailboat back. He wasn't very happy about it.''

"Does he know where we are right now?"

"No. He's on a business trip. He won't be back until Monday. But by then you'll be—"

"In Milan with you."

"What?"

Meghan forced an friendly smile. What she was considering was improbable, maybe even impossible, but worth a try. "Think about it, Cole," she said softly, seductively, playing on his emotions and making her voice sound as much like Heather's as she could remember. "Isn't that what you wanted? For the two of us to go away together? Now's your big chance. Your father need never know. We'll hide from him together.''

Cole looked puzzled, as if he were hearing words he'd longed to hear, but thought it impossible. Encouraged, she gently pressed onward. "He's wrong about you, you know. You're smart, suave, successful, and nobody's fool.''

He squinted at her. He seemed to be concentrating on her eyes. She moved so that her back was to the water, Cole's face illuminated by the halogen lamp behind her. Keeping her face in shadow, Meghan prayed her voice would have the desired effect. "In fact," she crooned, "I've been looking all my life for a man like you, Cole.''

"Have you really?" He sounded like a little boy in desperate need of love, affection . . . and acceptance.

She softened her voice even more. "Of course I have. How could you think differently? You're the most handsome, talented, and exciting man I've ever known."

Unbridled longing entered Cole's eyes. "You *do* care. I knew you would if I could get you alone. . . ." He frowned. "Why are you throwing your life away on that no-good—"

Smiling, Meghan realized Cole had slipped into the past. "He's nothing to me, Cole. Nothing. He never was. I only used him to get you to notice me." She pouted provocatively. "You're always so busy, and the girls at The Wharf adore you."

His response was fervent. "Oh, but I did. I noticed you the first night I saw you. I was standing by the bar, and you looked over at me and smiled. That smile did something wonderful to me. It made me feel like I was the only man in the room; like I could take on the world and win. I knew then we were meant to be together."

Meghan slipped further into the role of Heather. "What took you so long to tell me?"

Cole eyed her suspiciously. "I tried—on *Candida.*"

She tensed. She'd forgotten about the three days Heather had spent imprisoned on Cole's yacht. She tried to imagine what had happened between them. "I was frightened, Cole. You were so . . . intense. I didn't realize how you felt. I'm sorry I underestimated you. I'll never do it again," she said demurely. "It's not too late, is it?"

"Too late for what?"

"Too late for us. We can still go away, can't we?"

She saw him break into a sweat.

"Can't we?"

He nodded vigorously. "Of course we can."

"What about the gun?"

Cole looked down at the gun in his hand as if realizing for the first time he held one. "Oh, God. I'm sorry. I never meant to hurt you." His voice reeked of remorse.

"It's all right," she soothed. Cole wouldn't hurt her as

long as he thought she was Heather, and willing to run away with him. "I understand why you did it. But you won't be needing the gun now. Give it to me." She held out her hand, willing it to remain steady. "I'll put it somewhere safe."

He stared at her outstretched hand. She kept her face lowered. After an endless moment, he placed the gun in her hand.

"I love you, Heather," he whispered. "I'll make you happy, I swear I will."

Meghan stood stock-still, too drained to move. Her fingers closed around the cold metal of the gun, and her heart ached. For Heather, for Ralph, for Nick, and for Cole, who'd let his feelings of inadequacy and a high school rivalry drive him to murder and madness.

A flicker of movement behind him caught her eye, and she knew they were no longer alone. She inched backward. Suddenly the parking lot was flooded with blinding light. Meghan blinked rapidly.

"Police! Freeze!"

Cole snapped back to the present, unadulterated hatred filling his face. *"You lying bitch!"*

He lunged for Meghan. In a move she'd learned from Jason, she ducked and spun away. A large uniformed man leapt out from behind a nearby row of garbage cans and hit Cole with a flying tackle. Cole fought him like a madman, his screams of betrayal echoing across the water. Two more officers joined in the fray, one of them subduing Cole with a roundhouse punch to the jaw.

As they stood and dusted themselves off, Meghan numbly stared at Cole, lying unconscious on the ground. She'd never seen anyone lose it so completely. Mutely she handed the gun to a fourth officer who appeared at her side, watching as the paramedics loaded Cole onto a stretcher.

"Are you all right?" the sheriff asked gently.

"I'm fine," she answered distantly, all too aware she might not have been, had things gone differently. Turning away, she reached into her blouse, pulled out the thin wire taped to her skin, and handed it to him. She'd had him call the state police to come and wire her before her meeting with Cole, but hadn't been able to notify them she was leaving the house so they could follow her. "I hope you found out what you needed to know."

"Yes, ma'am. We got it all on tape. From the moment you left Ashton. Miss Peabody called us. She saw you leave with Benson. We had a tail on you before you crossed the bridge." He shifted uncomfortably. "I'm sorry I didn't believe your story at first."

"It's all right."

He looked as if he was about to say more, then curtly tipped his hat. "I'll be getting back to the station now. You can come in and make a statement when you're ready to leave. Just ask any of my men to bring you."

She nodded, and the sheriff strode away, leaving Meghan to slowly scan the commotion around her. The van that had followed her off the highway and three state patrol cars had arrived with the ambulance. Police radios squawked, red and blue lights flashed everywhere. A second man stopped beside her, and Meghan looked into the dark, furious eyes of Nicholas Hawkinson.

"Nick?" Relief swamped her, making her knees weaken.

"You don't need anybody, do you?"

Stunned by his hostility, she stared. "What are you talking about?"

"You. Single-handedly taking on a man you *knew* was a dangerous killer. A man who murdered your own *sister*." He raked a hand through his hair and began pacing. "Dammit, Meghan, here I was, terrified he was going to shoot you, and you were chatting him up as cool as a cucumber. First you got him to confess, then you got him to hand over that gun like he was passing potatoes at a Sunday dinner!" He stopped pacing and glared at her. "Christ, woman, is there *anything* you can't do?"

She simply continued staring, shaking her head. "Cook?"

"Oh, Meghan." He hauled her into his arms, nearly crushing her in the process. She held on tight, suddenly needing every ounce of his warm, solid strength. They were both trembling by the time he pulled away, holding her by the elbows to steady her.

"Dammit, Meghan, when Sheriff Taylor told me what you'd done, I wanted to strangle you both."

"You came with the sheriff?"

"I had to. He knew where you were, and I didn't. I was damned lucky to catch him as he was leaving the station to follow you." His anguished eyes bored into hers. "Why did you do it, Meghan? You could have died if we hadn't gotten here in time."

Tears pricked the backs of her eyes. "She was my sister, Nick. I had to know."

His face filled with compassion . . . and a dark, desperate need. Sliding his fingers into her hair, he kissed her deeply, almost fiercely. If she hadn't felt so emotionally drained, she would've responded to his need, but as it was, the best she could do was hold on and be thankful they were both alive.

Nick pulled away slowly, his eyes searching hers. Apparently not finding what he was looking for, he released her and stepped back, his voice holding an unsettling flatness. "I suppose you'll be going home now. Back to Washington."

Confused by the sudden distance he'd placed between them, she answered slowly. "I suppose so. Maybe not tonight, but in the next day or two. Jason and my parents will need to be told about Heather and . . . well, I've got some work to catch up on. I, uh, sort of left a few people in the lurch when I came here."

Nick looked away, his features set, his hands flexing at his sides. "Would you consider coming back afterward?"

Her heart dipped. "To you?"

He looked back at her, his dark eyes unreadable. "I know it's a lot to ask, and maybe this isn't the right time, but I think we need some more time together."

"As?"

"Friends, lovers, whatever you want."

But not husband and wife. Meghan forced herself to ignore the stab of pain she felt. "For how long?"

"I don't know. We'll . . . have to see what happens."

So. He wanted her to stay, but he wanted to keep his options open. She couldn't accept that. She'd already been discarded once by a man, and not even for Nick would she set herself up for it a second time. It would kill her to leave him, but she wanted all or nothing.

"I don't think so, Nick."

The look in his eyes was bleak. "I didn't think you would."

"Miss Edwards? Would you like a ride back to Ashton?"

She looked over to see Seamus O'Reilly standing nearby, hat in hand, then looked back at Nick. There didn't seem to be much point in discussing things further. He'd offered his terms, and she'd rejected them. "Are you ready?" she asked quietly. "I'll need to get my things from your house."

They rode back to the house in strained silence, looking out separate windows while Seamus drove. When they pulled into the driveway, Nick got out of the car and went inside, leaving Meghan to thank Seamus again and ask him to tell Sheriff Taylor she'd be by as soon as she could. As he drove away, she turned to face Nick's house, and felt hot tears well in her eyes. So this was how it ended. With both of them hurt and angry, and neither of them understanding why.

Squaring her shoulders, she went inside, only to find Nick nowhere in sight. Meghan didn't know whether to be disappointed or relieved. Reluctantly she gathered her things and set them by the front door, then went looking for him. Her heart might be breaking, but it wasn't in her to leave without saying good-bye. She found him standing in the loft, silhouetted by the moonlight as he looked out over the lake, a bottle of bourbon in his hand.

"Celebrating?" she asked quietly.

He didn't turn around. "Not quite."

She crossed the loft to stand beside him, her hands jammed into her skirt pockets. The silence that stretched between them was so acute, she could hear faint strains of music from The Wharf across the lake. When the song ended, she turned to Nick, who continued staring out into the chilly night. She ached to touch him, but was afraid it would only make matters worse.

"Listen, Nick. I'm not sure why you're so upset with me, but I don't want to leave with bad feelings between us. Not after what we've been through . . . not after what we've shared."

He looked at her then. "And what exactly was that?"

She hated the distance in his voice and longed to tell him she loved him, but her pride refused to let her. He didn't love her. He only wanted to sleep with her awhile longer. When he'd finished restoring his house, chances were he'd sell it as planned and go back to Houston. She'd seen him reading the real estate booklets, scouting the local market. She couldn't bear the thought of sticking around and watching her dreams die.

"I don't want to go, Nick. I have to."

"Why? Is it because your family would disapprove of me?"

She stared at him, shocked. "Of course not."

"Then what's wrong? I thought we were . . . getting along."

She swallowed, wondering how to put it without making it seem like an ultimatum. Marry me or else. "I need more, Nick."

He looked out over the water again, his jaw working. Finally he turned back to her, his emotions once again under control, his eyes dark and serious. "I know you do, Meghan. I have from the start. It's one of the reasons I didn't want to get involved with you in the first place. But I did, and now, God help me, I don't want to let you go."

"Nick . . ."

He held up a hand. "No. Hear me out. Please. I know I don't lead the kind of life or make the kind of money you're used to, but I've got some saved up and I've been checking around. City couples are always looking to buy old farmhouses and fix them up. The first few houses, I'd probably have to buy myself, then sell them when they're done, but after that, I'm sure I could keep the work coming in. . . ." He paused, taking a deep breath. "Especially if I had the right photographer taking my before-and-after pictures."

He met her eyes, his softly beseeching. "I don't want to tie you down, Meghan. I just want to be a part of your life. You can come and go as you please. Just don't go permanently. I need you too much."

"But you said . . . I mean, I thought . . ."

"Thought what?" he prompted quietly.

"I thought you only wanted me to stay for . . . for as long as it lasted."

His eyes darkened, his voice deepening. "I do. But how long it lasts is entirely up to you, Meghan. Personally, I'd prefer until death us do part, but that's up to you, too."

Suddenly she could barely breathe. "You'd marry me?"

"In a minute. I love you, Meghan."

"And we'd live here? In Ashton? In your house?"

"Unless you'd rather live somewhere else. I could move to Washington if—"

He never got to finish his sentence. Meghan threw herself into his arms and kissed him like she'd never kissed him before—with pure, unrestrained joy. By the time she was finished, Nick was backed against the wall and breathing hard, Meghan pressed as close to him as she could get, and the bottle of bourbon was soaking the floorboards.

"We're not moving anywhere, you impossible man. Not when we've got one room with sailboats on the wall and another done up in violets and eyelet lace to fill up. And after that—well, I'm sure you know how to put on an addition or two."

Nick looked stunned, then thrilled. "You mean it?"

Her eyes softened at the sheer happiness she saw in his. "Every word of it. I love you, Nicholas. I'd be honored to be your wife, live in your house, and have your children. Whatever made you think I wouldn't be?"

Smiling, he slowly shook his head. "A bad case of

nerves and insecurity, I guess. I've never felt about a woman the way I feel about you. It's scary as hell.''

"So you were willing to let me go, rather than tell me you loved me?"

"Not really." He reached into his back pocket and pulled out a small card. "While you were out talking to O'Reilly, I went into your purse and filched one of your business cards. As soon as I finished up here and sold the house, I was coming after you. Thought maybe I'd try to talk you into taking a sailing trip with me, maybe getting lost for a few weeks, maybe getting married somewhere along the way."

Meghan smiled, delighted by the idea. "And if I said no?"

Nick grinned. "I thought maybe I'd give you this, then ask you again."

Meghan gasped. In his palm was a diamond solitaire, exquisitely cut, nestled in an antique gold setting. For the longest time, she could only stare. "Oh, Nick. It's beautiful."

"It was my mother's. I found it in an envelope in the bottom dresser drawer. She left a note, telling me to make sure the woman I gave it to knew she wanted her to have it." Taking Meghan's hand, he slowly slipped the ring onto her finger, kissed her knuckles, then smiled gently. "I told you she was big on tradition."

"You knew," she whispered. "You knew all along I'd follow you up here tonight."

His eyes dark and solemn, he shook his head. "No. I just hoped you would." Drawing her closer, he rested his chin on her head and closed his eyes and sighed. "I just hoped you would."

Meghan didn't make it to the sheriff's office until morning.

SHARE THE FUN . . .
SHARE YOUR NEW-FOUND TREASURE!!

You don't want to let your new books out of your sight? That's okay. Your friends can get their own. Order below.

No. 132 ASHTON'S SECRET by Liana Laverentz
Meghan vowed to uncover Nick's secret, with or without his help!

No. 1 ALWAYS by Catherine Sellers
A modern day "knight in shining armor." Forever . . . for always!

No. 2 NO HIDING PLACE by Brooke Sinclair
Pretty government agent & handsome professor = mystery & romance.

No. 3 SOUTHERN HOSPITALITY by Sally Falcon
North meets South. War is declared. Both sides win!!!

No. 4 WINTERFIRE by Lois Faye Dyer
Beautiful NY model and rugged Idaho rancher find their own magic.

No. 5 A LITTLE INCONVENIENCE by Judy Christenberry
Liz faces every obstacle Jason throws at her—even his love.

No. 6 CHANGE OF PACE by Sharon Brondos
Can Sam protect himself from Deirdre, the green-eyed temptress?

No. 7 SILENT ENCHANTMENT by Lacey Dancer
Was she real? She was Alex's true-to-life fairy tale princess.

No. 8 STORM WARNING by Kathryn Brocato
Passion raged out of their control—and there was no warning!

No. 9 PRODIGAL LOVER by Margo Gregg
Bryan is a mystery. Could he be Keely's presumed dead husband?

No. 10 FULL STEAM by Cassie Miles
Jonathan's a dreamer—Darcy is practical. An unlikely combo!

No. 11 BY THE BOOK by Christine Dorsey
Charlotte and Mac give parent-teacher conference a new meaning.

No. 12 BORN TO BE WILD by Kris Cassidy
Jenny shouldn't get close to Garrett. He'll leave too, won't he?

No. 13 SIEGE OF THE HEART by Sheryl McDanel Munson
Nick pursues Court while she wrestles with her heart and mind.

No. 14 TWO FOR ONE by Phyllis Herrmann
What is it about Cal and Elliot that has Leslie seeing double?

No. 15 A MATTER OF TIME by Ann Bullard
Does Josh *really* want Christine or is there something else?

No. 16 FACE TO FACE by Shirley Faye
Christi's definitely not Damon's type. So, what's the attraction?

No. 17 OPENING ACT by Ann Patrick
Big city playwright meets small town sheriff and life heats up.

No. 18 RAINBOW WISHES by Jacqueline Case
Mason is looking for more from life. Evie may be his pot of gold!

No. 19 SUNDAY DRIVER by Valerie Kane
Carrie breaks through all Cam's defenses showing him how to love.

No. 20 CHEATED HEARTS by Karen Lawton Barrett
T.C. and Lucas find their way back into each other's hearts.

No. 21 THAT JAMES BOY by Lois Faye Dyer
Jesse believes in love at first sight. Will he convince Sarah?

No. 22 NEVER LET GO by Laura Phillips
Ryan has a big dilemma. Kelly is the answer to *all* his prayers.

No. 23 A PERFECT MATCH by Susan Combs
Ross can keep Emily safe but can he save himself from Emily?

Meteor Publishing Corporation
Dept. 293, P. O. Box 41820, Philadelphia, PA 19101-9828

Please send the books I've indicated below. Check or money order (U.S. Dollars only)—no cash, stamps or C.O.D.s (PA residents, add 6% sales tax). I am enclosing $2.95 plus 75¢ handling fee for *each* book ordered.

Total Amount Enclosed: $_____.

____ No. 132	____ No. 6	____ No. 12	____ No. 18
____ No. 1	____ No. 7	____ No. 13	____ No. 19
____ No. 2	____ No. 8	____ No. 14	____ No. 20
____ No. 3	____ No. 9	____ No. 15	____ No. 21
____ No. 4	____ No. 10	____ No. 16	____ No. 22
____ No. 5	____ No. 11	____ No. 17	____ No. 23

Please Print:
Name _____

Address _____ Apt. No. _____

City/State _____ Zip _____

Allow four to six weeks for delivery. Quantities limited.